SECRETS
IN THE HALLS

KAREN L ROSE

To my grandchildren:
Daliyah, Bentley, Natalie, Asher and our Bella angel.
To read is to broaden your world a thousand times
over again and again.

CHAPTER 1

"Let's go! Clear the halls and head to your homeroom! I mean *now!*"

While the students scattered and tripped and dodged each other throughout the crowded halls, Mrs. Waverly snickered. She loved the first week of school when her young buggers, as she liked to call them, listened and followed the rules.

It won't last, she thought. *It never does, but this week will definitely set a tone. God, I love this job. No, it's not a job; it's my life passion. I love seeing their faces when they're learning something new and it connects somewhere in their cerebral hemisphere. But then again, I have always been such a nerd.* She chortled out loud and looked around to see if anyone had heard her.

Neva Waverly had been teaching for almost twenty years, and the thrill of a new year was just as exciting to her as Christmas morning was when she was a kid. It was the fresh start, the different classes, the new students, as well as some of the students she'd had year after year, and even the smell of her new books!

Cindy Newport did not see Mrs. Waverly. She was busy staring down the hall, which looked too long and too foreboding. She took a deep breath and pushed her short bangs up over her forehead—an annoying habit her mother reminded her over and over again not to do. *"You're going to get pimples all over your forehead, young lady! I swear to good God, no matter how many times I tell you . . . Well, that's it. I'm done!"*

Her mother drove her crazy. Every day, Mattie would shake her finger in Cindy's face to chide her for some habit of hers that was either disgusting or lazy or ignorant. For Cindy, school was her refuge, her sanctuary. She was away from the negative vibes at home, where she was always made to feel worthless. But today, the foreign landscape of the school left her in a brand-new kind of panic.

Cindy was so focused on staring at the end of the hall that she didn't notice the looming figure coming at her from the classroom door. "Umph!" Cindy mumbled as she barged right into Mrs. Waverly. Of course, Cindy didn't know who she'd just collided with, but she looked up into the most intense green eyes that flashed with anger.

"Jeez, I'm so sorry."

"Yes, you should be, young lady! And what is your name?" Mrs. Waverly stood taller than her normal five feet six inches in her three-inch heels. As she towered over the shrinking student, the girl's face emerged, nearly the color of paste. "Again! Your name!" Mrs. Waverly was not going to be bumped into and ignored to boot—especially on the first day of school.

"I . . . uh . . . My name is Cindy. Cindy Newport, and I . . . I really am sorry, Mrs. . . . . Oh, jeez, I don't even know who you are!" Cindy crumpled to her knees. *This is not how I wanted my first day of high school to begin*, she thought as fresh tears promised to spill over.

The other students in the hall ran by quickly, not wanting to get involved with an incident that would make them late to homeroom. A few girls sneered as they sashayed by. One girl giggled out loud and said, "Oh no. Looks like Cinderella is already in trouble!"

Mrs. Waverly scoffed at the onlookers. "Now move on to homeroom, or you'll be with me after school!" The students politely ignored Mrs. Waverly and walked with more focus to their destinations. Mrs. Waverly reached down and gently touched Cindy on her shoulder.

"Hush, my young whippersnapper. Get up and come into my room until you can pull yourself together." Neva might've liked to appear as a major ogre in the school— after all, she did have her reputation to uphold—but she was not going to beat up on this crumpled student on the very first day.

Cindy was frozen. Her limbs were numb, and her head rang. She wasn't sure if she was hearing the school bells or just having an anxiety attack that had come on strong, fast, and ugly. She felt as though everyone could hear her heart beating against her chest. She'd sworn to herself she was not going to fall apart on the first day. She shook her head from side to side as if she could jostle her anxieties away. Cindy took a deep breath. *Slow down*, she thought. *Slow down and breathe.* Her therapist, Miss Anna, had taught her a few tricks, but when she was this deep in an attack, it was hard to pull out. She heard a voice, but it was muffled. She thought she heard laughing and refused to lift her head. Cindy wanted to morph into a puddle on the floor and slide away.

Mrs. Waverly had witnessed this before. How many teacher trainings had she gone to where they discussed a student in distress? A student having a major meltdown? What to do and how to avoid causing more anguish for the student? Neva squatted next to Cindy. "It's okay, Cindy. I'm here for you. No one else is in the hall now. How about you get up and come with me? You're not in trouble. I promise." Neva used her special comforting voice that always seemed to ease a conflict, and it was working. Cindy lifted her head to look at her.

"I'm so sorry." Cindy hiccuped. "I'm too embarrassed to get up. I just want to crawl into a hole."

Neva reached out to take Cindy's hand. She stood up, and Cindy uncurled her body and slowly, fearfully untangled her legs, grabbed her book bag, and stood up. She looked down the hall to her left and then to her right, praying she would not recognize anyone, but the hall had been emptied of students for some time.

Cindy, her head a bit dizzy and her chest still heaving as she took gulping breaths, looked at Mrs. Waverly again. "I have to get to my homeroom," she whispered in between jagged breaths. "I don't even know where that is . . . and . . . I . . ."

Neva tenderly guided Cindy into her classroom. Cindy stumbled through the doorway and almost collided with a student desk. Neva caught her and eased her into the desk. Cindy loved the familiar feel of the hard wood and let her hands grip the edge of the top of the desk. It made her feel solid and steady.

"I'm so sorry . . . and embarrassed. It's my first day, and I just wanted to get through it without anyone seeing me fall apart."

Neva looked down at this student who needed support, not a screaming lecture about missing homeroom. "Cindy," Neva said softly, "my name is Mrs. Waverly, and I am a ninth-grade teacher. You must be a new ninth grader at Wells High. So, let's start with your schedule, which I believe is that piece of paper crumpled up inside your fist. Why don't you pull it out, and we can figure out where you need to go right now. Homeroom is extra-long today, so you still have plenty of time to get there."

Cindy looked down at her right hand, which was balled into a tight fist. She stared at it as if she were seeing it for the first time. Slowly, she unfurled her hand to reveal the white paper schedule with her name on it and the list of classes underneath. She placed it on the desk and tried to iron out the creases and breaks in the paper with her hand, but it was unreadable.

Neva gazed at the new high schooler in front of her. *She is going to have a rough four years ahead of her if this is how she deals with a minor glitch on her first day.* Cindy's hair was askew, and her oversized glasses slid down the tip of her nose. A fresh crop of pimples peeked out on her forehead. *Oh my*, she thought. *This girl is a prime candidate for future bullying. I'm going to have to keep my eye on her.*

"You know what, Cindy? Let me take your schedule and go over to my computer to print you out a new one. How does that sound? Huh?"

Cindy raised her head, pushed her glasses back up her nose, and nodded. Snot bubbles slipped from Cindy's nose, and Neva quickly got up and whipped out a tissue from the top of her desk. Without saying a word, she placed it in Cindy's hand.

Cindy sniffed. "Thanks. My mom would have made me so conscious about that, but you . . . you . . . Well, thanks."

Neva smiled. *This poor child.* This was why Neva had chosen to be a part of the new mentoring program this year. *She is going to be my number one project!*

Neva found Cindy's schedule in the computer, printed it out, and walked over to her with it. "Now, Cindy, do you remember the Wells High summer programs? Where you came for an introduction to Wells and the subjects you'd be taking, along with all the extracurricular activities you could become involved in? Do you remember coming to that orientation?"

Cindy shook her head. "No, my mother wouldn't allow me to come. She said I had better things to do than start school any sooner than necessary. That's why I was so lost this morning, I guess."

Neva clucked quietly. She stowed the mother information in the back of her head for later and said, "Okay, no biggie. Let's take a look at your schedule for now, and then we can walk over to your homeroom. They're handing out some important papers you are going to need, and I don't want you to miss out on those."

Cindy smiled weakly. *I guess I have to leave this room some time.* She shoved her bangs up again. Cindy took a deep breath and felt a bit calmer. Her heart wasn't banging into her chest anymore, and the ringing in her ears was gone. She stood up and noticed for the first time all the cool posters all over the room. *This is a good place*, she thought. *A safe place.*

Cindy followed Mrs. Waverly down the hall, trying to take note of all the room numbers, the hall names. This was a big school. She wished her mother hadn't been so adamant about not letting her come to orientation. Cindy always felt like she was one step behind the others.

In just a few minutes, Mrs. Waverly had reached Cindy's homeroom. Neva could sense the tenseness in Cindy's body movements as they approached the door. Mrs. Waverly stopped a few feet from Mr. Tannereck's room. Sam taught math and was a good colleague of Neva's. She looked over at Cindy and said, "It's okay, Cindy. Mr. Tannereck is your homeroom teacher, and he will be very kind to you."

Cindy gulped. "Everyone is going to laugh at me. I know it. They always do. It happens all the time." Cindy was about to turn around when Neva took her by the elbow and gently guided her through the open door.

Mr. Tannereck stopped talking and looked over at his new student being escorted in by Mrs. Waverly. He'd always liked Neva. She was a good teacher and a professional colleague who did not gossip like some of the other teachers in the building.

"Good morning, Mr. Tannereck. How are you doing today?"

"Well, hello, Mrs. Waverly. I am doing just fine here with my new ninth graders, who are so excited to be here." He turned to his class and nudged them on. "You are all so excited to be here with me, aren't you now?"

There were a few nervous snickers and some coughs, but otherwise, the students just stared at the doorway, trying to figure out why Cindy, of all people, was being personally accompanied to her homeroom.

"Well, Mr. Tannereck, I have one of your incredibly talented students with me right now. I was in a bind trying to get my bulletin board completed when I saw Cindy in the hall and asked if she wouldn't mind helping me for a moment. Not only did this great new ninth grader jump to my aid, but we were so busy chitchatting that the late bell rang before I knew it, and I didn't want Cindy to be in any trouble for arriving to homeroom so late."

Mr. Tannereck smiled. He knew Neva was putting on a show, and perhaps later, she would fill him in. But for now, he welcomed Cindy into his room.

Neva watched as Cindy found the first empty desk to sit in. Before Neva turned away, she exclaimed, "Thanks again, Cindy, for all your help. Please come back and visit with me anytime!" And with that, she scooted out the door and back to her room.

Cindy felt her face turn red.

One of the girls behind her whispered, "Oooh, Cinderella is *sooo* special!"

Cindy rolled her eyes. *This year has to be better*, she prayed. *It has to be.*

CHAPTER 2

Neva walked through the halls, gazing at all the decorations hanging on the wall. Here it was, the beginning of the year, and already, so many colorfully decorated posters were advertising the first football game, soccer game, and numerous cross country meets. The race for class president posters adorned bulletin boards, making promises most high school students would never notice whether they came true—promises for better cafeteria food, more computers, and more dances ranked the highest. Popular names with pimple-free faces and long dreadlocks or wavy curls smiled back at her. This was important. This was critical. Neva sighed. Thinking back to her own high school days only made her sad. She had not been one of the popular girls. She'd had a face full of pimples and frizzy hair that refused to obey any hair product on the market. And then there was that awful day in gym class . . .

"Okay, girls, off to the locker room. We're done for today. And remember, everyone—and I mean everyone—you better be in that shower room when I get in there!" Mrs. Hinnock had screamed.

Neva always did as she was told. She'd been brought up to obey. And, by God, if that meant taking a shower after gym class, well, she was going to do it. The locker room was incredibly old but clean, barren with a musty smell from oversprayed armpit deodorant that hovered like a noxious cloud above the locker tops and never left. Neva walked to her locker and methodically stripped off her one-piece butt-ugly green gym suit. It was the single most unattractive piece of clothing she had ever worn, but rules were rules. Neva picked up a towel that would never cover her bumpy body. She was developing slowly, but her stomach was too big, her hips jiggled when she walked, and her boobs were still hiding somewhere, not overly eager to make an appearance. Neva hoped all the other girls had made their way through the shower line and left her a modicum of privacy. She hoped. She prayed. But her prayers were never answered.

"Look out, everyone! It's Neva! Neva been kissed! Neva been touched! Neva gonna be anything!" Sally Wagner chanted. At fourteen, Sally was tall and blonde, with deep Scandinavian blue eyes and a mouth that could slice you into more pieces than a food processor. Neva had always shied away from her, but somehow, Sally was always right there in front of her, tormenting her.

"Aw, leave her alone," begged Gina Moller.

"You're such a goody-goody, Gina. Neva deserves to be picked on because she's so *incredibly* ugly! We have to toughen her up in preparation for the rest of her life!" Sally's commanding voice demanded obedience from everyone, and no one even tried to defy her.

Neva hugged the towel close to her chest, trying to cover up what didn't exist there. The shower line zigzagged through a channel of showerheads designed to spray every part of your body no matter how hard you tried to escape the pelting cold shards. Neva picked up her pace, but when she was about to emerge from the nightmare tunnel, her body betrayed her. Her left foot hit a slick of something slippery, and before she knew it, her eyes were staring upward at the freezing streams of water as her back and butt smacked hard on the cold tile floor. Shock waves of pain and embarrassment ripped through her. She wanted to crawl deep into the drain currently digging curvy marks into her soggy skin.

Please, God, let me just die here and now. I don't want to get up. I want to die and come back as a horse and gallop away. Far, far away where no one knows my name. Please, God. Tell me I am not lying on the shower floor while everyone laughs so hard they're crying.

Sally was the loudest. "Look out, everyone! Neva can't even walk through the showers without tripping and falling. She's the number one disaster in our school! Be careful. She's contagious, and you do not want to catch her nerd disease!"

The tears flowed uncontrollably. Neva hated this part of the bullying—always the tears, which revealed her weakness. If only she could laugh it off. Her lack of self-confidence screamed to everyone that it was okay to make fun of her, that it wouldn't matter. Why was the world so unfair? Neva's tears mingled with the cold shower water that brought on an uncontrollable shivering.

Neva pulled her legs under her and, stumbling a bit, managed to get up. She was soaked, humiliated, and worn out. To make matters worse, Neva's towel was drenched and had a small bit of blood on the corner. She groaned. She had split her knee on the drain but knew the girls would immediately come to another conclusion. Neva took a deep breath and shuffled out of the shower hallway.

She'd hoped she could slink over to her locker and get dressed in private, but as she emerged from the showers, she heard a collective whisper. The girls who always made fun of her stood in a semicircle, awaiting her arrival. They were already dressed and ready to leave, but wait . . . They all had one arm behind their backs. Before Neva could retreat, the girls screamed in unison, "GET HER!" and the air was filled with various spray scents from their united cans of deodorant. Neva closed her eyes as the spray burned and stuck in her nose, in her hair, and sluiced down her shivering body in gooey rivulets that stuck to different parts of her.

"Aim it at her armpits!" someone screamed. "We have to make sure she smells good." Peals of laughter pierced the thick fog of Ban, Degree, Suave, Dove, and goodness knew what other brands landed on Neva.

Neva just stood there, frozen in place and unable to move. She wanted to scream at them, but her vocal cords lay limp in her throat. She wanted to run to her locker, but her body would not listen. And then it happened. Oh God, someone saw it. And it wasn't the *it* they were thinking, but that didn't matter to any of them.

"Oh, my God!" one of them shrieked. "Look at her towel! There's blood on it! She's got her period, and she's bleeding right here on the locker room floor! Run for your lives, everyone. It's Neva-used tampons!"

And right at that horrific moment came the sound she prayed for: "All right, girls!" shouted Mrs. Leanore Hinnock. "Party's over. The bell rang a few minutes ago, and you need to get moving. Now!"

Mrs. Hinnock walked over to Neva, put her arm around her, and guided her toward her locker. "C'mon, Neva. Let's get dressed. I see your knee has a scrape on it. After you get dressed, come see me in my office, and I'll bandage you up."

After what seemed like forever, Neva left the gym office and walked to her next class. *When will this ever end?* she thought desperately. It was always the same. Mrs. Hinnock was always so nice to her, and that was what hurt the most. She wanted Mrs. Hinnock to like her because she was a good student, not out of pity.

Neva squeezed the late pass in her tight fists. *I'm so sick of this. One day, I'll get back at girls like Sally. I won't forget.* Neva brushed a tear that slipped down her red swollen cheeks. She took a deep breath, opened the classroom door, and walked in, pretending nothing had ever happened to her . . . again.

CHAPTER 3

Beverly Winewrought sat on the big sofa in the teacher's lounge. She wanted to make sure she could see everyone who came into the room and where they sat. There was an added room over to the left where teachers could make phone calls in private, although most teachers used their own cell phones. *I would never do that*, thought Beverly, running her long fingers through her short black hair. She wasn't fool enough to let parents know how they could get in touch with her any time they wanted. *Forget that.* She snickered to herself. Beverly tugged at her sleeves, pulling them down over her wrists and hiding the bruise blossoming into an array of blues and purples and greens.

"Damn it!" Ted had screamed that morning.

Teddy Winewrought—tall and angular with a large hook nose and dark brown eyes that never softened—lifted his arm toward Beverly's face, thought better of it, and grabbed her wrist instead. Beverly had winced in pain but did not scream out. She refused to, and this had only angered Ted more.

"Why the hell can't you make breakfast for me when you know I have to leave so early? I hate these frozen waffles. They taste like cardboard, and I have an important meeting this morning. If my stomach starts making noises . . . Damn it, Bev, I'll be the laughingstock of my firm!"

Beverly was tired of him. Tired of his pouting, his whining, his demands. Sometimes she wished she'd never set out to meet him after connecting on that awful dating site. But she had, and she'd married him after only a year of dating—a year of kisses and roses and romantic dinners and promises of a wonderful future together. *Ha,* she thought. *Future, my ass.* Ted had turned into the biggest, neediest baby Beverly had ever met. And when he didn't get his way, he loved to grab her so tight it left a mark. *A mark I have to hide.*

She didn't know how much longer she could take his abuse, and she didn't know who she could trust to ask for advice. Beverly ran out of their house early every morning and faked extra activities at work so she could be away from home. As for breakfast . . . *Shit, he can make his own damn eggs.*

"Morning, Beverly."

Beverly sat up on the sofa and stared at Carl DeWitt, a sweetheart of a teacher but so young. Beverly was still a new teacher by the system standards, but she had put in seven long years, and Carl was just starting his third year—young, naïve, and way too connected with his kids. He knew everything about his students: where they lived, who their siblings were, and if they had issues. And if they did, well, he loved to help solve them. Not Beverly. No way. She taught biology and wanted nothing to do with her students beyond their forty-five minutes with her. *The less time the better*, she mused.

"Oh, hi, Carl. I guess this is your new off period, too. How is your day going?" Beverly didn't really care, but she loved to hear what every teacher was doing and know everyone's gossip. She spread most of the gossip. It gave her a small thrill when the gossip rumors got back around, and when the other teachers confided in her, Beverly just shrugged as if hearing it for the first time.

"Morning, Beverly. Golly, I really love my schedule this year. I have all ninth graders, and I think they are totally awesome!" Carl's grin showed white shiny teeth. Beverly swore he had to have them professionally polished.

"That's so cool, Carl," Beverly cooed with as much syrup in her voice as she could muster. "Just think, you will start them off on their high school career with your positive teaching style and get them motivated and interested in pursuing history as a career. How many of your students may end up in politics or even become our President someday? Huh?"

Carl wasn't sure if Beverly was being sincere or sarcastic, but he was just so thrilled to be a teacher he let her babble on. "I wonder, twenty years from now, where some of my kids will end up. You never know, but that's an amazing thought—the President? Wow!"

Carl found the big recliner in the corner of the lounge, sat down, and leaned back in his chair, his long legs outstretched and a bottle of Dr Pepper in his hands. He took a deep sip, suppressed a belch, and wiped his mouth with the back of his hand.

Beverly did not miss any of Carl's annoying habits. *Guys,* she thought. *They are so gross.* If he weren't such an easy target to make fun of, Beverly would have completely ignored him.

The door swung open with a loud swish. Barbara Atkinson, Assistant Principal, stood in the doorway, not moving. Her large hands rested on her hips, her feet wide apart, and the black clunky shoes she wore dimpled with splattered mud. Ms. Atkinson's bulky black glasses rested low on her pointed nose, and her brown eyes glared into the room. She shook her head, as if to make sure none of her short-cropped brown hair was out of place.

"Mr. DeWitt!" she exclaimed in her accusatory tone. "I need to see you in my office immediately, if not sooner." And with that, she turned around, almost tripped over her feet—which did not turn as gracefully as she expected them to—and walked away, letting the heavy door close with an ominous thud.

"Oh, my!" clucked Beverly. "I guess the old Battle Axe is on the warpath again!"

"Battle Axe?" Carl looked at Beverly. His eyebrows

scrunched upward, and his forehead became a trail of meandering lines. "Why did you call her that?"

"Her initials are BA," said Beverly. "She's always after somebody, ready to bring the axe down on them. She earned that nickname years ago, and it just stuck. So, Carl, I think you better go see what the old Battle Axe wants with you. If it's okay with you, I'd rather she not return to our one sacred place in the whole building. I need to chill for a few minutes before my next class."

"Oh, okay." Carl got up, screwed the top back on his Dr Pepper, and slipped it into his backpack. "I have no idea what she wants. It's only the first day of school. I couldn't have screwed up that much already. I'm feeling a bit nauseous. Is that normal?"

Beverly stared at the poor guy, who was overwrought by being called down to the assistant principal's office. She guessed he never got into trouble as a student. The way Atkinson had stared him down might have made him wet his pants.

"I'm sure it's nothing major. Atkinson likes to feel important, so she probably wants to ask you to do some extra lunch duty coverage or something ridiculous like that. Take a deep breath and feel good about yourself, dude. I'm sure you'll come back and tell me she needed an extra guy covering the locker room. Go on, get out of here."

Carl felt a little bit more confident, but he didn't rush out the door. He put his hand on the door handle, turned back to Beverly, and said unconvincingly, "Yeah, you're probably right. Something mundane, I guess. Okay, good talk. Have a great rest of your day. See you after school at the staff meeting."

The door had barely closed when Beverly pulled out her phone and texted her group:

Man, oh man! You are not going to believe what just happened. Old BA stormed into the staff room and demanded that Carl DeWitt rush to her office right away! What do you think Carl did now? More to follow as soon as I find out!

Beverly clicked off her phone, packed up her bags, and stood up.

"Time to check out my next group of exciting teenagers," she said out loud to nobody. "What a wonderful day it is!"

CHAPTER 4

Riley Maddox sat in her foods class and looked around at everyone. "I hate the first day," she muttered to herself. She shook her head from side to side, as if shaking it would erase the real fears that stemmed from not knowing anyone around her. This was her private anxiety, and nobody was ever going to find out. Not if she could help it. Every year, she pushed away the palpitations in her chest, the dryness in her mouth, and the dizziness that came and went all day long. This always happened on the first day of school. No, that wasn't right. It happened on the first day, *and* it happened during every new event in her life. And that meant it happened more often than she cared to admit.

Riley could not let anyone know her weakness. She had a reputation. Some of the other girls were afraid of her. Some of them even turned around and walked the other way when she came down a hall or even when they saw her strolling through the mall. She tried not to think about it, because it made her feel powerful inside—a special power that masked her real terror of being found out. So she pushed it deep inside her and tried to forget it.

Riley stared at the posters stuck on the concrete walls around the classroom. There were posters of the various food groups and pictures of famous chefs she'd never heard of and exciting restaurants she would never visit. *Ugh*, she thought. *What a waste of a class.* She was never going to eat anything she made in this class, and she sure as hell was never going to touch something one of the geeky kids made. *Ycccch.*

"Good morning, class," Ms. Saper began hesitantly. "I want to welcome each and every one of you to the most exciting period of your day!" Ms. Saper's initial awkwardness dissolved into her enthusiastic display of the items on her desk.

"Now, I know most of you think you know a little bit about cooking," she continued with a passion in her voice that made Riley blurt out a small "Hmph," at which Ms. Saper looked at Riley and smiled. "Oh, I see we have an expert with us today! And you are?"

Riley swallowed hard. She hadn't meant for her reaction to be so vocal. She didn't want to be put on the spot, but she had no choice but to demonstrate her displeasure. "I'm Riley Maddox. And I do know how to cook, so this class might be a waste of time for me, but go ahead, continue with your lecture."

Ms. Saper walked over to where Riley was sitting and looked at her from head to toe. "I am so happy to have someone in the class who will be my right-hand person then, Riley. Why don't you come up here to the desk to help me as we explore all the exciting cooking implements?"

"No thank you." Riley tried to be as cool as she possibly could, realizing the snickers and giggles around her were getting louder and louder.

"Yeah, Riley," shouted some guy in the back. Riley had no idea who he was. "You lead the class with all your know-how, and I'll make sure to order from you when I see you flipping burgers at McDonald's!"

The entire class of ninth graders burst out laughing. Riley squirmed in her seat and tried to shrink into herself. This wasn't going well at all. *I think I'm going to throw up.*

The girl with huge hoop earrings behind Riley whispered in her ear. "I think you better go on up to the front before we all find out you're a big nothing phony."

Riley spun around, and her hand raised, ready to slap the girl. Cell phones lifted in the air as if everyone was prepared to witness a girl fight. Riley lowered her hand and turned back to Ms. Saper.

"All right. I'm coming up. I will be glad to help teach this group of know-nothings how to cook." And with that, Riley gathered her false pride, stood up, and defiantly walked up to the front of the room. She stood next to Ms. Saper, who smelled so sweet from baking something that Riley felt like she was about to gag until, suddenly, the fire alarm sounded.

All at once, the students grabbed their backpacks, phones, and water bottles and stood up.

"Okay, everyone!" Ms. Saper barked out in that teacherly

voice of authority. "Follow me to where my room number is out on the field. Let's go!"

And with that official order, everyone followed Ms. Saper quickly—especially Riley—as they filed out of the room to the field behind the school.

Once outside, Ms. Saper walked up and down her line of students, taking attendance carefully because, being the first day, she did not know everyone's name and had to call out all the students on her roll. When she called Riley's name, Ms. Saper smiled as she looked straight at Riley and said, "Well, I guess I already know who you are, don't I?"

Riley smiled weakly and quickly turned around, her eyes scanning the field.

Ms. Atkinson walked by and demanded, "Ms. Saper? Do you have your attendance sheet for me? Have you completed it correctly, or do I need to go over it with you?"

Ms. Saper looked at her students and smiled gently, ignoring the caustic comments from her administrator. "Why, Ms. Atkinson, so good to see you this morning. Here is my attendance sheet, all filled out correctly. Is there anything else you need from me today?"

Ms. Atkinson glared at Ms. Saper over her thick black glasses. Riley, keenly aware of the tacit disgust some teachers had toward certain administrators, smiled. She understood sharp sarcasm when she heard it and knew there was more to this interaction than what was being presented out here on the field.

Ms. Atkinson turned abruptly, her thick-soled heels

causing a divot in the beautifully manicured football field, and marched over to the next teacher and class.

Ms. Saper looked over her students and shrugged. "Well, I guess we won't have too much time left in our class period by the time we get back today. I hope you are all as excited as I am to get going with our fantastic meals!"

Some of the kids shouted out some comments like "Yeah!" and "Awesome!" but Riley was too cool to join in. Ms. Saper noticed how Riley just stared off into space. She tucked that back in her "teacher log of important stuff" and walked over to Arthur Avari, the veteran music teacher who was in the line next to her. With their heads close together, they did that teacher talking thing where no one could hear them but knew they had to be gossiping.

Riley spotted her best friend, Jilly, a few rows over. Jilly and Riley had been best friends since third grade when Jilly moved there from the West Coast. Jilly was pretty with long blonde hair and so Californian Riley thought she was the coolest friend she'd ever had. Jilly didn't always agree with the way Riley put down other students, but she had put up with Riley because Riley, after all, was her first friend, and Jilly was loyal if nothing else.

Riley waved at Jilly, but before Jilly could wave back, Lucas Cannon, the big freshman quarterback of the football team, had slipped his hand over Jilly's shoulder and turned her around so she didn't see Riley waving.

Ugh, thought Riley. *Why does that big lug have to ruin everything? Jilly can't really like him. He's a football player.*

A dumb jock. No, I'm not jealous; I'm pissed off! They were supposed to go to the mall that weekend. *I guess that's not happening now . . .*

"Riley! Riley Maddox!" shouted Ms. Saper. "Don't you hear me, girl? I said it's time to return to the building. Let's go. Stop staring into outer space!" And with that, Ms. Saper turned and led the class back into the building. Riley, who had been first in line coming out, retreated to the back of the line and shuffled in, her face burning red from embarrassment, humiliation, and anger.

Once they were all back in their seats, Riley laid her head on her desk and sighed. *This is really the worst day of my life*, she thought, *and it's only just the beginning.*

Ms. Saper looked at her eager students minus Riley and smiled. "We are in for an amazing semester. You are going to love being here, and tomorrow, get ready to learn all about what we call 'mise en place.'"

Before the "huhs" could puff out of their open mouths, the bell rang, and everyone grabbed their stuff and stomped out.

"Uh, Riley," Ms. Saper said, "would you come here for a moment, please?"

"I . . . uh . . . I can't be late for my next class," said Riley as she swallowed her voice. She might have acted tough in front of the other students, but when a teacher called her out privately, her pretend nerves of steel just slid away.

"I won't keep you long, Riley. It's just, this class is always a favorite for everybody, and I was a bit surprised that you, well, you blew it off. Is something bothering you? And besides, this class is an elective. You chose it. So, what's the deal, huh?"

Riley looked down at the floor and shuffled her feet, staring at her worn sneakers. If only she'd had the money to buy those cool turquoise ones at the mall. She and Jilly had gone shopping just last week, and Riley always pretended she didn't like anything, when the truth was she didn't have the money to buy anything. That wasn't really true. Riley did have all the money she needed. Her parents gave her a credit card, but she liked to play the poor girl. She did not want to be that pathetic little rich girl.

"I don't know. I don't know. Why are you picking on me? I gotta go." And with that Riley turned around and left the room as quickly as she could.

Alisa Saper slumped in her chair. "She's going to be my challenge this semester for sure," she said to herself. "I have a feeling there's a bit more to that girl than meets the eye, and I'm going to find out what's beneath that tough veneer." Alisa had always liked to take up the quest when it came to students who seemed to be covering up what was really hiding underneath.

CHAPTER 5

Carl DeWitt looked up at the clock in his classroom. "Oh, shoot!" he exclaimed to himself. He had already forgotten Ms. Atkinson had demanded his presence in her office, but between his last class and the fire drill, going to her office had completely escaped his mind.

Carl shut down his computer, scooped up his planning book, and walked swiftly out of his room and down to the main office.

The main office was situated near the front of the school so all visitors could be seen approaching the building. Whether that was intentional, no one ever knew since the building was so old. Carl pulled the door open with such force Cassandra Conway startled behind her desk.

"Why, Mr. DeWitt," she said, "are you okay today?"

Carl, out of breath, gulped for air and replied, "Sure, CC. It's just I'm late to see Ms. Atkinson, and she insisted I see her immediately if not sooner."

Carl loved calling her CC, and she seemed to blush every time he did so. He enjoyed staring into her deep brown eyes and at her long auburn hair she always kept in a ponytail with some big material thing, which she once told him was called a scrunchie. Carl thought about asking her out on a daily basis, but he was too scared, afraid she might say no. He was even more afraid she might say yes, and then he would be totally clueless as to what to do next. He kept saying he was going to work up the nerve to ask her, but he always choked on his words before he had the chance. The students often used the expression "choked on the cheddar," and that seemed to fit him perfectly.

Carl looked straight into CC's chocolate-colored eyes and whispered, though only because he couldn't find his voice: "I'm okay. Just a little out of breath and wondering why she"—Carl pointed toward Ms. Atkinson's room— "wants to see me."

"Oh," answered Cassandra. "She seems to be in a real snit today, for sure. Don't know what she put in her coffee this morning, but it sure wasn't sugar. Well, go on back now, and then if you want, you can tell me what the problem was . . . If you want to, of course."

Carl smiled weakly. "Thanks, CC. You've really helped me calm down. Okay, here I go. No wonder the kids hate coming down to see her. I think I know how they feel."

Casandra chuckled. "You are right on point with that thought. Now go on back before the bell rings for your next class!"

And with that, Cassandra's phone rang, and she was back in her zone dealing with parents.

Carl trekked through the maze of offices. The principal's

secretary, Amelia Goddard, sat at her desk in front of the principal's office, working on her computer, and gave Carl a quick smile as he strolled by. The principal, Lila Libertino, was in her office when Carl walked past. Her short gray hair rested in a perfect wave. Her glasses sat on the top of her head, and her clear gray eyes focused on the pair of parents in front of her, her hands doing all the talking. She nodded at Carl as he walked by, and he quickly nodded back without disturbing her conference. Carl continued down the hall past another administrator's office, but the door was closed, and the lights were out. Finally, the last office on the right was Ms. Atkinson's. Carl took a deep breath, straightened his shoulders, and walked in.

Ms. Atkinson jerked her head up as if an alien had stomped into her office.

"Excuse me, Mr. DeWitt!" she demanded in an outraged tone that sliced like ice shards through the air. "Would you please go back outside my office, knock on the door, and then wait to be invited in?"

Heat rose in Carl's face, turning it several shades of crimson. His shoulders sagged. "So sorry." Carl turned around and banged his shoulder on the doorway. "Shit!" he muttered softly and walked down the hall.

He spotted Cassandra again, but she was speaking with a student who was crying, so he turned around and stood against the wall for a moment. He took a deep breath, looked around to see if anyone had noticed he was just lurking about, and then shuffled back to Ms. Atkinson's room.

She was bent over her desk, pulling out some files, her back to him. For a split second, Carl felt like walking in and pissing her off again because he found her so rude, but he held back from being childish. Instead, he raised his hand and rapped on the doorjamb.

Ms. Atkinson didn't even look up as she yelled, "Come!"

Carl strode into the office and stood in front of her desk. Normally, he would be more casual and sit right down, but considering how formal she was, he decided to wait to be invited to sit. Far be it from him to assume she was going to be informal now after she'd reprimanded him only moments before.

Ms. Atkinson turned around and wrinkled her brows so tightly Carl thought her eyes were going to pop out. She looked up at Carl. "Sit down, Mr. DeWitt."

Carl sat down slowly, as though sitting in her office was a huge honor that he did not want to disrespect. He didn't know why she had such power over him—after all, she was only another educator, just like him—but she loomed large and loud, and he felt very insecure.

"So, Mr. DeWitt, how long have you been teaching now? A year or two, is it?"

"Uh, actually this is my third year, Ms. Atkinson." Carl took a deep breath and released it so he would not appear so nervous. It really bothered him that she made him feel so anxious. No wonder the kids squirmed about coming in here. She probably chewed them up and spit them out for dessert.

"Oh, my. Third year, is it? Time does fly by because it

seems like only yesterday I was giving you a tour of the building and letting you know what our expectations are here at Wells."

"I remember that, too." Carl wasn't sure where this conversation was going, but he didn't feel it was necessary to engage in much of the back-and-forth dialogue.

Carl looked around the room so he would not have to stare back at Ms. Atkinson. Her beady eyes squinted at him and made him squirm. The bookcase behind her held numerous artifacts that he guessed reflected her career as an educator. Proud displays of awards, certificates, and degrees adorned the shelves. Maybe she had to look at them now and then to remind herself how important she was.

"Mr. DeWitt!"

Carl looked back at Ms. Atkinson. "Oh, yes . . . I was just noticing all your accomplishments behind you."

Barbara Atkinson cracked a smile, her thin lips barely covering her teeth and the smudge of red lipstick on her upper tooth. "Why, yes, thank you. I have worked very hard, indeed, Mr. DeWitt. And I assume you will be in possession of these and many more at the rate you're going. That being said, let me explain why I asked you to come see me."

Oh, no. Here it comes, Carl thought. *This is where she lowers the boom, and I either lose my position or who knows?*

"Mr. DeWitt. Carl. Dr. Libertino has suggested that you be involved in our new mentoring program we're starting in a few weeks. She would like you to head up the program. You'd be checking in with me all the time, of course. I have also asked Mrs. Waverly to guide you along, as she has had much experience with these young students."

Ms. Atkinson folded her hands. "This would be a huge commitment on your part as well as the school's. We want this program to be a major success, and you seem to have a great rapport with the ninth graders."

"Wow . . . I mean, thank you," replied Carl. "I don't know what to say. I . . . uh . . . think this would be an awesome challenge, and, well, you know, I'm totally up for it."

Damn, thought Barbara. *When are these young teachers going to learn how to speak clearly and concisely?*

"So, does that mean you accept this new position? There will be a stipend, of course—well, a small one, anyway—if you take the job. What do you say? Are you up for this? Do you want it? Let me know now, or else I will have to tell Dr. Libertino that you declined and then find another teacher, and—"

"No, Ms. Atkinson—I mean, yes. I want the position, and no, you don't have to look any further. This is so cool. Yes, I am up for this challenge. I have so many ideas, and I—"

Ms. Atkinson put her hand up. "Stop. I've heard enough. I have work to do now. You can go. See my secretary as you leave and set up an appointment with her next week so we can go over the details and get this program moving. And stop by and have a chat with Mrs. Waverly so she knows you have accepted the position. The two of you can start planning. Thank you for coming by. Have a good day."

And with that, she turned in her chair to face the back

bookshelf and pulled out a huge binder, then placed it on her lap. She waved goodbye without turning around. Carl got up carefully so as not to knock over the vase on the table next to him. He bent over and picked up his book bag, slung it over his back, and eased himself out of the office quietly and quickly.

Carl went straight to Joanne Cumberly, Ms. Atkinson's secretary, and stood quietly in front of her desk. Joanne had gentle green eyes and soft auburn hair that bounced on her shoulders. Her face lit up in a smile whenever she talked with someone, and she always seemed to wink at just the right moment.

"Well, hello, Mr. DeWitt. I see you survived your meeting over there, huh?" Joanne smiled and winked at Carl.

"Whew. It wasn't easy. I can assure you!"

"It never is, Mr. DeWitt, it never is. Now, I bet she asked you to set up some weekly appointments."

"How did you know?"

Joanne laughed, her sea-green eyes twinkling and her shoulders bouncing up and down. "Why, Mr. DeWitt, I have been here a long time, and I've learned to roll with the punches, if you know what I mean. Her bark is way scarier than her bite once you get to know her, which I'm guessing you will! Now, let's look at your calendar and mine."

Carl just smiled and took a deep breath. Talking with Joanne put everything back into place, and he felt relaxed once more.

Later, much later, when he was alone in his classroom, Carl jumped up and shouted and laughed, thinking how scared he had been before and how excited and determined he was now to make this new program a fantastic success!

CHAPTER 6

Lunch was always a challenge for Cindy. Where to sit? Who to eat with? Nobody. Who to say hello to that would say hello back? Lunch was easier in elementary school because they'd had assigned seating. Even if nobody talked to you, at least you didn't have to sit alone. And then there was middle school. That had been awkward every day. Cindy had always made an excuse to eat as fast as she could while standing and then asked the teacher in charge if she could go to the media center to complete an assignment. This became such a routine that eventually, the teacher would just nod at Cindy as she approached her. It was a cursory nod, and Cindy would then make a quiet beeline to the media center. There was always a book to read, a computer to use, or she'd sit in the corner and listen to music with her secret headphones, which could have earned her a detention if she'd been caught.

But high school was so different. One lunch. One school. Four grades. That meant two thousand students walking around the building, eating, talking, texting, socializing.

All at once. Some snuck outside to smoke, to vape, to take a quick toke. In math class, she had overheard a few kids talking about meeting over the hill.

Cindy knew all this was happening. She wasn't stupid. She was just a loner. She liked it that way. It was easier than trying to be friends with someone and then having to explain why everything was a trigger, that everything made her heart go zigzag and made her want to throw up. Actually, she did throw up, but she always made it to the girls' room in time. *Damn it*, she thought. *Do I even know where all the bathrooms are in this building?*

Neva Waverly always enjoyed coming to the library during the lunchtime. She knew it was called the media center now, but calling it the library was "OG," and she liked that expression. Neva was well aware that kids who came to the library during lunch often used it as an escape, a hideaway from the chaos of the rest of the building. Yes, there were those kids who loved to read or use the computers or who just needed to feel the quiet, but Neva knew there were also those who used this secluded place as a security blanket of some kind.

At the beginning of every year, Neva would search the library looking for those ninth graders who were in need of belonging. These were the outcasts. Even the geeks had each other. Neva knew all about cliques, though she was never included in any growing up. There were the drama freaks, the girl jocks and the guy jocks, the brainiacs, the computer nerds, the music kids, the druggies, the students who didn't know English, the couples, and especially the mean girls. And then finally, to the school media center flocked the ones who didn't fit into any of those groups, no matter how hard they tried or how much they wanted to belong to any one of them.

So Neva would scoop up these lost souls and invite them to her room for lunch talks. Sometimes they would come to see what she meant by "lunch talks," and sometimes they were just curious as to why *they* had been invited to something. A few were so paranoid they thought she was trying to trick them into spontaneous counseling and never showed up. But Neva was always hopeful.

Neva spied Cindy in the corner of the library tucked behind the old reference books that no one used anymore. She knew Cindy had had a rough morning since she'd personally escorted her to her homeroom class, but goodness knew what had transpired since then. Neva wandered over to Cindy so quietly Cindy didn't notice her approaching.

"Cindy? Hi, remember me? I'm Mrs. Waverly. We met this morning outside my classroom."

Cindy jerked her head up as if an alarm had gone off. She stared up into Mrs. Waverly's clear green eyes that twinkled with sincerity. Cindy had a flashback of her morning episode, and for a quick minute, her stomach churned, and bile threatened at the back of her throat.

"Cindy? It's okay, hon. You're not in any trouble. I just saw you here, and I wanted to say hello again."

Cindy focused on the green-and-gray carpet. Specks of mud were scattered around her feet, and she counted them as a way of calming herself. Her therapist had suggested this technique—focus on something nonconfrontational and nonemotional, and let your breathing return to normal.

Mrs. Waverly waited patiently. She recognized that Cindy was working on some self-help routine by the way she waved her hands in front of her head and closed her eyes.

After a few minutes, Cindy looked up at Mrs. Waverly. She attempted to smile, but before she could commit to a relaxed moment, she had to glance surreptitiously around the media center to make sure no one was staring at her. *Phew*, she thought. *I escaped that major disaster!*

"Hi, Mrs. Waverly. Yes, I, uh, do remember you. And thank you again. I really appreciated your help this morning."

Mrs. Waverly grabbed the opportunity to have a conversation. "Do you mind if I sit down next to you?" And without waiting for an answer, Mrs. Waverly pulled out one of the dark green plastic chairs and eased herself down. "So," Mrs. Waverly continued as if the two of them had been talking for a long time, "how has the first day been going for you? First days can be a bit rough, I know, but I was hoping that by lunchtime, you would be starting to feel like your old self."

Cindy shrugged. "It's okay. I like my classes. I recognize some of my classmates from my middle school. It's just so big here."

Mrs. Waverly smiled. "Yes, a bit too big, if you ask me. But then again, nobody has asked me." Mrs. Waverly chuckled at her attempt to crack a joke. "Actually, Cindy, I was hoping to see you again today and invite you to come to my classroom during lunch break. I know so many of the students here like to roam the halls or stake out their favorite spot for the next four years, but there are some students who are not comfortable with those choices, so I offer another option."

Cindy wrinkled her nose and squeezed her eyes. *So now I'm a charity case. That's just great. One mistake this morning and I'm labeled for life.*

"Uh, thanks, Mrs. Waverly. That's very nice of you. I, well, I kinda like coming to the media center. I do my homework because I have so many other things to do when I get home."

"Oh, my, that is wonderful, Cindy. So, what do you do at home?"

"I, uh, well, you see, I . . ." Cindy struggled to find the words. How could she say she hurried home to sit in her room to avoid arguing with her mother all evening?

Mrs. Waverly picked up on the stalling tactic. "Hey, Cindy, it's all good. Listen, I have to go, but I did want you to know that I have students who like to come and chill in my classroom every day. They listen to music, do homework, talk about stuff, text—you know, whatever. The invitation is always there for you. Have a great rest of the day, and I hope we meet up again."

And with that, Mrs. Waverly got up, pushed the chair back, and continued walking around the media center. There were a few more students she wanted to invite to her room, and odds were they were sitting somewhere along the edges just like Cindy.

Cindy stared at Mrs. Waverly as she combed the room, stopping every now and then to speak with a student or two. The worried faces of those students slowly melted into smiles. *What's wrong with me?* Cindy thought. *I'm not the only kid she came to see. Maybe I will . . .*

Cindy placed her nose back in one of her Harlequin romance novels.

Mrs. Waverly waved goodbye to Donnie Skaler, the media specialist. "Thanks for your help, Donnie. Talk to you tomorrow!"

Neva had barely turned around to exit the media center when Beverly Winewrought plowed into her.

"Oh, Neva, I am so sorry!" whined Beverly. "I didn't realize you were there. I was so preoccupied with my phone. Oh, wow! I sound just like the kids, don't I?"

Neva did not like Beverly. She was a gossip and was always looking to stir up trouble.

But there were times when Neva felt there was something dark and secretive about Beverly, almost as if she were holding back something she didn't want anyone to know. A secret of sorts—or maybe more of a sad shadow that she hid under.

"You're fine, Beverly. I was just heading back to my room."

"Oh, and did you hear? Did you hear the latest? Why, I was sitting in the lounge minding my own business, of course, when that ol' Battle Axe Atkinson stormed in and read Carl the riot act. Goodness knows what kind of trouble poor Carl is in, and does he even have his tenure yet?

I don't know what he did, but I hope he doesn't get into too much trouble—"

Neva interrupted Beverly before she could finish her outburst. "I'm sure he's fine, Beverly. Did you actually hear what Ms. Atkinson said to Carl?"

"Well, no, I didn't hear her say anything specific, but, well, you know how it is! And the way she blew into the lounge and demanded to see him right away—I mean, she practically accused him of something. I'm sure of it."

"I'm sure it was nothing serious. Sorry, Beverly, I must get going now. Talk with you later." And with that, Neva pushed through the exit door and headed back to her room.

Beverly stood there, hands on her hips, and said in a threatening whisper to the closing door, "Tsk, tsk, tsk, you old woman. You think everyone is a goody-goody. Well, let's see how this debacle turns out. That Carl thinks he walks on water because everyone likes him, and now, well, he might need a new pair of water shoes!"

CHAPTER 7

Mattie Newport stared at her daughter, Cindy, as she entered their small home.

"How was your first day of school, baby?"

Cindy did not look at her mom. She hated these questions. Every. Single. Day. *What did you do today? Who did you see? What happened? Did anyone bother you? Did anyone make fun of you? Did you have any episodes?*

Cindy walked quickly to her bedroom and gently closed the door. Slamming it would only bring on the wrath of her mom, and the questions were tough enough without her losing her temper and screaming and banging on the walls. So Cindy retreated to the sanctity of her bedroom for peace. The soft blue walls were covered with posters that reflected Cindy: a sunset at the beach, snow-covered mountains, paths through the forest at fall, and her favorite, a full-blown poster of the cast from *Game of Thrones*. She dreamed of being Arya Stark, the girl with grit and strength. Sometimes at night, Cindy pretended she was

Arya and told off every mean girl who had ever looked at her with pity or disdain. Cindy was shaken out of her daydream by her mother's whiny voice.

"Cindy! Come out here right now, young lady! I need to talk to you. I received a phone call from your school today, and we need to talk. And I mean now. Don't make me break down your door . . . again!"

Cindy sighed. "Jeez, Mom. All right. I'm coming. I'm just changing my clothes. I'll be right out. Okay? Okay-a!"

Cindy threw her book bag on the floor next to her desk and undressed, changing from her everyday jeans and tee to her comfy sweatpants and her favorite but ripped Justin Bieber concert T-shirt. She would never be allowed to go to a concert, so Cindy bought the shirt at Target one day and pretended she went to see him on her own. It was a lie—a big lie—but it was one she loved to tell. It made her feel grown up, as if a big weight had been lifted off her shoulders. Cindy took a deep breath, opened the door, and prepared herself for yet another showdown with her mother, which always ended with her mother crying.

Mattie was waiting for Cindy in the kitchen. She had a fresh cup of coffee in her hand and was munching on a piece of day-old crumb cake she'd bought at the grocery store. She always got the best deals at the grocery store, mainly because she had been their best cashier for the past seven years.

Mattie took a sip of coffee and stared into space. *Yes, I'm the best cashier at the store because I'm the smartest one there.* Mattie had quit college after her first year. She'd gotten pregnant and had no choice. Her parents said she could stay home until the baby was a year old, and then she had to get out and get a job. *So much for my future career.*

The line was "I coulda been someone," and Mattie always said to herself, *Well, if you hadn't been stupid enough to get pregnant . . . But you were, so you deserve what you got!* She wasn't even sure who the baby daddy was.

Mattie tried not to get too caught up in her past. She still had dreams, and she'd always promised herself that when Cindy was grown up and ready to leave the house, she'd go back and get her degree. *I'm not done; that's for sure!*

Cindy slid into the kitchen and stood there scrutinizing her mother. Her mom was still young at thirty-three, her skin clear and unwrinkled, her dark brown hair pulled back with a scrunchie (did moms really wear scrunchies?). Her makeup accented her deep brown eyes, and although her trim figure was hidden underneath her store apron she always left on, Cindy's mom was someone men always stared at when they thought Cindy wasn't looking.

Her mother had had a rough go at it. Cindy knew it wasn't easy being a single mom, and though there were times she blamed her for not giving her a daddy, for not having enough money, for not having all the nice things her peers had, she knew her mother loved her. Loved her enough to make her crazy, but she knew deep, deep down inside that her mom worshipped her. Cindy hoped that one day, she could make her proud.

"Hey, Mom," Cindy said softly so as not to startle her. When her mom was deep in thought and Cindy snapped her out of her daze, she would jump a foot in the air and get all shaky and angry.

Mattie closed her eyes and opened them slowly. "Hey, baby girl. I was hoping you would come talk to me. I got a phone call from your school today."

Cindy was curious. She had done nothing wrong, so why on the very first day was her mom getting a call? "Yeah. So who called?" Cindy tried to act nonchalant about it, but she was getting that nervous sensation, and her heart fluttered out of control.

"Come sit down next to me, my girl. Let's talk about your day. Seems you had a bit of a rough start. That is, according to this teacher who called me. Her name is Weaver or Waver or something like that."

Cindy sighed. *Really?* This was what happened because of a simple problem like not knowing where to go because she was unfamiliar with the high school. Lost because her mother refused to let her go to freshmen orientation in the first place. *Ugh. Here we go.*

"Her name is Mrs. Waverly, and she was very nice to me. She helped me find my class this morning. Remember when *you* wouldn't let me attend the freshmen orientation because . . . I don't even know why anymore!"

Exasperated, Cindy walked over to the fridge and yanked it open, then pulled out a bottle of store-brand soda. "Yuck. Can't we ever buy real soda like Pepsi or Dr Pepper or anything other than this cheap stuff?" Cindy was losing it and fast. She didn't want to start hyperventilating but felt like she was spiraling out of control.

"Cindy, honey, it's okay," said her mom. "She wasn't upset with you at all. This teacher just wanted to make sure you were okay. She also wanted permission from me for you to attend some kind of program after school. Seems like some other teacher is putting together a thing of some sort—damn, I don't know what she called it, but it seemed like something that could really help you. She was really just calling to introduce herself to me, and—Cindy, what's wrong?"

Cindy was busy focusing on breathing. She took a slow, deep breath in and let it out, then did this several more times until the room stopped moving and the ringing in her ears ceased. She hadn't heard what her mom said, but at least she wasn't yelling at her. Cindy regained control of herself and sat down next to her mom.

Mattie took Cindy's hands in her own and held them tight. "Cindy, I know I should have let you go to that freshmen orientation. That's on me. I'm sorry. Part of me is afraid to let you go because, well, I still think of you as my little girl and—"

Cindy sighed. "Mom . . ."

"Okay, I know. I know. I have to realize you're in high school, but baby, it's not easy on me. At any rate, did you hear what I just told you? About the thing, I don't know what it's called. It's a thing Mrs. Waverly wants you to be a part of, and you know, honey, it might be a good thing for you. Especially if it gets you to be a part of something at the school. I want you to belong to something, Cindy. It's important." Mattie squeezed her hands. "How about we start dinner together and you tell me about your day? Huh? How was it? Did you like it? Did you like your teachers? What did they say? Who did you talk to today?"

Cindy moaned.

CHAPTER 8

The first week of school was finally over, with two successful fire drills, a few too many lost schedules, two fights—one of which included two girls and a boy—one distraught teacher, four super cranky parents, three suspensions, one overly demanding student government president, two whiny teacher representatives, and the ultimate pep rally to kick off the fall sports season.

Not a bad start, thought Lila. This was her tenth year as principal of Ida B. Wells High School, and she loved her life. She didn't mind it when she heard her students making fun of her school's name with comments like "I Bee Well" and "Wella, wella, wella here we are" because deep down inside, she knew how important Ida B. Wells was in history. After all, Lila was a former history teacher.

Lila Libertino, born and bred in the Bronx, New York, met her activist husband when he was involved in a civil rights protest at Columbia University. Lila, 99 percent Italian, blended exquisitely with Darrius Rummond, her

African American husband of twenty years. Undergraduate school, graduate school, and finally a doctorate in education completed her educational circle. But what she cherished most was the beautiful biracial family she and Darrius had created. Twelve-year-old Bessie and fifteen-year-old Benjamin, both named after famous African American firsts in their fields, completed Lila's dream of family and career.

Lila pushed her chair away from her desk, smoothed down her pants, and slipped on her special "walking the halls" shoes. She glanced at her family picture on her desk as she grabbed her walkie talkie and marched out of her office.

Amelia heard Lila approaching before she reached her desk. She looked up and smiled. "Heading out to check on the troops?" Amelia adored her boss. Lila was well respected by the staff, the students, and the community. She was all business, but her rapport with everyone was genuine and caring, and the atmosphere she oversaw was one of positivity and success. Every year Lila felt it necessary to have the newest educational quotes posted on the classroom walls and in the PTSA newsletters because she believed in them, and that transferred to everyone around her. These maxims were the cornerstone of her mission as a leader of the school; it grounded Lila and drove her to push her students and staff to the best of their abilities.

"I have my walkie turned on," Lila said. "If you need me, don't hesitate to give me a holler." She grinned at her secretary. Lila had arranged for Amelia to transfer with her to Wells after she was appointed principal. This job was so important, and Lila had worked side by side with Amelia for a few years at her previous school. Lila had known that Amelia would be the perfect balance she needed. She had placed the utmost trust in Amelia, and Amelia never let her down. Many teachers and especially parents would try to pry information from Amelia, but she was extremely skilled at safeguarding everything of Lila's, from private emails to classified conversations to confidential files that landed on her desk on a daily basis.

Lila waved goodbye, then greeted everyone she passed in the office before striding out into the hallway. The building was over fifty years old, but her maintenance crew kept it shining like new. Because of the way the building looked, everyone took pride in keeping it clean. So many things were critical to Lila, but few rarely saw the day-to-day list of these crucial items she attended to. This allowed others to focus on their jobs, from teaching and supporting to maintaining and feeding to coaching and more.

As Lila traveled the halls, students and staff alike waved, said hello, or high-fived her, and she loved every moment of it.

Lila made a point of visiting every classroom in every hall, if not all at once, at least by the end of each week. By week's end, she made sure she was visible in every corner and classroom and studio that existed in her building, along with the gym and cafeteria. Only one area bothered her. In the lower level, which housed the fine arts and music rooms, a hallway took a sharp ninety-degree turn and led to a steel door that opened to the extra storage containers. Lila did not like this corner; it was dark, isolated, and there was no camera back there that allowed her to observe any inappropriate behaviors such as drug deals or make-out sessions. One time, she found an empty wine bottle. So Lila made every attempt to make her way down to what was unofficially referred to as the "dark hall."

The late bell had sounded, so all students should have been in their classrooms, but Lila spied a young lady and a young man dashing down the hall, unaware their principal was only thirty yards behind them. Lila clicked the switch on her walkie and whispered, "Security. I need someone down in the storage back entrance. Now!" Lila switched her walkie off because she didn't want the response to tip off the two students as she approached.

As Lila turned that infamous corner, she heard giggling and shuffling and a few "umphs" and an "ouch!"

Lucas Cannon had his precious quarterbacking-callused hand all the way up the front of Jilly Castings' brand-new sweater that had cost her mom more money than she could afford to part with. Jilly swayed side to side as though she were drunk while Lucas's lips pressed against hers, causing them to relax and go slack, allowing him to slip his tongue inside her mouth. At the same time, Lucas fumbled his way up her stomach and lifted her bra, which she'd bought with her babysitting money. No one had ever touched Jilly that way, and it was exhilarating and frightening and painful all at the same time. Lucas's hand was so rough that Jilly felt like five nail files were crawling up her chest.

Girls LIKE this? she thought to herself. And more importantly, she pondered, *I wonder how many other girls have had his hand up their sweater—and on their breasts. Is he going to talk about this at football practice?*

So many thoughts ran through Jilly's head, while on the outside, she giggled (because she was too scared to push away and risk humiliation) and squirmed as Lucas made moaning sounds she had never heard before. Then her world turned ice cold.

"EXCUSE ME!"

Jilly and Lucas both turned their heads at once to see Dr. Lila Libertino staring at them with the coldest steel-gray eyes that could burn laser bolts into both of them and melt them right to the floor.

"And where do both of you belong, may I ask?" Lila asked in her most professional yet authoritative voice possible.

Before either student could respond, Lila's most trusted security leader, Scottie Sheldrake, along with his partner, Pauline Clifton, arrived on the scene.

"Take those hands off her, young man, and back away!" bellowed Scott, staring at Lucas with daggers in his eyes. Scott had retired from the police force a few years before and had worked in the sex crimes department for the past ten years of his career. He'd retired as a lieutenant, and the pain and suffering he had seen during his work would last him a lifetime.

Lucas froze. He looked at Jilly and realized his hand was still clutching her breast as though it were a lifeline.

He pulled his hand down her sweater and stuffed both his hands into his jean's pockets. Jilly's face burned with embarrassment, and she tried to adjust her loosened bra with one hand.

Pauline gently touched her on the elbow and softly said, "Come with me, girlfriend. You have some fixin' up to do, and we don't need to do that here."

And with that, Jilly was escorted away from Lucas, her principal, and the head of security. She wanted to collapse right then and there in the hallway, but Pauline held her tightly so she could lean on her. "It's okay, girl. PC is with you. Now come along, and we'll get you cleaned up right quick. What were you thinking back there, girl? You're not even old enough to be hiding down in that hallway, let alone with some boy playing around with you like that. Didn't your mama teach you right?"

Jilly's entire body was covered in chills. She was cold and shaking. She had never, never, ever been in trouble in school before. What had she been thinking? Had it really been just a few minutes ago that she and Lucas were in math class writing down their homework assignment? When the bell rang, Lucas had reached for her hand and pulled her so close to him she could smell his cologne. At that point, she'd lost all her self-control.

"Hi, Jilly," Lucas had murmured to her, grabbing her hand as they both walked out the door. "Uh, excuse me." Lucas bumped into Riley, who was trying to nudge herself in between Lucas and Jilly.

Riley snapped at Lucas. "Excuse me yourself, you big jock. This is my friend, and we are heading to our next class . . . *together*, if you don't mind." Riley was getting sick and tired of this guy who thought he was Mr. Cool and a bag of chips. Who was he to get in the middle of her and her best friend?

Just as the three of them were about to be in the throes of something destined to explode, Cindy tripped over her shoelace and collided into Riley's back.

"Umph!" Cindy blurted out. "I'm really sorry. I . . . uh . . . I tripped. Are you okay?"

Riley gathered herself after maneuvering and twisting her body so she wouldn't fall onto the floor, then looked up to see Cindy hovering over her bent body with smudgy glasses teetering over her greasy nose. Cindy's pinched face promised to unleash a torrent of tears. "Get out of my way, you nerd!" Riley slung her book bag over her shoulder and scanned the crowded halls, but Jilly and Lucas had melted into the swarm of students, and Riley could no longer see them.

"Argh! You really pissed me off! Get out of my way!" Riley stormed down the hall, bumping and knocking anyone in her way. She ignored the nasty comments hurled at her; she didn't care. Her best friend in the whole world had just dumped her for some guy. For some guy she barely knew! This was her worst day. Ever.

Cindy pushed her glasses back over her nose, unaware of the stares burning into her back. She slid over to the wall and crouched down to tie her shoe . . . again. "How many times a day do I do this?" she mumbled to herself. With her shoe tied, Cindy took a deep breath, let it out, and merged into the thick crowd, trying as best she could to become invisible once more on her way to her next class.

Jilly tittered. Lucas slyly slipped his hand into hers and guided her down the hall.

"It's okay," he promised. "I want to show you something."

Jilly had never received attention from a guy before. And especially not from one as popular as Lucas. She seemed to lose all self-control whenever he was near. It was like an out-of-body experience. She could not say no to him, and even when her best friend, Riley, tried to squeeze in between them after class, Jilly felt weak and unable to argue. She wanted to shout, "Hey, this is my best friend, Riley," but the only thing that came out was another stupid giggle.

Since when do I giggle? thought Jilly. *That's positively the grossest thing I have ever done.*

When that weird girl—Jilly didn't even know her name—tripped into Riley, Lucas took that as his cue and snatched her away, and they fled down the hall. It seemed as though the seas parted when she was with Lucas. *So this is what it feels like to be popular*, she mused. *And I'm with him!*

Lucas tightened his hold on Jilly and looked into her eyes. "You're the most beautiful girl I have ever seen," he said without taking a breath as they ran. "Your eyes look like the Emerald City in *The Wizard of Oz*!"

Not the most romantic description, thought Jilly, but he

was complimenting her nonetheless, and she was not used to such admiration from anyone.

Jilly dropped her head and held on to Lucas as he careened through the hallway. She couldn't talk as he hurled her along with him, as though she were the football he was trying to carry down the field for a touchdown. The hallways and the students around her became a blur until they both came to a halt. She wasn't sure where Lucas had taken her. The short hallway was dark. There were no windows along the walls, and at the end of the miniature hall was a heavy metal door held closed with a chain and a lock.

"Where are we?" She looked up at Lucas, but his eyes were glazed, as if he were deep in thought.

"Don't talk," he said breathlessly. He pulled Jilly close to him, and she could smell the minty Tic Tacs he must have eaten recently. She could count each of the long dark eyelashes that covered his deep blue eyes, which reminded her of ocean pictures from some faraway island. On his forehead were dried-up pimples she assumed were from wearing his helmet. He smiled and lifted her chin with his hand. The rough calluses on his hands rubbed against her smooth skin.

As Lucas leaned toward Jilly, his right hand tugged at her sweater, and she gasped at the thought of what he was about to do.

"It's okay, Jilly. It's okay. I think you are so pretty." And then his lips touched hers. He pressed hard against her mouth, trying to part her lips. Jilly's lips went slack, and his tongue penetrated her small mouth, scraping her teeth.

She giggled. *Why am I giggling?* Her cheeks were blazing, and his hardened hand lifted her bra, and—

"EXCUSE ME! And where do both of you belong, may I ask?"

CHAPTER 9

Jilly was ushered into Ms. Atkinson's office. She did not remember the long walk from that dark hallway to the girls' bathroom with Ms. Clifton, where she was allowed her to wash her face and adjust her bra and sweater.

Ms. Clifton had leaned against the bathroom wall and watched Jilly. She'd seen this all too often—the big popular jock drags the pretty innocent little nothing into a hallway and has his way with her. *When are girls going to learn that teenage boys do not use the brains God gave them until they are maybe thirty-five? Maybe.*

Pauline moved closer to Jilly. Jilly was starting to cry, and Pauline didn't want her to go completely ballistic right there in the bathroom. She put her arm on Jilly's shoulder.

Jilly could smell the scent of clean body wash and sweet lotion on Ms. Clifton. Her curly black hair was shiny, and her big gold earrings reflected the overhead bathroom lights.

"Jilly. Girl, it's going to be okay. Hey, the only thing you did wrong was allowing that boy to drag you someplace you shouldn't have been. You shoulda been in class. That was your first mistake. And your second mistake was letting a boy tell you what to do. Now finish washing your face and fix your sweater. It's all twisted in the front. Yeah, that's good. Now you listen to me. If ever you're not sure about what to do while you're here at Wells, you just say to yourself, 'What would Ms. PC want me to do?' And from there, it will be easy peasy. You hear me? You use my name any time you want to. You tell that person that Ms. PC is gonna get ahold of them, call their mama, and get them in a world of trouble."

Jilly looked up into the deepest darkest brown eyes she had ever seen. Ms. Clifton had the smoothest mahogany-toned skin. Without any hesitation, she reached up and hugged Pauline as tightly as she could. Pauline just smiled, her one gold-capped tooth shining.

Pauline stepped back and looked at Jilly. "Well, I guess you're not disheveled anymore, so it's time I took you over to the main office."

"Thank you, Ms. Clifton. Thank you so much. I was so scared. Well, I guess I really wasn't so scared until all of you showed up. I got carried away. I have never done anything like that in my life. What's going to happen to me? Are they going to kick me out of school? What . . . Oh, God, will my parents find out?" Jilly felt dizzy and on the brink of hyperventilating.

"Whoa, girl. Relax. PC is gonna take good care of you. Now breathe for me. That's it. Take a slow, deep breath—in, now out. Good girl. Okay. Another one. There you go."

Pauline gently brushed Jilly's blonde hair out of her face. "You going to be fine. Now let's see what the damage is going to be. I'm gonna have to take you to Dr. Libertino. She's a good woman. She's not going to drop you like a rock in the ocean. But whatever happens, just be sure to thank her and tell her you will never do anything like that ever again. You hear me, now?"

Jilly nodded up and down so hard her neck cracked. She followed Pauline out of the bathroom like a robot and all the way to the office. Jilly stared up at Ms. Clifton as they were coming around the corner to the main office. She was the nicest woman Jilly had ever met. Jilly was not the kind of student who knew all the security guards. She'd barely known who the principal was back in middle school, and now she was sitting in the assistant principal's office, where the principal had pretty much dumped her and told the assistant principal in their code to deal with her.

What did that mean? Did administrators have a secret language that only they knew? What was going to happen to her? Was she going to be suspended? Maybe expelled? She had never even thought of the consequences. *Oh crap. How could I be so dumb? So stupid!* To think Riley had been trying to save her, and she had completely ignored her best friend. If she still had a best friend . . .

Jilly stared into space. She didn't notice all the diplomas hanging on the wall testifying that Ms. Atkinson was indeed qualified for her position as assistant principal. She didn't observe the framed pictures of former students, an astronaut hugging Ms. Atkinson, other pictures of unknown adults and Ms. Atkinson, or the ceramic bowls and vases that lined her bookshelves. No, Jilly was utterly unaware of any of the décor Barbara Atkinson had so carefully arranged. Barbara wanted her office to look official yet friendly, casual yet filled with memories of important people and her special connections. None of these attempts were successful when it came to Jilly, who swayed back and forth in her chair awaiting her sentence and silently praying for compassion, hoping this administrator, whoever she was, would be kind and understanding of her stupid mistake.

Jilly was very grateful there had been no students in the hall when she was escorted to the office while classes were in session. Where she should have been! How could she have allowed Lucas to take her to a secret hallway? And then? He had kissed her. Really kissed her. Jilly touched her lips, unaware she was doing it in front of Ms. Atkinson. Her lips felt swollen. Bruised even. How was she going to explain that to her mother? Her father? And then his hand. *Oh, no! Oh, no!* He had put his hand on her breast! No one had done that to her. Ever, ever, ever.

Ms. Atkinson handed Jilly the phone.

Jilly looked up. "Huh?"

"It's your mother, Jilly. She wants to speak with you. Now."

"What? I . . . I can't talk to her. I can't . . ." Jilly's eyes filled with tears. What was this woman trying to do to her?

"Jilly"—Ms. Atkinson raised her voice—"take the phone now and talk to your mother. She's waiting."

Jilly mechanically raised her hand and took the phone. "Heh . . . heh . . . hello?"

Jilly listened to her mother on the other end of the line, her eyes filling with tears and overflowing onto her reddened cheeks.

"Yes, Mom. Yes, Mom. I know. I'm sorry. I'm so sorry." Jilly couldn't handle any more conversation with her mother. She stood up and gently placed the phone handle on the desk, then sat back down, her head falling into her hands and her shoulders heaving up and down with her sobs.

Ms. Atkinson talked quietly to her mother. "Hmm, yes. Okay . . . Yes, that's something I really want to discuss with you. We can talk tomorrow. Yes, thank you. Goodbye."

Jilly could not lift her head. She was so humiliated and embarrassed and angry with herself.

Barbara Atkinson looked at the young ninth grader. How many times had she had to deal with this same scenario? As much as she respected Lila, she didn't appreciate that she always dropped these cases on her desk. Why not give this to Jeff Stineman? He was such a weasel assistant principal; he always slithered out of these difficult cases.

Barbara stood up. She came around her desk and pulled the other chair close to Jilly. Barbara hated being labeled as a softy and had embraced the nickname she heard others call her: Battle Axe. As if she didn't know what the staff called her behind her back. And she would not give them the satisfaction of discovering the nickname they were so fond of was anything but the truth.

"Jilly," Barbara began her reprimand. "Do you realize how much trouble you're in?"

Jilly looked up, her lips and her eyes swollen from crying to the point that Barbara wanted to call the nurse in to make sure Jilly was okay.

Jilly nodded and hiccuped. She wanted to say something, but the words lodged in her throat, drowning her. She wanted to say how sorry she was, how stupid a mistake it was, and that she would never do this again, but when she opened her mouth, nothing came out.

"Okay, Jilly, here's the deal. I want you to stay with Ms. Clifton for the rest of the afternoon because you are in no condition to go back to class. Then I want you to go straight home, and first thing tomorrow morning, you are to report back to me with your parents."

At the mention of her parents, Jilly's puffy eyes blinked uncontrollably. "Why do they have to come in?"

"Well, Jilly, first, I'm glad you've found your voice. Second, there is the matter of your actions today, and quite honestly, I'm not sure you are completely aware of the many rules you broke. I don't want to keep you after school today, but I'm going to present something to your parents tomorrow that I am hoping they will accept. In other words, you should be suspended for your actions today. Let's see, cutting class, hiding in the back hallway with a boy while committing inappropriate behaviors per our school handbook. However, this was your first infraction; therefore, I would like to discuss a special opportunity we have here at Wells with your parents. It is a program I want you involved in. They will need to give permission for you to join, but I feel this is the best decision for you. Do I make myself clear?"

And with that, Ms. Atkinson got up, pushed her chair back, and grabbed her walkie talkie. "Ms. Clifton," she barked into that black box, "I need you to come to my office immediately."

CHAPTER 10

Lucas Cannon slouched in his chair inside Assistant Principal Jeff Stineman's office. Scott Sheldrake, head of security, leaned against the window box in Jeff's office, his muscular frame blocking the few rays of the late sun. He glared at Lucas, hoping his laser beam dark brown eyes were burning a hole in the back of the young teenager. Scott was supportive and understanding of the students, but he rarely felt compassion when a teenager was found taking advantage of another, especially a female who was an innocent victim.

Jeff Stineman leaned back in his executive chair, his pudgy fingers linked together behind his balding head. At fifty-five years old, Mr. Stineman was a career assistant principal with no hopes of ever running his own school. He didn't care. *Let the stuff float up,* he always thought, *so I don't have to be left holding the trash.* He was not a team player. It didn't matter to him what school he was working in or what principal he was working for because at some point, the tides always changed, and he was content to drift along for the ride. He might have been at Wells for over twenty years, but his loyalty was not sewn into the purple-and-white school jacket he wore every day regardless of the weather.

Jeff's wife had left him—how many years had it been now? Maybe seven or eight. And with his two adult children out on their own, he was all alone. He only saw his children on his birthday and maybe a holiday now and again. It didn't bother him. A few emails and texts here and there were more than enough communication to keep him feeling involved.

Jeff eyed Lucas. The brown curly hair on top of Lucas's head fell in small coils over his forehead, covering his eyes. Lucas let his head drop onto his chest, appearing defeated. At least that was the impression Jeff assumed Lucas was going for at the moment. He knew the game Lucas was trying to play—subservient, apologetic, passive, even a bit obsequious. It wasn't going to pass muster with Jeff. He looked over at Scott. Both men knew the drill; they had delivered this tête-à-tête numerous times over the years.

"Well, Mr. Sheldrake," began Mr. Stineman in his outraged disciplinarian tone, "tell me about young Lucas here. What's his story?"

Scott stood up from his perch by the window, adjusted his uniform pants, and walked over to Lucas. "You see, Mr. Stineman"—Scott cleared his throat as though a long-winded explanation was about to commence—"Lucas is no stranger to me. Even though we are still early in the first semester, Lucas was brought to me several times over the summer during football practice."

Scott looked down at Lucas, waiting for Lucas to acknowledge this introduction. Lucas refused to lift his head, so Scott continued. "There was a horrible incident this summer in the boys' locker room. Seems several of the freshmen had painted some awful racial slurs on a few specific lockers in the football section. Of course, we could not identify any of the culprits because, well, you know, we cannot have cameras placed anywhere in the locker room according to code.

"We interviewed the entire junior varsity team, Lucas included. And wouldn't you know, Lucas Cannon's name was brought up multiple times as being a ringleader in this activity. That is according to several of the boys who were willing to fess up as long as they were not going to get caught for 'snitching.'"

At this point, Lucas's head shot straight up, his blue eyes tinged with broken red lines and a sneer so tightly pressed his lips were void of all color. "I . . . I was not . . ." Lucas slumped back in his chair, as if any conversation at this point might open a door he was not willing to go through, implicating him in something far worse.

"The coach," continued Scott, "felt that Lucas, while a strong leader on the field, might need some off-the-field time and gave Lucas a week off. Lucas was sent to the security team for the week to help us prepare the lockers for the opening of school."

Lucas, squirming in his seat, looked bitterly at Scott.

This was not going well, he thought but continued to remain silent. He hated being away from football, and working for security was not his idea of a good time, especially considering he didn't get paid to do their dirty work.

"Lucas fulfilled his part of the deal, which was to help our security team out for the week before he could return to summer practices. He wasn't the most congenial helper, if you know what I mean . . ."

Lucas looked up at Scott and scrunched his eyes. He did not know what *congenial* meant, but he was sure it wasn't a compliment.

"At any rate, Lucas did his time and returned back to practice the next week. Unfortunately, we have had a few other instances of vandalism which I did not report to you, Mr. Stineman, because I was hoping I could investigate them on my own. Looks like we resolved the issue, I think."

Lucas sat up in his chair, this time rounding his shoulders and clearing his throat. "I was nowhere near the back wall of the gym."

Scott eyeballed Lucas, then turned to Jeff. "I never said where the vandalism was found." Scott tilted his head in Lucas's direction. "We have power washed the area and have installed new cameras at the back of the building, so I know there will be no more incidents."

Lucas knew his face was flushed, and he rubbed the palm of his hand over his forehead, collecting small droplets of sweat, which he quickly wiped on his pants.

"So, Lucas has not been what we call in the business a 'model student,' and today he was caught cutting class, hiding in the hallway near an emergency exit with a female student. In addition to those infractions, I believe I was told there were some inappropriate activities going on between the two of them. Am I correct in all of this?" Mr. Stineman asked.

Before Scott could answer, Jeff interrupted and added, "Lucas, I need you to respond to this. Is everything I just said true?"

Lucas focused on Mr. Stineman, trying to appear nonchalant and rather offended that he was even being pressed to explain his actions. "Yeah."

"Come again?" said Mr. Stineman. "I could not hear you very clearly."

"I said, yeah. I was in the hall with some girl. What of it?"

Scott edged closer to Lucas. He didn't like the tone of this arrogant student who was in no position to come across this way.

Mr. Stineman had had enough. It had been a long day, and he wanted to leave early because he had to return that evening for a PTSA meeting. "Okay, Lucas. We're going to be done here in just a few minutes. You're racking up quite a bit of negative points with regard to your behavior here at Wells. As of now, you will be serving five after-school detentions with no football practice this week."

Lucas rose from his seat. "But I—"

"Sit down! Another thing I want to make perfectly clear to you: if your behaviors do not change—and I mean as of today—we will begin paperwork to have you transferred to another school. I believe the kids refer to that school as 'the institution for the best of the worst,' and right now, you are heading in that direction. Do I make myself clear?"

Lucas glared at Mr. Stineman.

"I don't believe you answered my question, young man. Do I make myself clear?"

Lucas sneered. "Yeah, as clear as mud, man."

Scott wanted to take this presumptuous student outside and tell him a thing or two, but that would never be allowed, so he took a deep breath and looked at Jeff. "Do you want me to take him back to class, Mr. Stineman?"

"No," replied Jeff. "I think he can spend the rest of the day with security in your in-school program. I'm sure he'll have some work to catch up on after today. That's all, Mr. Sheldrake. Thank you for your assistance in this matter." His gaze hardened a fraction. "And Lucas? I hope this is my last time seeing you for disciplinary matters."

Lucas grunted, stood up, and followed Mr. Sheldrake out of the office.

Jeff sighed. *I have a feeling I'm going to see a lot more of that boy before too long.* And with that, he picked up his phone and called Lucas's parents to explain what had just transpired.

As Lucas was walking out of the office, he noticed Jilly sitting in the other assistant principal's office, her head in her hands and her shoulders bobbing up and down. Lucas assumed she was crying. *All girls gotta do is cry, and everyone feels sorry for them. Gets them out of trouble. Me, I'm in trouble now, and God knows what's going to happen when I get home.*

CHAPTER 11

Jilly's parents had not been to the high school in quite a few years. Jilly was their fifth and youngest child, with a ten-year gap between her and the twins. Jilly's mom, Jackie, and her dad, Alfred, had thought the twins were the end of their child-bearing years, and Jilly was definitely a surprise. Jackie's once shiny blonde hair was now a lackluster yellow, and her green eyes were no longer bright as emeralds. She was tired, and Alfred, with his silver hair and hazel eyes that still twinkled when he smiled, was not much help. A great dad when it came to playing ball with the boys, Alfred was a hands-off dad when it came to Jilly, claiming ignorance with young girls—especially teenage ones.

They were completely flabbergasted when a Ms. Atkinson had phoned them yesterday and described what Jilly had been found doing in some hallway with some boy when she should have been in class. That was not the Jilly they knew—the Jilly who still had her American Girl dolls lined up on her dresser and a stack of *Seventeen* magazines piled in the corner of her room. Boxes of doll accessories lined her closet, and sweatpants, biking shorts, and Skechers were strewn across the floor. When had she grown up? When had teenage hormones burst onto the scene, making her lose all sense of decency and morality?

They'd barely spoken to Jilly all night. They guessed she was embarrassed, humiliated, and too ashamed to talk to them, so Mom and Dad gave her space. But before they did, they'd demanded she turn over her cell phone and unplug her laptop. "No social media tonight," they'd said. "You don't need to pour out your heart to anyone who will listen. You need to reflect on your actions and pray for forgiveness."

Now Mr. and Mrs. Castings opened the door to the main office and stopped at the first desk. Cassandra Conway—according to her nameplate—greeted them with a smiling and compassionate face.

"Good morning. You must be Jilly's parents." Cassandra studied the two parents. They were uncomfortable and tired-looking, and she assumed they wanted to be anywhere other than where they were standing. Jilly was quietly standing behind her parents attempting to be as invisible as possible.

Jilly's parents nodded in unison. "Yes, we're here to see Ms. Atkinson."

Cassandra nodded and smiled. "I'll tell her you're here. Why don't the three of you have a seat over there and relax? Ms. Atkinson is probably in the halls right now."

Jilly tugged on her mother's light blue sweater. "Mom, come on." Jilly could barely get the words out.

Jilly's mom turned and followed with Alfred in tow. Alfred had wanted to go to work this morning instead, but Jackie had admonished him. "How dare you try to avoid your daughter at this crucial time in her life? For God's sake, Alfred, the girl needs us both right now. Perhaps if you had given her some of your precious attention, she wouldn't have begged for it from some boy!"

Alfred, feeling completely out of his element, plodded slowly behind Jackie and sat with his two ladies, as he'd liked to say before all of this happened. Now he didn't know what to say or how to feel.

Jilly sat between her parents, her knees shaking up and down. She was nervous, and that stemmed from being a pleaser. She wanted to please her parents, her friends, and hell, even Lucas.

Jilly stared blankly into the dark blue carpet until somebody came to stand in front of her. Jilly looked up to see a male teacher she did not recognize. Being a freshman, she didn't know all the teachers in the building. She didn't mean to stare at him, but she was curious. He had on beige Dockers, a button-down white shirt, and a dark purple sweater with the letters *WHS* stitched in white. His brown hair suggested he did not know how to use a brush, and his thick black-rimmed glasses reflected the overhead lights, preventing Jilly from seeing his eyes.

"Uh, good morning, Mr. and Mrs. Castings," he said to

her parents. Carl DeWitt had slipped into the main office, and after a few moments of chatting with Cassandra, he'd asked where the Castings were. Cassandra had quickly pointed to the corner, and Carl had walked over to greet the family.

"My name is Carl DeWitt. I teach social studies. And I—"

Before he could say anything else, Ms. Atkinson burst into the main office. Her hair was askew, as though she'd run down the hall, and her suit jacket was missing a button, allowing her blouse to spill through the opening, adding to her disheveled appearance. "Hello. Good morning," she snapped a bit too loudly. "You must be Jilly's parents. I'm Ms. Atkinson. Can you please come along with me?"

Barbara Atkinson barely acknowledged Carl, but as she turned, racing toward her office, she put one hand up in the air and called out, "And Mr. DeWitt, if you please, come along as well."

Ms. Atkinson's office had been rearranged to allow everyone to sit at her round table in the corner. She pulled the walkie talkie out of her waistband, clicked it off, and set it on her desk. Then she walked over to her door, gently closed it, and stood looking at the group.

"Good morning, everyone. Jilly, Mr. and Mrs. Castings, I am so glad you could come this morning. Oh, in case you have not met Mr. DeWitt, I have invited him to our meeting as well, and I'll explain why in just a few moments.

"Now, to the heart of the matter. Jilly, I don't know if you had a conversation with your parents last night. I truly hope so, but regardless of that, I need you to explain what happened to Mom, Dad, and me—oh, and Mr. DeWitt, of course."

Alfred Castings seemed a bit put off. "Excuse me. I know we're here to discuss Jilly's inappropriate actions yesterday, but is there some reason her teacher needs to be here as well?"

Carl adjusted himself in his chair, feeling a bit awkward, especially considering he wasn't completely sure why he was there either. He'd received an email that morning telling him—not asking him—to report to a parent conference with Jilly Castings and her parents first thing before school started, no explanation included.

"Mr. Castings, if you wouldn't mind giving me just a few moments prior to explaining Mr. DeWitt's role in this matter. And Mr. DeWitt does not teach Jilly this semester."

"So why is he part of this?"

It peeved Barbara to no end when she wasn't given the opportunity to explain herself. She glared at Mr. Castings, who promptly zipped his lips in response.

"And so, Mr. and Mrs. Castings, as I stated earlier, I would like Jilly to explain exactly what transpired yesterday. Jilly? You may begin now."

Jilly lifted her trembling chin and looked at her mom, then her dad. Her pale green eyes immediately swelled with tears that overflowed onto her reddened cheeks. She tried to speak, but her lips quivered uncontrollably.

Mrs. Castings reached over for her daughter's hand and

held it tightly. This was too painful for her to bear. Her daughter had never been in trouble in school and rarely caused problems at home. To see Jilly so shaken in front of everyone caused an ache in her heart.

Barbara reached for the box of tissues she kept on her desk and placed it on the table. She wasn't heartless, but she had seen this scene play out too many times, and it didn't move her as much as it might move someone else.

"Okay, Jilly, take a breath now and let's get this out. You have had all night to think about what happened. It isn't the worst thing in the world, but you broke several rules yesterday. Let's start with the first one."

Jilly looked at Ms. Atkinson. *I want to crawl under this table and never come out again.* She'd messed up yesterday and had cried all night. Couldn't she just leave her alone?

"You skipped your math class yesterday. Is that correct?"

Jilly let her chin fall to her chest. She nodded.

"And you went with another student. Is that correct?"

Again, Jilly nodded.

"And, well, to save everyone from further embarrassment, I believe that when Dr. Libertino found you at the end of the hallway where there are no cameras, poor lighting, and an emergency exit, you were in a very compromising position with another student. A boy. Is that correct?"

Jilly scrutinized Ms. Atkinson. She did not see a compassionate adult in front of her. Instead, Jilly saw a cold statue who might actually be enjoying this horribly uncomfortable encounter. Jilly pulled her shoulders back and squared her face. She wasn't going to give in to this person who did not know her and, from the looks of it, was relishing putting her through this torture.

"Yes!" Jilly's voice cracked a bit. "Yes, okay? I cut class and ran down the hall with Lucas, and yes, we were in that dark hall, and he was holding me and . . . and . . . Are you satisfied now, you—" Jilly stopped there. If she'd kept going, it would not have been something she could have ever recovered from. Jilly snapped her mouth shut and stared at Ms. Atkinson.

"Well, I think that about sums it up. Thank you, Jilly." Barbara turned to Jilly's parents. "And now, Mom and Dad, while everything that Jilly stated is correct, I want you to know that there are very specific consequences for her actions. Actually, everything from after-school detention to suspension."

At that, Mrs. Castings gasped. "But—"

Ms. Atkinson intervened. "Look, Mr. and Mrs. Castings, I remember your twins, Timmy and Jimmy. I worked with them all four years. Great boys. I hope they're doing well."

Mrs. Castings looked at her husband and then at Ms. Atkinson. "Why, yes," she said. "They are both incredibly involved in their careers and . . ." Mrs. Castings stopped there. She didn't want this to become a comparison study of her family. "So, what consequences will my Jilly have to deal with at this point?" She was tired of seeing her daughter treated like a criminal and wanted this conference to be over.

"I'm glad you asked," Ms. Atkinson said. "And that is

why I've asked Mr. DeWitt to attend this meeting. I have asked Mr. DeWitt, along with another veteran teacher, to head a new program for our students. This program will begin next week, and I would like to forgo any of the usual consequences for Jilly if she agrees to be a part of the program."

Jilly's eyes widened.

"You see"—Ms. Atkinson's voice had an overabundance of excitement in it now—"Mr. DeWitt and several other faculty members will be extending an invitation to select students to join a mentoring program. We want our students to be a part of a much bigger mission than just attending school. The program has many merits, but I don't want to steal Mr. DeWitt's thunder. He and Mrs. Waverly, an English teacher, will be heading the program, and I think Jilly would enjoy the interactions of this group.

"Mr. DeWitt, I want to turn this next part over to you so you can share the vision of your program and why, after hearing about Jilly's mistake yesterday, you think she might benefit from being a member of this new group."

And with that, Ms. Atkinson got up, grabbed her walkie talkie, and left the room. Mr. DeWitt stared after her with a dumbfounded expression. He was not prepared for this at all and had to get ready for his first period class, but he'd been left holding the mic, so to speak.

He turned back to Jilly and her parents, and for the next twenty minutes, he shared exactly what he was hoping to accomplish. Afterward, he, Jilly, and her parents exited Ms. Atkinson's office.

Mr. DeWitt turned to Mr. and Mrs. Castings and shook their hands. "Thank you for listening to me. I look forward to working with Jilly this year. And thank you for believing in the program. And Jilly . . ." Carl turned to her and said softly, "You did fine back there. I'm very proud of you. I know we're going to get along just great. Now, you have a good day, and I'll see you soon."

Carl DeWitt left the main office and whisked down the hall in a hurry to get to his classroom.

Jilly turned to her mom and grabbed her in a bear hug. "Thanks, Mommy," she said through more tears. "For being here for me. I won't let you down. I promise."

Mrs. Cumberly waved her over. "Hi, Jilly. I'm Ms. Atkinson's secretary. Here's your pass to class. The bell just rang, honey, so hurry up and get going. Say goodbye to Mom and Dad for now."

Jilly took the late pass, waved to both her parents, scooted out of the office, and raced down the hall.

Mr. and Mrs. Castings stood in the office, frozen for a moment. It had all happened so quickly. They were still not sure what was going to transpire, but for now, they were relieved it was over. Mr. Castings, in a new gesture, took his wife's hand in his, and they both walked out of the office.

CHAPTER 12

As Neva walked into Carl's room, she smiled at the poster on his podium:

EVERYONE
is welcome here

She sat down at the round table across from Carl. She'd known Carl since he'd started teaching at Wells. He was an eager, passionate young teacher who loved his subject and his students and reveled in his role as deliverer of knowledge. She looked around his room and made a quick inventory of the kinds of posters, decorations, and artifacts that defined Carl DeWitt. Neva had always believed the way a teacher embellished their room was a clue to how deep their love of teaching ran. The classroom was a mirror to an educator's soul. She observed how eclectic Carl's choices of posters were, covering almost all the wall space available.

The various artwork ranged from portraits of Martin Luther King Jr. and John F. Kennedy to Famous Women in Sports and Women's History Month: Famous Firsts to numerous maps of the United States and the world. There was a poster declaring that *Diversity creates Dimension in our World*. Other posters advertising the historical theme of the month hung over low shelves of books. Finally, Neva spotted a poster depicting the local Maryland politicians hanging side by side with a copy of the Constitution and the Declaration of Independence. She smiled to herself as she studied the poster of politicians and reminisced over the familiar faces she recalled from her youth.

"So, Mr. DeWitt," Neva began. "I am very happy to be working with you on this mentoring project. I've been wanting to start this for the last few years, and finally, I was given the go-ahead from Ms. Atkinson. I knew I couldn't do this great work alone, so I asked for another teacher to help me." Neva smiled. "Actually, if you want to know the truth, Mr. DeWitt, I specifically asked for you."

Carl sat up, and his eyes opened in surprise. "Wow. I mean, that's really cool. I appreciate your belief in me. Can I ask why me? I mean, there are so many other teachers in this building who have been here for years and know the ropes and—"

"Carl," interrupted Neva. "Can I call you Carl?"

Carl nodded vigorously, almost knocking his glasses off his nose.

"You see, Carl, I have been here for a long time, and I know many, if not all, of the teachers at Wells. And there are a goodly number of teachers; however, I wanted to include a teacher whose passion for our kids was obvious. I can see your love of teaching when you interact with your students in the halls, in the cafeteria, and especially in the classroom. When I walk by your room and hear you lecturing with such finesse and love of your subject, well, my heart swells with pride. I've heard the students laughing at your comments or calling out with enthusiasm. It's very clear to me how much they respect and enjoy your class."

Carl was nonplussed. "I, uh . . . I can't thank you enough. I do love teaching. I always have. I knew I wanted to teach ever since I was a little kid and set up my own classroom just for my brother and sister in our basement. Hell, I had so much fun back then, I couldn't think of any other job I wanted to pursue."

Neva sat back, crossed her arms over her chest, and smiled. "And that's exactly why I want you to be a part of this program. Now, let's get started."

For the next two hours, Neva and Carl talked, laughed, planned, scribbled notes, and got to know each other's desires and visions for making the mentoring curriculum a huge success.

Beverly Winewrought walked down the hall by herself. It was after four o'clock and time to go home, but she was in no hurry. *Why rush home only to have to deal with Teddy?* It didn't matter what she cooked for dinner or what plans she had to share with him; if he was in a mood, Beverly wasn't going to have a good night. She had thought he was different. She'd thought he would be a good partner. *Boy, was I ever wrong!*

Beverly heard laughter coming from Carl DeWitt's room. She couldn't imagine what was going on this late in the afternoon in there. She slowed her pace to almost a crawl as she reached his room. She didn't want to intrude—after all, she had no clue who was in there—so Beverly gently placed one hand on the wall next to the door and leaned in as closely as she could without tripping into the room.

She took out her phone and texted:

> You are not going to believe what I am hearing!

Beverly stood outside Carl's room and listened to a private conversation that, taken out of context, gave a very wrong impression.

Neva Waverly laughed about a student. *How inappropriate*, thought Beverly, but she continued to eavesdrop.

"And then," said Neva, "the salesman asked her for the bracelet in her backpack, and that's when she crumbled to the floor crying."

"Oh, no!" exclaimed Carl, laughing hard. "How could she have talked her way out of that debacle!"

Neva dropped to a whisper, so Beverly couldn't hear what else was said, which meant she missed some important context. "My sister was so bad as a young girl that my mother and father were clueless as to what to do," Neva said. "Her shoplifting stories are indeed very funny, but she could have been arrested that time and so many other times. She was skilled at lying and weaving these incredible stories. But as funny as some of her illegal escapades were, I was very worried the storytelling would not always save her. That's when I knew I had to get involved with her. To this day, she still calls me her savior. I think that's a bit much, but it certainly left a mark on my life. Maybe it was a calling, or at least a clue, as to what I wanted to do with the rest of my life. I love helping kids. I love letting the light shine in on them so they can see there is more to them, more for them to grab hold of, and especially more for them to achieve if only they believe in themselves."

"And what is your sister doing now?" Carl asked softly in case the response would bring more hurt.

"I'm glad you asked. My sister, the storyteller, is a journalist for a big newspaper on the West Coast. She found her calling, and I am so, so proud of her."

Carl nodded, his eyes glazing over as a sudden rush of memory flooded his mind.

I was sitting in the lunchroom by myself—always by myself as the new kid in school. Mom and Dad, who always argued with each other, had decided a temporary separation was the only answer, so we left Dad to live on his own in the house for a while. Mom took me, my brother, and my sister, and we moved back to the home where she'd grown up, only now, it was just her father—my grandpa—there. He was ancient to me then. He could barely hear me, and his quick hand would smack my head if I wasn't fast enough with the paper or his pipe. Grandma had passed years before of a painful cancer that ate her body and her soul. Mom still cried when we went to the cemetery—deep, gulping sobs that made her shoulders tremble. Eventually Mom and Dad got back together and bought a summer home with the hope to rekindle their relationship.

As I sat at the lonely table in the lunchroom, different boys walked by me and slapped me on the head when the teachers were too busy chitchatting to notice. "Hey, Carl da NitWitt!" they teased—a daily torment because I was unable to keep up with them on the playground. I was not very coordinated, but I could embarrass them in the classroom, and that only infuriated them even more.

"Carl," called Neva. "Are you all right? I thought I lost you for a moment."

Carl closed his eyes tightly, then opened them to see Neva staring at him with a worried expression.

"Oh, I'm okay. I guess your story about your sister had me thinking back to my own childhood for a second."

"Well, some of our stories are indeed funny," remarked Neva, but seeing the heartbreaking forgotten look in Carl's eyes, she added, "and some of the events in our past are sad and hurtful."

Carl nodded and got up. He went to grab his water bottle from his closet by the door and heard a shuffling sound in the hallway. Carl stepped out into the hallway to see Beverly Winewrought on her knees scooping up several notebooks scattered on the floor.

"Here, let me help you," Carl said, his voice tight as if

he were having trouble catching his breath. He dropped to his knees and started picking up student notebooks when he noticed Beverly's cheeks were quite flushed. "Are you okay?" he asked.

Beverly was embarrassed to have been found right outside Carl's door, much less on the floor with her student work scattered across the hallway.

"I, uh . . . I must have tripped over myself as I was walking by," muttered Beverly.

Beverly cradled her cell phone in her hand. It sounded like it was blowing up with text messages, as though a statewide emergency were in effect.

"Is everything okay?" questioned Carl. Beverly's cell phone was always attached to her hand as an added appendage. He couldn't see the text messages on her phone, but they were lighting up like a series of fireworks.

"Of course!" snapped Beverly. "I just have a lot going on right now. And besides, the noise coming from your room distracted me as I was walking by, and that's why I tripped, and . . ." Beverly stopped, frozen in her bent-over position as she saw Carl staring at her forearm. Beverly always wore long-sleeve blouses or large sweaters to cover up any telltale signs of what she called "Teddy Tantrums," but it was too late. A bruise, only a few days old, in varying shades of blues and purples, roped around her forearm like a tattoo gone wrong.

Beverly quickly pulled her sleeve down over the markings, but it was too late. Carl's eyes widened, and he gasped.

"Beverly . . . Have you had that looked at by the nurse?"

Carl probed cautiously; he knew from prior experiences what the mark was quietly screaming. Beverly had been abused. *By whom?* he wondered. But he knew it was not his place to question or push.

Beverly ignored Carl. She grabbed the rest of the notebooks on the floor and shoved them into her satchel. She looked at Carl for a brief second, her eyes pleading for him to not ask any more questions. Then she reached out for the few notebooks he had picked up, and Carl, fumbling with his load, almost dropped all of them. He adjusted his hands to gather the notebooks and gently handed them to Beverly.

"Thanks," she whispered, but then her tone shifted from shame to anger as she spoke with a threatening and flat affect. "And next time I find you busy laughing about our students, I'm going to report you, Carl DeWitt!" She stood up, turned around, and dashed down the hall as though her life depended on it.

Carl stood up, totally flummoxed as to exactly what had just transpired. "Huh?" he said. *What the hell was that all about?*

CHAPTER 13

Riley flopped forward in her seat with her head resting on her crossed forearms so she could cast a furtive glance at everyone around her in English class. Two rows over was Lucas, the dumb jock who had gotten her best friend in a world of trouble. Three seats behind Riley was Jilly, who sat ramrod straight in her chair. Jilly was not talking to Riley, no matter how many texts Riley had sent her.

First, it was simply *hey, how r u?* This was followed by *where r u?* Then, *r u even on ur fone?* Riley had been about to give up when she finally got her answer: *This is Jilly's dad. Jilly does not have her cell with her, so please stop texting. Phone is off!*

"Excuse me, Ms. Maddox!"

Glazed-eyed Riley didn't hear Mrs. Waverly calling her name. Riley felt a sharp jab on her shoulder. She turned around to see Junay Phame, class president and all-around teacher's pet in every single class.

"Riley!" hissed Junay. "Pay attention! Mrs. Waverly is talking to you!"

"Huh?" Riley turned back around to find Mrs. Waverly hovering by her desk, her large hands resting on her hips, her head cocked to the side and her lips a bit pinched.

"Welcome back, Riley," said Mrs. Waverly, trying very hard not to sound too sarcastic. "As I was saying to Riley"— she paused and looked around as she sauntered to the front of the room—"sometimes, no matter how hard we prepare for something, no matter how much time and effort we put into, say, a project, well, sometimes, it just doesn't turn out the way we hoped it would." Mrs. Waverly surveyed the class. "So, in the poem *To A Mouse* by Bobby Burns, what happened?"

Her students were so young, and many of them were genuinely interested in learning what she had to impart to them, at least she hoped they did, but she felt like she was banging her head against a brick wall. She wanted to reach out and shake them and tell them the lessons she wanted to share would last them all of their lives. No, she wasn't the pope or the president, but she wanted them to feel the pain and anguish of a character in literature or what greed and selfishness could lead to or . . . or . . . maybe that love conquers all.

Damn, she realized, *who am I kidding? They are fourteen years young and way more interested in their latest text, newest TikTok, the best video game on the planet, or who scored in the last game.*

"Okay, everyone," she interrupted her own train of

thought. "Let's take a look at the title of the book we're going to read. Cindy, what's the title?"

Cindy looked up. Her cheeks flushed. She hated being called on in class. *I know this! I know this. Don't stutter.* "Uh . . . The title is . . . uh . . ."

"Uhhh, yeah, cool . . . What a great title for a book!" Lucas laughed.

A few students snickered, but Mrs. Waverly gave everyone that special teacher look, and there was silence.

Cindy was humiliated, but she gathered up some hidden courage and blurted out, "It's *Of Mice and Men* by John Steinbeck."

"Thank you, Cindy." Mrs. Waverly smiled. "And Lucas, today after school at your special session with security, why, I have an additional assignment for you."

Lucas sneered. He hated the class. He hated the school. He hated everybody. He was about to make another snide comment but decided against it. He was already serving after-school detention for playing around with that girl—whatever her name was—and he was missing football for no good reason.

Lucas might've been missing football, but he wasn't missing time with the guys. He waited in the locker room after each of his stupid detentions. It was there that Lucas had bragged to all his friends about what he "did" with that girl. None of it was true, but the guys didn't care. He was their hero—suffering after-school detention because he was found with a girl during class.

His crew loved hearing about his escapades with girls.

They would laugh, slap him on the back, and make lewd gestures with their hands as they grabbed their crotches and made varied groaning noises that sounded more like wounded dogs in heat. Lucas enjoyed exaggerating and filling in all kinds of details he knew nothing about because he'd never actually experienced any of it. He used his imagination and limited knowledge from gaping at pictures of naked girls in the magazines he kept hidden under his bed.

Mrs. Waverly continued with her lesson. "We have already discussed the plot of the poem by Bobby Burns. And, yes, it is sad and depressing. But are we just talking about a mouse here? C'mon, now. Think. Think. The bigger question is, why would Steinbeck use a line from a very, very old poem for his novel?

"Now, I don't expect you to know that answer right now. Instead, I'm going to revisit that question when we finish the novel in about a week. For now, let's get back into your groups so you can finish the worksheet, which includes some vocabulary. Feel free to use your cell phones, but only—and I mean *only*—use them for the purpose of defining these words."

Desks shuffled and squeaked. Chairs clanged into one another, and book bags clunked and thudded as they collided on the floor while the students rearranged their desks from rows to quads. They were used to shuffling and reshuffling and finished the task in just a few moments.

Cindy liked her group. She was comfortable sitting with Junay, Aiden, and Roland. They were quiet and easygoing and never made her feel unease. Cindy looked around the room. *Thank goodness I don't have to sit with Lucas*, she thought. *I could never do it.*

Junay, her long black hair pulled back with a bright blue scrunchie that matched her sweater, took control of the group. "So," she said, her voice sharp and confident, "let's take a look at what words we need to look up first and get that out of the way."

Roland bent over his chair to grab his worksheet out of his book bag while sneaking one finger up his nose. Picking his nose was more of a habit than a voluntary action—something he did without even realizing it.

Riley, always observing others, noticed Roland's finger placement right away. "Oooooh, you are the grossest, most disgusting human being on the planet! Get a tissue, you freak!"

A few kids heard Riley and joined in with groans and gagging sounds.

Roland, embarrassed and ashamed, pulled his finger out, wiped it on his pants leg, and mumbled, "Sorry . . . My bad."

"You are gross AF," muttered another student.

"Okay," said Mrs. Waverly. "Let's all focus on our assignment." She hated distractions. *Picking noses? Really? I may just walk out and throw up if I have to see that one more time.*

Riley turned back to her group. She wasn't interested in talking with any of them, especially since she was stuck with Lucas in her group. She glared at him. He thought he was so cool. *What's the line? Oh yeah—too cool for school.*

But Riley had known Lucas since elementary school. Way back in, what was it—third grade, maybe?—Lucas's parents were the gossip for a long time. They had divorced. No big deal. Divorce had happened to several of Riley's classmates. The tough part was that his dad moved somewhere in the South, and Lucas rarely got to see him. And then it happened. His mom met a guy, and they got serious, and after a year or so, they married. Lucas was still struggling with this relationship. *Hey*, thought Riley, *who of us wouldn't be struggling in that situation?* Riley figured Lucas wasn't too keen on his stepdad because, although he was a quiet and small boy, he was suddenly picking fights with the older kids, arguing with the teachers, and refusing to do his schoolwork. When Lucas's stepfather came to school to sit with him in class one day to see why Lucas was misbehaving so badly, Lucas had pulled the fire alarm, and when they all went outside, he ran home.

Everyone figured Lucas was going to be sent away, but his new dad was a police officer in town, highly respected, and he'd managed to work things out with the school. Riley knew it was Lucas who was vandalizing the high school with racial slurs. She didn't tell anyone because, one, she was not a snitch and two, Lucas's stepdad was black. She figured Lucas was releasing his anger, and since he wasn't beating anyone up, she ignored his lashing out. In time, she felt Lucas would deal with it in a more mature way. So what was the big deal? Lucas was white, his mom was white, and his stepdad was not. Lucas was not coping very well.

Anyway, that was his problem, and Riley was still pissed

off because her best friend wasn't talking to her, and all because Lucas thought he was Mr. Cool. Riley stared at Lucas, who sat there acting like this class assignment was a great imposition on him.

"So, like, what are the answers, group?" he asked, looking at Riley and the other two girls. Sondra and Whitney were popular girls; they didn't need Lucas to enhance their popularity status. Lucas gave Sondra and Whitney his special wink, as if that would make them melt and hand over the answers.

Sondra Brewer flicked her black shoulder-length strands back and forth. The multicolored string that wrapped around one of her dreadlocks shimmered in the sunlight filtering in through the window. Her brown eyes squinted at Lucas, and if she were magical, her eyes would have lasered a hole right through the middle of his forehead. Sondra's deep copper-colored skin was flawless, and when her temper flared, flecks of gold appeared on her cheeks.

"Don't wink at me like I'm some cheap hussy you can order around, Lucas Lowlife. I know your mama and your daddy. They might think you're something special. I don't."

Whitney did not possess the silky way with words Sondra did, so she just nodded, her frizzy brown hair bobbing up and down. "Yeah, like that."

Lucas just clucked his tongue and murmured, "Whatever."

Riley enjoyed watching the back and forth, especially because she respected Sondra and seeing Lucas being put in his place was plain fun. "Anyway," she said, "since I had nothing to do last night, I sorta went ahead and finished the vocabulary. Here it is." Riley pushed her worksheet into the middle of the quad formation.

"You're awesome," Lucas said. "Ya know, if you ever—"

"Don't!" Riley hissed at him. "Don't you come at me after what you did to my best friend."

"What are you talking about?"

"You know damn well what I'm talking about. You and Jilly, in the dark hall during class. You got her in so much trouble, I . . ."

Mrs. Waverly seemed to appear as if on cue. "Well, hello, group," she said in a calming, smooth voice. "How is this team doing today?"

Sondra looked up at Mrs. Waverly. "We are doing just great, Mrs. Waverly. And thank you for asking. In fact, we're done with our vocabulary and are about to start on some of the questions."

Mrs. Waverly nodded. She seemed to know just when to show up to a group of students and redirect them. For now, she was content to move on to the next group.

All three girls stared at Lucas, scrutinizing him as if he were on trial, then tightened their lips as a way to hold back some ugly comments.

"Whatever," Lucas mumbled as he copied the definitions from Riley's paper.

Jilly was watching the entire scene from her group. She willed Riley to look at her, trying to use telepathy to tell her best friend how sorry she was, how stupid she'd been to get into so much trouble, but she had not had a single moment to talk to Riley. But honestly, Jilly felt different. She wasn't sure how, but things weren't the same anymore between her and Riley.

Riley's ears burned, and she turned to see Jilly staring at her, eyes watering. Riley mouthed to Jilly, hoping Mrs. Waverly did not catch her. *"After class!"*

CHAPTER 14

The bell rang. Students quickly returned their chairs and desks to their proper places in the rows. Riley shoved her chair under her desk, flung her book bag over her shoulder, and rushed out of the classroom in hopes of finding Jilly.

Jilly, her blonde hair swinging back and forth in her throwback ponytail, was already halfway down the hall when she heard Riley's shrill voice calling her name.

"Jilly! Hey, Jilly, wait up! C'mon, slow it down!"

Jilly had been avoiding Riley since the—what could she call what had happened? The incident? The event? It wasn't a make-out session. Maybe some would call it getting felt up, but Jilly barely remembered any of it. It was all a blur. And the worst part of it, the absolute worst part of the entire episode, was that Lucas—the jerk—hadn't called her or acknowledged her. Hell, he wouldn't even look at her. What a complete and utter jerk. *And to think I fell for it!*

And now Riley wants to grab hold of me and squeeze every detail out like the ketchup packets in the cafeteria. Jilly slowed down, if only to catch her breath, allowing Riley to close in on her.

"Hey, Jilly!" Riley called breathlessly. She finally caught up and locked her arm in Jilly's. "Jilly . . . Jilly, I've been trying to talk to you for days. I texted a zillion times, and then your dad answered and said you weren't allowed on your cell. I was so worried about you. I was trying to find out what happened. What *did* happen? Everyone is talking about it. They're saying you and Lucas were having sex down in the dark hall. All the kids say it's *the* place to hide when you want to skip class or do something with someone.

"What did you do? Did you really have sex? Oh! My! God! Tell me you did not have sex in the school hallway. They say the principal caught you right in the middle of it, and then security grabbed you and hauled you down to the nurse, and apparently, Lucas had his crew there watching, and then the police came for him, and they handcuffed him and—"

Jilly stopped in her tracks. "Stop. Stop it right now! Are you kidding me? Do you really think I would have sex, let alone in the freakin' school hallway? I don't care if it was a dark hall with locks and bolts and chains. Really, Riley. Don't talk to me right now. I can't talk to you anyway. I have to stay after school." Jilly turned abruptly into Mr. DeWitt's room.

Riley was dumbstruck. "What do you mean you have to stay after school? Are you in detention? Are you being suspended? Please call me tonight. *Puh-lease!*"

Riley felt as if her shoes were stuck in wet cement. She couldn't move. All around her, the school halls were filled with students laughing and shouting. Some were running to catch their bus; a few were strolling with friends with nowhere to go. School was over. Athletes meandered to their gym lockers to change, the drama kids flocked to the auditorium for rehearsals, and many others headed to their various clubs and organizations. But Riley had nowhere to go, and worse, she was all alone.

She stood staring at the classroom door Jilly had slid into. More kids zipped past Riley to get through the door.

Cindy Newport saw Riley outside the door to Mr. De-Witt's room. She wanted to say hi, but Riley had never been one to say hello unless she had a reason to or if it was someone popular—and that was not going to be Cindy. Still, Cindy was working on some of the strategies suggested by her therapist. Her therapist was young, savvy, and in tune with what teenagers often went through. She made Cindy feel comfortable and at times, even brave. Cindy was going to see her tomorrow, and she wanted to be able to tell her she'd tried—tried to make friends, tried to reach out to other students even though she was terrified to do it, tried to overcome her fears.

"Uh, hello, Riley," Cindy said, her voice trembling with uncertainty.

Riley ignored Cindy. Cindy was one of those girls who always had problems, and Riley wanted nothing to do with her.

"I said, hello, Riley," Cindy repeated, this time with more emphasis in her voice, hoping against hope she would not be ridiculed.

Riley sighed. What did this girl want? *Wait a second,* thought Riley. *She's going into the same room as Jilly. Cindy doesn't get in trouble. What's going on in there, and why can't I go in?*

"Oh, hello, Cindy," Riley said so sweetly she thought she might get an instant cavity.

Cindy stood up a little taller. She looked into Riley's amber eyes and smiled. *She knows who I am.*

Riley carried on as though they were two friends sharing something in private. "So, Cindy, what's the deal here? What's going on in Mr. DeWitt's room? How come you're here with the others? Are you in trouble? Did you do something really stupid? Huh? You can tell me; we're friends, right?"

Just before Cindy could say a word, Mrs. Waverly whisked by. "C'mon, Cindy. It's time to start our group. Let's go." She gently reached for Cindy's arm. "Oh, hello, Riley. Nice to see you so soon after class. I'm sorry, but our after-school program needs to get going now. See you tomorrow. I hope you enjoy reading *Of Mice and Men* tonight so we can have a great talk in class about it. Take care, hon." Mrs. Waverly, with Cindy in tow, swooped into the room and closed the door.

"Well, thanks a lot to the both of you!" snapped Riley. "I am sick and tired of not knowing what's going on around here!" Riley turned and stomped her way down the hall, hoping to disrupt any other groups meeting without her.

• • •

Mr. DeWitt and Mrs. Waverly stood in front of the dozen students seated in a semicircle facing the front of the room.

"Good afternoon, everyone," began Mr. DeWitt, "and thank you for being here today. Mrs. Waverly and I are extremely excited to begin this very special program with you. I know how much this is going to help each and every one of you." Carl turned to Neva. "So, Mrs. Waverly, do you want to say a few words?"

She looked around the room and smiled. Her electric emerald eyes lit up when she smiled, and her voice was as soothing as a fur-lined blanket. "Well now. Where do I begin? Yes, Mr. DeWitt and I are incredibly happy that you're here. You have been invited to be a part of this group, and I'm so thankful you agreed to be here."

A few of the students shuffled in their seats, and a few mumbles and a "Yeah, right" could be heard.

"Now, you might be thinking, 'Why *was* I picked to be a part of this group? Am I in trouble? Are my grades so bad that I need help?'"

Jilly stared at her desk. She refused to look up. She did not want to be there, but she knew attending these stupid after-school sessions was the only way she was going to be excused for her inappropriate actions and, according to her parents, the only way they would eventually forgive her.

With her head tilted downward, Jilly shifted her eyes to see who was seated around her. Thank goodness Lucas wasn't a part of this. She recognized a few students, but because Wells pulled from several middle schools in the area, there were students she didn't know. *Thank goodness for that as well.*

Mrs. Waverly continued, "Sometimes we need support, a sympathetic ear, and on occasion, we need advice on how to handle things. Such things as—well, I don't want to get too far ahead of myself here. For now, I'll say this—and Mr. DeWitt and I mean this from the bottom of our hearts—what we are doing here is for *you.* To help you because we share your pain, your confusion, and your frustrations. We are not here to judge you, and neither will we let you judge one another.

"So, yes, we did select you because your teacher may have shared some concerns about how you were adjusting to high school life. This isn't a study hall, and this isn't a therapy session, although at times, you may feel like it is."

A few snickers could be heard, but Mrs. Waverly let them pass. She smiled again, warming the room instantly as she did. "I love teaching. I always have, and I know Mr. DeWitt feels the same. We have learned over the years that sometimes, being a ninth grader can be overwhelming, and we want to be there for you to make sure you're not feeling that tremendous sensation of failure.

"So here is how we will begin. At your desk, you have a composition book. We'd like you to take the first page and create something on the page that defines you. You can draw a picture, create a design, doodle, write your name a hundred times. It doesn't matter. In other words, take the next ten minutes and fill up that page with whatever comes into your head that shouts, 'This is who I am—pimples, frogs, braces, glasses!' and whatever else floats your boat!" Mrs. Waverly clapped her hands together. "Now get to it. Mr. DeWitt, the background music, if you please, sir."

Carl walked over to his Bose speaker, turned it up, and using his cell phone, tuned into the latest songs.

CHAPTER 15

Riley, totally defeated, headed down the hall, ignoring the raucous laughter and fits of playful yelling in the various classrooms where groups were meeting. They were having fun, and she was lonely and on her way home to an empty house. Her parents were both doctors in different practices, and inevitably, they were never home. She had no brothers or sisters, and when she met Jilly, she'd felt an immediate bond. Maybe it was more than just a girlfriend, but nonetheless, Riley felt like Jilly filled a hole in her lonely life that she'd never realized existed before. Jilly was the sister she'd never had, the best friend she'd always wanted, and a confidante she sorely needed. And now this Lucas guy was squeezing her out as though she were a dry piece of wood. He was hammering a wedge in and splitting her and Jilly in two.

"Hey."

Riley looked up just before she bumped head-on into Lucas. He wore his purple-and-white school athletic jacket with his book bag slung carelessly over his shoulder. His dark brown hair hung over his deep blue brooding eyes, and his squared jaw munched on those wintergreen hard candies that left sparks in his mouth when he spoke.

Riley stopped in her tracks. She gave Lucas the once-over. He wasn't bad-looking, but she didn't get all googly-eyed over him like all the other girls did. She didn't know why. It bothered her sometimes, but maybe guys like him didn't do anything for her. Maybe it just guys in general.

"Hello, Lucas," Riley responded as dryly as she could. She didn't want him to ever think she was interested in him or wanted to befriend him. "Shouldn't you be at football practice or something else jocks do when they're not in class?"

Lucas had known Riley forever. She was a pretty girl, with her bobbed brown hair and deep brown eyes. She had a sharp wit and never gave him any of those girly looks he was used to getting from all the other girls.

"Yeah, I should. But I'm stuck in stupid after-school detention for a few weeks because . . . Well, because . . . And that witch Waverly gave me an extra assignment to work on in detention hall. Did you finish the book for her? Maybe you could give me the answers to the questions. I hate reading, and I'm never going to finish that dumb book."

"First of all, the book isn't dumb. Second of all, Mrs. Waverly isn't a witch. She's probably one of the best teachers at school. And most important of all, I wouldn't give you the time of day, let alone the answers to questions about a book you need to read. Maybe reading some literature will keep you off the spray-painting kick you seem to be enjoying this year."

Lucas contemplated pushing her, but she was a girl after all, even if she was pissing him off. "How do you know anything about the walls? What are you, a spy for the school?" Lucas's hands squeezed into two hard fists.

"You're lucky I don't report you, Lucas Cannon. You haven't grown up since I knew you in elementary school. Getting all angry at me because you got in trouble. You got my friend in trouble, too, and now I can't even hang out with her. You're bad news, dude. Go away from me."

Lucas took a step closer to Riley. He could smell her sweet fragrance, like cotton candy at the beach, and for a split second, he wondered what her skin felt like. He'd always wanted to touch her, but she was always cold and distant to him. Maybe he could, just this once . . .

"I said back off, you dick-for-brains! I am in no mood for your tricks." Riley's voice grew louder, then shriller. "You might fool half the girls in this school, but not me!"

"Why, hey there, you two! What's going on here?" someone with a booming, gravelly voice called. "Shouldn't you be safe at home playing a video game or in some after-school activity?" Beverly Winewrought, with her hands on her hips and her face pinched with concern, stood in between the two teens as if anticipating something dangerously wrong was about to take place.

Beverly had seen these situations erupt before. A boy and a girl disagreeing over something so innocuous and benign—or so it would appear—and then, before they could blink, their bodies would react like a flint, flinging sparks, and a fire between them would ignite. Beverly was in no mood to disentangle these two from a fight. She had a sixth sense when it came to these confrontations, and she could sense this argument was not a young lovers' quarrel but a nasty, angry altercation between two nonfriends.

Lucas's brain went red hot, and he lost all sense of reason. It was the same sensation he felt whenever he argued with his stepfather. Lucas should have liked him; his stepfather was kind and reassuring and so understanding, everything his real father wasn't. His real father drank all the time, had moved to another state, and never bothered to call—not even on his birthday. But Lucas refused to believe his father was gone forever. He searched for him on social media and tried calling his grandparents for information but had had no luck. His grandparents had written his father off as a deadbeat dad, a lazy good-for-nothing son, and wanted nothing to do with Angelo—especially since the only time he called was to ask for money.

Lucas's last memory of his dad, almost six years ago, was the worst of all. Angelo had come home late at night when his mom, Julie, was already sound asleep. Angelo had snuck into Lucas's bedroom, got undressed, and slid into bed with him. "Jeez, Daddy, get out of my bed! Go to your own room. You smell! You smell like you've been drinking that yucky stuff. Go away!"

But Angelo grabbed Lucas, gently at first on his shoulders and then harder as his hand moved around to the front of Lucas and reached for—*no!* Lucas screamed protests in his head. Angelo kissed Lucas on the back of his head, murmuring softly, "It's okay. It's just you and me, and you will like this. I promise. Now, hush . . . Shhh. Don't squirm, my little man. Your daddy is going to make you feel just fine. I'm not going to hurt you."

Lucas froze. He didn't know exactly what was happening, but he knew it made him feel uncomfortable and sick to his stomach. He wiggled and twisted and freed himself from his father's grasp, his father too drunk to know what Lucas was doing. Lucas let himself fall to the floor and away from his father's large, callused hands that had left a burning imprint on his body.

Lucas crawled to his dresser, ignoring his father's moaning and groaning. "Come back. Looky boy, it's just Daddy. It's okay. I'm not going to hurt you. C'mon back, boy, before I get angry and whip you for not listening to me."

Lucas did not look back. He grabbed his sweatpants and twisted his legs in, then slid his sweatshirt on. Still on the floor, Lucas crawled to his door, and on all fours, he slipped out. He hurried to the front door where his sneakers sat and quietly slid them on. Once outside, Lucas ran. It was a frigid night, and the stars and the moon were hidden behind snow-filled clouds, but Lucas didn't pay any mind to the frosty temperature. He kept running, his lungs burning with the icy air rushing in. *Keep going!* he cried in his head. *Don't stop. Don't ever stop.*

Lucas didn't remember how he had ended up at the

elementary school playground that night. He only remembered the school maintenance worker, Billy, nudging him the next morning.

"Hey. Hey . . ." Billy shook the little kid. Lucas something, he thought the kid's name was. "What the hell you doing here in the log house? Boy, you know it's Saturday and we don't have school. And it's snowing! Man, you're lucky I'm here trying to shovel. Did you run away from home? C'mon, little guy. Come inside where it's warm, and we can—"

Lucas startled awake. He was freezing cold, and this man was reaching for him, and . . .

"Don't touch me! Don't you fucking touch me! I swear I will kill you! Go away! Go away! I hate you! I hate you!" Lucas shook uncontrollably—whether it was from the cold or the fear or the shame or all three, he didn't know.

Billy pulled back. He knew something was terribly wrong with this young boy. He didn't want to subject him to anything that might scare him, so he backed off and pulled his cell phone out of his pocket and dialed 911.

Lucas squirreled himself into the farthest corner of the little log house he often played in with his friends during recess. Lucas was unaware of the hour or the day. He only knew he had to get away from . . . from that monster. Now this stupid log house on the playground felt like the safest place on the earth. He heard a siren in the distance. It got louder and louder. He shook his head. *Maybe they're coming for my dad. Maybe they're going to lock him up. I'm sorry, Daddy. Daddy, I'm sorry I . . .*

He heard whispering and shuffling outside the log house, but he was too afraid to look.

"Lucas. Lucas, I'm a police officer. I'm not going to hurt you. Why don't you come on out of there so we can talk? I'm the good guy, son. I'm not going to hurt you. I promise. C'mon, Lucas. It's cold out here, and I brought you some nice hot chocolate. Here, I'm gonna leave it right by this opening, and you can get it all by yourself."

Walter Young had been working the night shift when the 911 call came in. He knew Billy Petrin, who was head of the elementary school maintenance department. Billy was a decent man, and when Walter had come racing onto school grounds, he'd explained the situation quickly and succinctly.

Walter was concerned about the boy hiding in the log house. Why was he there? Had he been there all night? Why? Was he a runaway? That was disturbing enough, but was there something else going on? Too many questions, and for right now, in this cold with the snow falling, he needed to get this boy to warmth. Walter would ask all the right questions soon enough.

Lucas, shivering now, crept toward the opening of the log house. His limbs were stiff, and he could barely feel them, but the thought of the hot chocolate was too good to ignore. With a shaking hand, he reached for the steaming cup and brought it slowly to his numbed lips. The hot liquid should have burned him, but he was so frigid that it slid down his throat with ease. The warmth cascaded down his chest and into his stomach. Lucas leaned back against the wall, allowing the nourishment to do its job. He held the cup with both hands, the heat melting away his almost frostbitten fingers. His eyes were half-closed, but he glanced out the doorway to see who had brought him the hot chocolate.

Standing outside the small door of the playground log house was a tall, thick-shouldered African American policeman. He held a wool blanket in his hands and was looking straight at Lucas. The policeman reached through the small gap where Lucas was kneeling and gently placed the blanket through the make-believe door of the house. He looked at Lucas with his large brown eyes and smiled. "It's okay, son. I'm here to help you. You're not in trouble. I'm a police officer. I'm not going to hurt you."

When Lucas heard the last line, he brought his knees up to his chest so quickly he spilled some of the hot chocolate over his upper body, then whimpered.

Walter's chest tightened. He took a step back. Sometimes, it took a little longer for them to trust. He had been involved in enough cases with young children to know he had to be patient. Something had triggered this little guy, and Walter didn't want to see him run off.

Lucas tried to catch his breath. The hot chocolate he'd spilled was turning to icy patches on his sweatshirt, making him even colder than he'd been before. Lucas saw that the policeman had stepped back, so he quickly reached for the blanket, pulled it in, and covered himself with it, careful not to spill any more of the hot chocolate.

Walter was pleased. This was a good step. *Now let's see if I can get some trust here.*

"Say, little man. Is this your school? Billy here says you're a great kid. Right, Billy?"

Billy, a few feet away from Walter, nodded his head up and down with such force his glasses flew off his nose.

Walter slid over to Billy and murmured softly so Lucas couldn't hear, "Listen, Billy, go back into the building, call your principal, and explain you got a kid out here by the name of Lucas. See if she can call his mom. Go quickly before I lose this kid. I can't bear him running."

Billy turned around and pretended to go back to his shoveling, all the while making his way quickly to the building.

"Lucas! Lucas!" Riley shouted in Lucas's face. His eyes were glazed, and she thought he was in one of those freaky trances like in those scary movies she watched.

Beverly Winewrought stepped in and gently pulled Lucas away from Riley. "It's okay, Lucas. I thought you were losing your grip there for a minute, and I did not want to see you explode. Hey, Lucas. Look at me. Look at me, young man, right now!"

Lucas snapped himself out of his dark thoughts. He shook his head as though he'd just been slapped in the face—hard. He looked down and realized his hands were balled so tightly in two fists that his knuckles had turned white from loss of blood.

"Lucas, where are you supposed to be? Huh? It's after detention time and—"

"I'm supposed to be with DeWitt and Waverly, but I'm not going in there. I don't like her. She's mean."

"What do you mean, Mr. Cannon? What do you mean when you say something like that?" Beverly asked him, ignoring the fact that Riley was plain staring at him, her mouth hanging open.

"I, uh, I don't know . . . I can't talk anymore. I gotta go. I gotta go right now." Lucas pulled away from Mrs. Winewrought, but not before turning to look at Riley with such hatred in his eyes she felt a chill run down her spine. Then Lucas, with his book bag over his shoulder, careened down the hall as though his life depended on it.

Riley was left there alone with Mrs. Winewrought. "Uh, I have to go, too, Mrs. Winewrought. I'm late, and my dad's supposed to be picking me up. See ya tomorrow." And with that, Riley turned and left the building, going in a completely different direction from Lucas.

Her dad wasn't going to pick her up. He never did. Neither would her mom. Their lives were too busy for them to remember they even had a daughter.

Beverly, nonplussed at what had just transpired, found herself back outside Mr. DeWitt's classroom. She strained to hear what was going on in there, and as she did, Neva happened to glance at the doorway window. She smiled and waved, then turned her back on Beverly and continued strolling through the classroom.

Beverly just stood there, her mind racing with so many different thoughts. *What the . . . ?*

CHAPTER 16

Lucas ran out of the building, not sure where he was going. He wasn't sure of anything anymore. He just felt he had to keep running. He was near the edge of the teachers' parking lot when he noticed the royal blue CR-V with bumper stickers on the rear of the car. He recognized the sign that promised peace and tolerance to all. It was Mrs. Waverly's car. Lucas had been in the parking lot one morning and happened to see her pull in.

Lucas stuck his hand in his pocket and pulled out his house key. He walked over to her car and pressed his key against the hard metal, hearing his key scrape into the deep blue shine, leaving a jagged scar that screamed his hatred, his anger, his jealousy.

Lucas turned around to check if anyone had seen him. *Damn it.* His mind exploded. There was Riley on the other side of the parking lot, staring at him, condemning him for his actions, knowing his secrets—all of them. *Why does she always see me for who I really am?*

He put the key back in his pocket and turned toward

the field, where his teammates were practicing, laughing, and hitting each other, barely keeping their male egos in check. And where was he? Standing around with his hands in his pockets wanting to cry because he wasn't a part of them. But he needed them.

Lucas wiped his nose. He sniffed, then spit out a snot ball. He couldn't be seen near the field, so he turned and went the other way, in no particular hurry to get anywhere. He didn't notice the streets he passed or the cars that honked at him when he wasn't paying attention as he crossed the road. And there it was. He found himself standing in front of the little log house at his elementary school.

Lucas looked to his left and then his right. Satisfied he was alone, Lucas crawled in through the opening. *It's so tiny*, he thought. He smiled, remembering how he'd imagined this house being larger than life once upon a time.

He shuffled over to the corner, put his book bag down on the cracking wood, and rested against the wall. So many images came flooding back, and he was afraid to allow those dark memories to seep in. But they were going to—had to—so he let himself be open to the darkness of that time. He felt dizzy as the events rushed to his head.

Most of it was a blur now. His mom had rushed into the log house where he was huddled in the corner, covered with a woolen blanket, clutching an empty cup. He wouldn't let go of the cup. She'd cradled him and rocked him, saying words he never could remember except that they were soothing and comforting.

He'd choked out the words to his mother: "Don't let him touch me. Don't let him touch me!" Lucas had coughed and sobbed and repeated those words over and over and over.

Walter, as big as he was, somehow climbed into the log house, and the both of them managed to calm Lucas down. *And I guess that's when the two of them . . . That's when they fell into each other like two missing pieces of a puzzle.*

Afterward, all Lucas could recall was that his mother, with her arms draped around him, had sat in his bedroom with him while Walter escorted his father out of the house in handcuffs. That was the last time he ever saw his father.

The scene came rushing in like waves that refused to subside, soaking him, drenching him with feelings he had locked away in a very deep and frozen place in his heart. And sitting here once again, with his heart beating wildly, the memories slipping out like icicles rushing down his roof, Lucas wept deep sobs that racked his shoulders with such intensity his head bumped against the worn walls as he cried.

He wasn't sure how long he sat there, cold and wet from tears that embarrassed him more than absolved his guilt. Lucas was better off away from his father, but a piece of him deep down yearned for the father he once knew. The one who'd played football with him, watched their favorite teams every week, and wrestled with him on the rug. The thought of that, however, now had a dark edge, and it sickened him to think about those times. Lucas spit on the floor as if to rid his body of the memory and the stink of it.

He wanted to like Walter. After the night Lucas slept in the log house, Walter befriended his mom. That friendship had led to dating, and that led to them getting married. The divorce was fast since the court had ruled his dad was an unfit father and needed to be in therapy, which, of course, he denied, cursed, screamed, threatened, and then finally, moved away.

Walter tried to be a father to Lucas, but Lucas wouldn't let him in. He knew he was wrong every time he wrote something derogatory on the walls at the school or in the mall bathrooms, but he couldn't help himself. He was filled with hate and jealousy and longing for something he no longer had, and vandalizing was a cathartic release for him. And damn if Walter always came to his rescue. He was the father Lucas should have had from the beginning. If only . . .

Lucas spit again and then crawled out of the log house. *I'm too old to keep coming here every time I feel sorry for myself.*

Dusk was falling, and the streetlights gave a misty orange glow as Lucas plodded home. He was disgusted with himself. He always was after he gave in to his anger.

"Shit," he muttered. He'd almost hit Riley right in the face.

She could have told everyone from security right up to the principal that she'd seen him that night spray-painting the walls near the gym. He didn't know what in the world she was doing walking around the building so late at night, but then again, there was a lot about Riley he didn't know.

She was really cute, he thought, *but not approachable*. She didn't flirt with him. In fact, he never saw her flirting with anyone.

• • •

Riley had spotted Lucas from across the parking lot, glad to be far away from him, but then she'd frozen in her tracks when the sunlight reflected off an object in his hand. *A mirror? A pen? No*, she realized. It was a key, and he was pressing it against a car. *Whose car is that?* She had no clue, but she could tell even from far away that he was keying the car and smiling while he did it. Not a smile, really. More like a smirk. What was he thinking? He was downright evil.

And to think Jilly liked him. Ycccccch. If she ever got to talk to Jilly again, she was going to have to sit her down and explain what Lucas was really like under his good looks and hot bod. What was it that caused some girls to lose all control when a boy so much as looked at them? Riley was never going to be in that situation. She had too much pride to allow some boy to change her entire personality just because he looked at her. Nope, not her. *No way, no how.*

Following his horrible act, Lucas took off down the street and out of her sight, and Riley's deep thoughts were broken apart by a whiny irritating voice.

"Hi, Riley. You still at school?"

It was Cindy.

"If I'm standing here, then I guess I'm still at school." Riley glared at Cindy, who shifted her body weight from her left foot to her right foot and blinked. Riley was losing her patience.

"Oh," said Cindy. "Yeah, right, I guess that was kinda dumb." Her face crinkled as if it were painful for her to have a conversation.

Cindy continued to engage Riley. Her therapist had told her not to give in too quickly when talking with another person. But trying to converse with Riley was not easy, and Cindy was breathing too quickly.

Riley tried to ignore Cindy. She was hoping to catch up with Jilly, but then she caught sight of Jilly getting into her father's car and leaving the parking lot.

"Damn it all to hell!" Riley muttered. "I can't believe I missed her." She looked over at Cindy and was about to curse at her for distracting her, but when she saw the look on Cindy's face and heard her hyperventilating, Riley took a deep breath and took Cindy's hands in hers.

"Cindy, look at me. Focus on me. Look. At. Me. Now!" Growing up with two doctors for parents had taught Riley a few things, and it was pretty obvious Cindy was having a panic attack.

Cindy's eyes fluttered, and even though she was being held by Riley, she started to sway backward. Riley grabbed her tighter and eyeballed her as hard as she could.

"Okay, breathe, girl. Just breathe, damn it. I don't want to call 911 on you now. Look at me and focus. C'mon, you can do this. I know you can. All right, Cindy. Together with me. Breathe in—one, two, three. Now breathe out—one, two, three. Again."

The racehorse galloping away inside Cindy's chest slowed. She stared into Riley's soft caramel-colored eyes and felt comfortable. Riley wasn't making fun of her or ridiculing her the way others had always done in the past. She had a soft, gentle touch that made Cindy relax. When she was able to breathe again with control, she pulled her hands away from Riley.

"I think I'm okay now. Thank you, Riley. I, uh . . . It's just that—"

"Look," Riley said. "I get it. You don't have to explain. I know you get panic attacks now and then. You just have to learn to control them. It's not easy. I used to get them, too, ya know. I just remember my breathing exercises, and it helps."

"Wow. I didn't know you—"

"Hey, that's not for publication, if you please. No one knows that, and I probably shouldn't have told you either. It's just that, I know how it feels when your heart wants to jump out of your chest, the ringing in your ears won't stop, and you want to crawl under a bush and cry. So, yeah, I get it, but this better stay between you and me. And I mean like forever. Got it?"

Cindy nodded so hard her glasses fell off. She bent down to pick them up just as Riley did, and they both bumped their heads.

"Ooomph!" Riley let out another expletive and wanted to smack Cindy, but Cindy's eyes were already watering, and she did not want to deal with any crying. Not now. She was in no mood. "I gotta go." Riley turned and started out of the parking lot. There was no ride for her tonight— or any night. Doctor Mom and Doctor Dad would be in their offices, and unless she stopped at Subway for dinner, it was a microwave night again.

"Uh, Riley. Can I walk with you? I'm heading in the same direction. I think we live kinda close to each other. Would it be okay if we walked together? We could just talk, ya know."

Riley was about to growl at Cindy, but then suddenly, a thought came over her like a lightning strike. "Sure, Cindy." Riley smiled. "Sure. But you have to tell me absolutely everything that happened in that after-school thing you were in today. I want to hear all the details. And don't leave anything out. Got it?"

Cindy nodded, this time with her middle finger pressed against her glasses so they wouldn't fall off again. She pushed her bangs up over her forehead and smiled.

CHAPTER 17

Riley sat by herself in the kitchen, picking at the Hot Pocket dinner she had microwaved for herself. It was after seven, and her parents had still not arrived home. She wasn't worried; she was used to her solitary lifestyle. Her parents gave her all the clothes and accessories she could ever want. Riley had a computer, the latest PlayStation, and her own smart television in her room. She should want for nothing. Nothing at all.

She twirled her short hair with her finger, rolling it tighter and tighter, thinking. There was a time when she wanted to cut herself. She had read some teens did it to release their pain. What was her pain? That she wished her parents paid more attention to her and that she and her mom could go shopping at the mall together? Instead, her mom had given her a credit card of her own so she could go online and buy whatever she wanted without ever worrying about the cost. She would buy totally rad shirts and bracelets and earrings. The sad part was, Riley would never wear any of those purchases. That wasn't what she really wanted. They were just things, and they didn't ease her pain. And to that end, neither would cutting. In the end, Riley had conceded she never wanted to cut herself, but the thought still crossed her mind now and then.

Riley's homework was strewn over the kitchen table, and her English assignment was almost completed. She wanted to read more of *Of Mice and Men*, fascinated by the lifestyle of men who would work at a ranch for a while and then leave and go to another ranch or just move to . . . wherever. No strings attached, no pressure—just do your work and nothing more. The relationship between George and Lennie intrigued her. She yearned for someone to feel that strongly for her. To think that someone—a friend—would do anything for you, no matter what the cost. Riley stopped reading. She didn't want to finish the book. Not just yet. She didn't want it to end.

For some reason, it made her think about Cindy. She didn't want to be friends with Cindy; being friendly was one thing, but she wasn't looking for a new BFF. Cindy had told Riley everything about the group meeting in Mr. DeWitt's room, and Riley hated to admit it, but she was envious. Why couldn't she be included in such a session? She wanted to be anywhere Jilly was because, well, because Jilly was her only friend. And what did Cindy mean when she said Mr. DeWitt and Mrs. Waverly wanted everyone in the group to stay with them as a team for the next four years?

Riley was deep in thought between her schoolwork, Jilly, Cindy, and then there was Lucas. Seeing him vandalize that car in the parking lot had sent chills up Riley's neck. What was wrong with him? And why did he hate so much? He had a mom who was always there for him and a stepdad who was such a nice guy. Riley had seen Lucas's stepdad at some school events wearing his police uniform and beaming with pride every time he saw Lucas. Where were her parents during those school activities? Working.

Yeah, they had very demanding careers, always taking care of others, but Riley felt she needed to be taken care of too. Well, sometimes at least.

"Riley? Where are you, hon? All the lights are off. Are you okay?"

Riley jerked up. She hadn't realized she'd been dozing on her arms at the kitchen table. The light in the kitchen was on, but she hadn't turned on any of the house lights.

"I'm in the kitchen, Mom." Riley quickly gathered all the loose papers and books into a pile and shoved them in her book bag.

Jeanine Maddox, Riley's mom, shuffled into the kitchen, the long day's work hanging heavily on her shoulders and her glasses perched on top of her head. Her hair, with many new silver strands, was pulled back in a bun. Riley knew not to ask her mom how her day had gone; she could read it on her face and in the way she carried her body. And judging from the looks of it, it had been one of those horrific days. Riley pushed her chair out from under her and cautiously inched up to her mom.

Jeanine looked at Riley and smiled wearily. A few more wrinkles had managed to sneak in around her mother's soft dove-gray eyes. Riley reached for her mom and the two embraced, both needing to feel the warmth of each other. Riley let her head rest on her mother's shoulder, breathing in the mixed scent of antiseptic chemicals and Chanel No. 5—her mother's favorite perfume.

"Where's Dad?" Riley asked, her nose still nestled in her mother's shoulder, not wanting to let go of her just yet.

"Your father's in a long surgery and probably won't be home for hours. There was an accident on the highway, and he was called in. He was on his way out with me, but he had to go back. Did you have your dinner?"

Riley nodded against her mother's shoulder. She closed her eyes to the rhythmic swaying her mother automatically fell into whenever she held her. They stayed like that for another moment or so, and then Jeanine pulled back, holding Riley by her shoulders and looking at her squarely in the face.

"Tell me about your day. I want to hear everything."

Riley smiled. Her mother was completely worn out and probably hadn't eaten all day. "I'll tell you in a few minutes, but how about I make you one of your favorite salads?"

Jeanine smiled, her eyes watering at the sight of her teenage daughter who knew her so well. "That would be absolutely perfect. Let me go change my clothes, and I'll be right down." Jeanine hugged Riley one more time before turning and plodding up the stairs to her room.

Riley sniffed back a few tears. *I'll make the salad,* she thought as she opened the fridge and pulled out the ingredients, *but I bet she never makes it back down to the kitchen tonight.*

Riley spent the next twenty minutes creating a beautiful, healthy salad for her mom. She never would've spent that time and careful dedication on dinner for herself, but Riley would do anything for her mom. She set the salad on the table, covered it with some plastic wrap, and cleaned up the kitchen from all of her cutting and shaving and dicing. By the time Riley had finished putting away all the utensils she had used, an entire hour had passed. Riley wiped her hands dry, picked up the picture-perfect salad, and stored it in the refrigerator. After glancing over at the sparkling kitchen, Riley headed upstairs.

Riley tiptoed into her parents' bedroom. There on the bed, lying on top of the blankets, was her mom, sound asleep. She had changed into her comfy blue sweats and oversized sweatshirt, but when she sat on the bed to put on her socks, she must have leaned back and closed her eyes. Riley snickered. There was one sock on and one sock off. It reminded her of an old children's story, but she couldn't remember which one.

Riley walked over to where her mother stowed the family afghans on a deep mahogany blanket rack. She selected the one her great-grandmother had made for her—rich in purples and blues—and tenderly placed it over her mother. She reached down and left a gentle kiss on her mother's forehead, then switched off the lamp on the nightstand and left the room.

It was getting late, and it had been a long day. Riley got into her pajamas, washed her face, checked for any new pimples, and brushed her teeth. Having completed her nightly rituals, Riley crawled into her bed, plugged her cell phone into the charger, and switched off her night lamp. She snuggled deep into her thick violet comforter. With thoughts of Jilly and Cindy and Lucas swimming in her head, Riley fell asleep, tossing and turning all night with images too bizarre to recall in the morning. Somewhere in the dream, she was with Lucas on a ranch, helping Lennie and George and looking for rabbits in the field.

When Riley's alarm snapped her out of her inexplicable dream, she rose more exhausted than she'd been when she went to sleep. She wanted to roll over and go back to sleep, but the thought of returning to those strange dreams propelled her to get up. She considered taking a morning shower to rinse away all the night cobwebs from her brain, but she was too cold and far too hungry to take the time. Riley slipped on her favorite jeans, Taylor Swift T-shirt, and extra-large sweatshirt that spelled *WELLS* on the front. Riley trudged down the stairs to an empty but exceptionally clean kitchen and decided cereal was in order for the day.

Chomping on Cheerios and Lucky Charms together in her favorite multicolored bowl, Riley started planning her day.

CHAPTER 18

Beverly Winewrought sat at her school desk, working feverishly on her computer. Her cell phone sat at her ready on the left, and an extra-large cup of steaming coffee sat on her right. She had a definite routine. She was, after all, a science teacher who lived and breathed by a scientific and logical approach to everything. At least that was how Beverly believed her life should be, even though it rarely happened that way.

Beverly consistently woke up at 4:30 a.m. sharp, hours before her husband, which for Beverly, was a blessing. Then came a quick blazing shower, makeup, hair, and finally, an outfit that would eventually be covered up by her perfectly ironed lab coat. After grabbing her nightly packed lunch from the refrigerator and her huge satchel stuffed with student papers, notebooks, and her planner, Beverly was out the door.

Once outside, she always took a moment to breathe in the air, regardless of the temperature. It was, for her, a sign of freedom from her house. The inside of her home choked her and made her feel insignificant and inferior, but once she stepped out into the open, she became the Beverly she's always known she was—confident, secure, smart, and ready to take on the world of teenagers.

Her first stop on the way to school was her favorite Starbucks. Although Beverly's best friend scoffed at her because she was supporting a franchise and not a local business, her daily dose of Starbucks ignited Beverly and made her feel like all was right with the world. By now, her local Starbucks barista addressed her by name and made her special concoction every day she arrived, which recently included weekends. Anything to get away from the house, even for a few hours in the morning.

Beverly's mind raced back to last weekend and Ted. She winced.

"What do you mean you're going to Starbucks now? It's Saturday. It's early, and I thought you and I could, well . . . We haven't in such a long time."

Beverly had interrupted Ted softly so as not to wake up the anger always brewing inside him. Anything could cause a volcanic eruption in Ted, and Beverly always seemed to be in the line of fire. Getting up and away from him each morning allowed her space and time to think, to feel and to know she was not the reason for his fury. Ted had his own demons, and although these terrors had been buried deep inside him—she suspected for years—it was only recently they'd resurfaced. She tried to get him to talk about his feelings and moods, but that only seemed to trigger him to explode into a venomous rage. Bruises, swollen cheeks, sprained wrists. Yes, she should have gone to her doctor, but she didn't want to report him. He had become an abusive, angry man, and she wanted to find out why.

Ted kept his emotions in check most of the time, but Beverly never knew what the trigger could be each day. Going out in the morning to get a coffee or go to the grocery store allowed Ted the time to wake up from his own nightmare and, hopefully, let whatever was clawing at him dissolve.

So, in response to his random urge, Beverly had affectionately whispered to him, "I'll be back soon, Teddy. I want to get you some of those warm almond croissants you love so much and a fresh bottle of your flavored cream. We'll have a wonderful morning. Hmm?"

Ted had seemed content with the thought of a hearty breakfast and didn't realize Beverly was just placating him. "But when you get back!"

Beverly nodded, pulling on her Saturday morning sweats and hoodie. "Of course, my love." And without so much as a hug or a goodbye kiss, Beverly had bolted out of the bedroom.

Those memories always caused Beverly to squeeze her lips together so tightly her teeth left indentations. Sitting at the stoplight, Beverly shook her head from side to side as if she could erase the memory like those erasable sketch pads she used as a young child. The light turned green, and it took a few friendly honks from the car behind her for Beverly to snap out of her dreamlike state and continue on her journey to Starbucks and school.

Now, with her Starbucks in hand and the memory of Ted sufficiently obliterated, Beverly sat in her classroom staring at the posters of the universe that covered most of her back wall. Daydreaming, planning, determined to make her marriage work, she envisioned life on the other planets where there was no anger, hostility, wars, or endangered climates.

Soft humming sounds escaped Beverly's lips as she sipped her steaming latte. Breaking the soft warm energy of the morning like a glass being shattered, the first bell rang, and the halls were suddenly filled with noisy teenagers who had more energy at 7:30 in the morning than any other creature on the planet.

"Ah, well," Beverly muttered aloud, "I best be up and about to welcome my cherubs." Beverly laughed at her own joke and was trying to finish a few last emails to parents when two of her best students, Junay and Sondra, pounced into the room.

The girls were so deep in their conversation they didn't bother to look up and greet Beverly. Beverly smiled to herself. Girls and gossip were a deadly combination! Beverly went back to banging out on her keyboard but couldn't help but overhear the dialogue.

"You have got to be kidding!" hissed Sondra.

"I heard it from a very reliable source. That man is dangerous. I'm so glad I don't have him for class," Junay said.

"He stares at your chest when he's answering you. At least that's what someone said."

"You know, I heard that, too. That girl who sits behind

us in here said she keeps her book standing upright on her desk so he can't look at her."

"That is absolutely the most ridiculous thing I have ever heard."

Junay nodded vigorously. "And there's more. That afternoon session he's having every week—well, I heard he's doing some weird stuff in there."

"Like what?" Sondra wanted details, specific information. "You can't go on such vague comments like that. We need to find out what exactly."

At this point, Beverly cleared her throat, causing both Junay and Sondra to stop talking and look up.

"Oh, good morning, Mrs. Winewrought," said Sondra sweetly. "How are you today?"

"I am just fine. Thank you for asking. Is everything okay, girls?"

The two girls shuffled their feet and unloaded their heavy book bags onto their desks. They were just about to speak when the classroom door was flung open and the other students poured into the room, talking, shoving, laughing—all typical of young high school students. Not necessarily eager for their first period science class but enthusiastic for another day with friends and all the demands of high school life.

Beverly looked back at the two girls. "Maybe during lunch you could both pop in here for a few minutes?"

Sondra nodded, while Junay stared at the floor. Both girls leaned on their desks and plopped down.

Beverly waited for the late bell to officially announce

the start of the school day and then belted out in her best first-thing-in-the-morning voice: "Well, a good day to all of you, and welcome to another Wacky Winewrought pop quiz!"

Moans and groans echoed, feet stomped, book bags thudded to the floor, and cell phones turned to silent as the class awaited their fate with yet another test of their knowledge—or not!

The class period flew by between collecting quizzes, answering questions, introducing the new topic of the week, and then the bell proclaiming class was over. The students filed out with a little less pomp than when they'd entered.

Beverly smiled and quickly called out, "Have a great day, and hey, do something nice for someone today!"

Some of the students heard her and nodded, but most were too busy on their cell phones, catching up with friends, or jostling each other out of the way, afraid to miss out on the excitement in the halls.

CHAPTER 19

Carl DeWitt jumped out of his chair as soon as the last student marched from his room. This was second period and his planning time, but he wanted to rush to the main office. Almost running, Carl couldn't stop himself from grinning. He had a plan, and he was praying feverishly that it would come to fruition.

Scott Sheldrake walked toward him as he made his daily rounds throughout the halls. "Hey, Mr. DeWitt."

Scott always had a smile and a handshake at the ready when he approached staff. When the school was humming and everyone was where they were supposed to be, Scott was a happy camper. He reached his arm out toward Carl, and the two men greeted each other with a strong hand-shake in the middle of the hallway.

The outside sunlight filtered in through the high win-dows, casting long soft yellow rays on both the men. Floating motes drifted over their heads, and one flores-cent ceiling light buzzed as though signaling something foreboding was about to happen. Had a movie crew been filming the scene, it might have looked a bit like two angels in heaven plotting a rebellion or a quick stopover on Earth for the desserts they longed for.

"What's shaking?" Carl enjoyed his casual friendship with Scott. There was a time in Carl's life when he'd even thought about joining the police force. The academy was a place of discipline, law, and order, and Carl had needed that direction—for a while, anyway. But in the end, he chose a different path. Nonetheless, he had the utmost respect for Scott, knowing his many years as a decorated police officer had been fraught with peril. Scott loved sharing his experiences with Carl, and there was many an afternoon where Carl could be found sitting in Scott's office as he regaled him with his adventures on the beat.

"You know, Carl, I've been thinking about giving up this job and going back to police work. I love the kids here, but sometimes I long to be back on the streets helping people and seeing the community."

Carl didn't want to be rude, but this was his planning period, and the clock was ticking. Having a conversation with Scott could take up his entire free time, and Carl was in a hurry—

The walkie talkie on Scott's belt sounded with requests for security and a nurse down in the gym ASAP.

"Sorry, Carl, my man. Duty calls. I'm outta here! Let's catch up later? Ten-four." Scott signaled for his team to join him with his walkie up next to his mouth and jogged down the hall toward the main gym.

Carl nodded and smiled, then turned toward the office once again. He walked as fast as he could without approaching a slow jog. He glanced at his watch as he opened the door to the main office. Yes, there was still time.

He was in such a hurry he didn't notice Beverly Winewrought slinking behind him.

Beverly's vigilant eyes had followed Carl all the way down the hall, observing him when he'd stopped to chit-chat with the head of security. Now, it looked like Carl was almost jogging down the hall. Hmm. Why? He wasn't dragging some misbehaving student with him. In fact, he didn't have anything in his arms, so he wasn't delivering something to the office.

Beverly was curious. *No, be truthful,* she told herself. She was downright jealous of Carl. He seemed to possess pockets filled with luck and good looks, and Beverly's jealousy was growing greener each day. She worked just as hard if not harder than he did, yet he'd gotten the special after-school program with Neva and Beverly hadn't. *I asked that ol' Battle Axe last spring if I couldn't be a part of some new program, and she swore she would look into it for me. Ha! That didn't happen.* And now Atkinson—the nastiest administrator she knew—wouldn't look her in the eyes. She knew she had done her wrong. *Just wait for the yearly survey to come out. Boy, is she ever in for a surprise when I say what's been on my mind.*

Beverly waited outside the main office for a few minutes before she opened the door. She didn't want Carl to think she was trailing him, even though she definitely was—surreptitiously, of course. Beverly yanked the door open, hoping to disrupt whatever action was happening, only to find Carl leaning over Cassandra's desk. *For a school receptionist, she sure has too much free time on her hands*, thought Beverly.

Cassandra smiled from ear to ear, as though Carl had just shared the funniest story of the century with her. Her cheeks were flushed, and she was so focused on staring at Carl that she didn't even look up as Beverly pounced in. Realizing Cassandra was not paying a bit of attention to her, Beverly ignored the two of them and hustled over to the small mailroom and stood in front of the news bulletin, hoping to hear some of their conversation as she pretended to read the information stapled to the board.

Other teachers walked through the mailroom, but Beverly only nodded and grunted as they greeted her. She didn't want to get into any long conversations with anyone else; she really didn't care what they had to say. What she wanted to know was what Carl was up to, so she positioned her face closer to the papers stapled to the board so anyone walking by would think she was too focused on something of importance to talk.

The period was almost over, and Beverly would have to leave to prepare for her next class, but so would Carl. She was getting annoyed that he was hanging around Cassandra for so long. What could he possibly want with her? She should've been answering phones and attending to parents who entered the office. Beverly reached for her phone and opened a new text.

What is Carl doing with Cassandra? Who knows what is happening here? Tell me, somebody, before I scream!!

Beverly heard Carl say goodbye, and as soon as he left the office, she casually strolled by Cassandra's desk. "Well, good morning, Ms. Conway," Beverly purred as though she were a cat looking for a treat. "Been a busy day so far?"

Cassandra held up one finger as if to say *Hold on a sec!* while she placed her finger from her other hand on the school's headpiece firmly tucked in her ear. Cassandra replied to someone on the other end of the phone while Beverly's own cell phone emitted all kinds of clicks and bells alerting her of text messages coming in.

It seemed like an hour had passed before Cassandra made a motion that signaled she had signed off with whomever she'd been talking to and smiled at Beverly. "Hello, Mrs. Winewrought." Cassandra's clear deep chocolate-brown eyes were filled with innocence and childlike purity. Beverly thought she was too naïve for this job.

"Was that Mr. DeWitt using up all of your time this morning?" Beverly wanted to sound firm and authoritative, but she wasn't in any position to come across in that manner. She looked around the main office to see if anyone had happened to walk by that she hadn't noticed, but the office was clear of other staff members.

Beverly suddenly felt emboldened and took a deep breath. She spoke as rapidly as she could before she lost the courage to say what she wanted to say. "You know, Ms.

Conway, I don't know what you two were talking about, but I sorta get the creeps when Mr. DeWitt talks to me. I mean, he's a nice guy, I guess, but I've heard some of my female students talk about him, and I'm not sure you—"

"What do they say about him, exactly?"

"Well, it really isn't for me to say, you know. I—"

"You started the conversation, Mrs. Winewrought. I did not. And if you're going to imply something derogatory, then maybe you need to be a bit more specific about what you're trying to say."

Beverly had not anticipated such an unpleasant response from Cassie. She'd thought the girl was more sheepish and insecure and not so assertive. Beverly took a step back, wrinkled her eyebrows, and replied with as much astonishment and outrage as she could muster. "The bell is about to ring, and I need to be prepared for my students. If you do not understand what I'm trying to tell you—what I'm hoping you will glean from my remarks—well, I don't know if I can help you, Ms. Conway. Goodbye."

Beverly turned around with such force she knocked the vase of day lilies from Cassandra's desk. The flowers tumbled right out of the vase. Water stains spread over Cassandra's desk while the rest of the water gushed out and spilled onto the floor. The sound of the vase shattering on the office floor made Beverly wince as a memory of something deep and dark inside her cracked open. Cassandra jumped up and grabbed tissues out of her decorated box, then tried to soak up the excess water that had covered all of her work papers and drenched her navy blue sweater.

Cassandra glared at Beverly with eyes that could send shivers up your spine, but Beverly's emotions hardened into marble.

Beverly eyed the mess she'd made. "See that the custodian cleans that up for you." And with that, she shoved the door open and made a mad dash for her classroom.

Once down the hall, far away from the main office, Beverly slowed her step to a crawl and took her time returning to her classroom. She had plenty of time, but she'd wanted to leave before she could say anything else that was just as untrue as the comment she'd left Cassandra with. Her students only had wonderful things to say about Mr. DeWitt, but Beverly was tired of hearing them put him on such a high pedestal. *No teacher deserves that much praise*, thought Beverly. Especially not one so green in the profession. He had only been teaching—what, a mere three years? And already, he was receiving accolades from administration along with offers for leadership roles. It pissed her off. She hated using that expression, but it captured her true and unadulterated feelings.

And what was Carl doing? Killing time with a school receptionist? Was he hitting on her, asking her out? Was he trying to get some dirt on other staff members or maybe parents? How about some kid gossip? This was not the time or the place to have such personal conversations. Who knew how intimate he was getting with her? What if a student had come in? What if a parent had? Totally inappropriate. Beverly had been within her rights to let Cassandra know that the big Mr. DeWitt was dangerous.

Beverly's hand buzzed as text messages piled in. She couldn't wait to get to her classroom and bask in the euphoria at the anticipated responses she was hoping to get from her friends.

CHAPTER 20

Cindy rushed out of her mentoring session with Mr. DeWitt and Mrs. Waverly. Her mom was waiting for her in the school parking lot, ready to take her to see her therapist. She loved Miss Anna because every time she left one of their sessions, Cindy believed she could conquer the world.

Miss Anna was young and pretty and very much in tune with teenagers. She never made Cindy feel like a loser. And the most important part was that Cindy could tell Miss Anna absolutely anything in the whole wide world, and Miss Anna would never think less of her.

Cindy and her mom arrived in the sprawling parking lot of the town medical center that loomed large and foreboding at times, but not today. Cindy hopped out of the car and waved goodbye to her mother. "See ya in an hour, Mom. Love ya!"

And before her mom could respond, Cindy was halfway to the front door with a skip in her step and a lightness in her heart.

Miss Anna's office was on the second floor, and today, Cindy decided to run up the stairs instead of taking the elevator. She was filled with energy and excitement and optimism and could not wait to share this new piece of her personality. Cindy opened the door to a small waiting room with a few chairs. It was empty—thank goodness. Cindy hated to have to make small talk before she saw Miss Anna. A few pictures hung on the wall: scenes from the beach, the mountains, even a large lake somewhere unbeknownst to Cindy. She knew the pictures were there for a calming effect, and they often helped Cindy breathe more easily before she met with her therapist.

The door to Miss Anna's office opened, and a smiling Miss Anna poked out her head. Her soft hazel eyes puckered in the corners as she waved Cindy into her office.

"Hi, Cindy!" Miss Anna's gentle, easy manner of speaking always lifted Cindy's spirits.

Cindy made a dash for her chair, anxious yet excited to be with Miss Anna.

Miss Anna gazed at Cindy. She thought she looked different today. Maybe it was her eyes. Cindy was looking straight ahead when normally, she avoided direct eye contact. Anna had been working on several things with Cindy to help with her panic attacks and anxieties, especially when they occurred at school.

Each session began with an opening statement such as, "Tell me what you're feeling today," and went from there. It had taken Cindy over four weeks before she could respond comfortably, and that was over a year ago. Now Cindy was able to jump right into their sessions and focus on various grounding techniques. Each session would end with positive statements to ensure Cindy left without worrying about tomorrow.

Miss Anna used to worry about tomorrow. She remembered that all too well.

"Anna," Bobby had cried to his older sister. "Please tell them to leave me alone. I don't want to play with those guys. They make fun of me . . . all the time . . ."

"Bobby." Anna had leaned over and hugged her younger brother tightly, breathing in his peanut butter breath while avoiding pressing against the sticky remnants on his face. "You don't have to play with them. If you want to stay home with me, you can. Mom and Dad are out somewhere, so it's just you and me. Why don't you help me make dinner, and then we can watch a movie?" Anna stood up and grabbed a paper towel. She dampened it at the faucet and gently wiped the last of his lunch from his face, staring into the same hazel eyes as her own.

"Are you sure, Anna? Are you really, really sure? Because if you want to have your friends over, it's okay. I'll stay in my room. I'm okay. I don't want you to—"

"Bobby!" Anna said with pretend anger in her voice. "I don't mind, and I mean it. Now go wash your hands, and later tonight, I'll let you make the spaghetti."

Bobby grinned. His two front teeth were missing, and sometimes he whistled when he spoke, and spittle would spill out when he cried. At eight years old, he was the cutest little brother she could ever imagine, but he worried her. He was keeping to himself more and more, and when she asked him why, he would just shrug and say he liked staying inside and reading his graphic novels about his favorite heroes.

Bobby no longer seemed to enjoy being outside with the other eight-year-old boys playing football or kickball. He hated sleepovers and hanging out with the other kids to play video games. Anna had come home from school one day and found him hiding in her closet playing with her old American Girl dolls she had packed away in a suitcase years ago.

Anna had tried to tell Bobby it was okay; whatever he liked to play with was perfectly fine, and she would be damned if she let the other boys make fun of him. But as time passed, Bobby withdrew even further. Her parents were in denial, no matter what the teachers tried to tell them.

"He'll grow out of it," they would tell his teachers.

"No," her parents argued. "He does not need therapy."

Bobby was a lost boy who was experimenting. That was all.

Bobby would call Anna on the weekends, but the number of phone calls lessened over time. He started writing to ease his pain. At first, it was just jumbled thoughts in a notebook with an emotional outburst here and there. Sometimes, his writing cursed at the gods—*which* god, Bobby wasn't sure, but he questioned what higher being would have created a human with such wrong thoughts.

Was it evil? Was it abnormal? Bobby wasn't sure who he was anymore, and he had no one to talk to about his feelings.

One day, while he was on his way home after school, another boy—someone who lived near Bobby but attended a private school—approached him. They started talking. At first, it was just careless unimportant chitchat about who lived on that street and the next street over. Bobby began to look for Matthew every day after school, and the two developed a friendship of sorts. Bobby held back, overly cautious not to say too much to a new friend for fear of being ostracized, humiliated, or worse—called out.

Anna was away at college and caught up in the excitement of living in a sorority house and dating a few different guys, and she often forgot to reach out to Bobby every weekend. Afterward, Anna blamed herself, no matter what she had read or had been told.

Bobby struggled in high school, and although he was a handsome teenager the girls *ooohed* and *ahhhed* over, Bobby wasn't happy. One night, he was caught by some friends in a stall in the men's room at the mall with another teenager. Bobby knew he was destroyed. He couldn't bear the shame or the pain of feeling different any longer. He went home that night and wrote two goodbye notes—one to Matthew apologizing for what they'd been doing in the stall and one to Anna, thanking her for the love and support she had always given him. After finishing the letters, he folded them neatly and placed them in his composition book filled with his personal reflections. Then Bobby snuck into his father's study, found his father's pistol, and took his life.

Anna was devastated. Her parents, who were still in some state of denial, had tried to rationalize that Bobby was too much of a lost soul, and that maybe, just maybe, he'd found peace.

Anna could not come to terms with losing her brother. The ache in her heart nearly destroyed her. She left college and moved to Northern California where she worked on a horse ranch for emotionally damaged kids, some of whom were physically disabled as well, and almost all were underprivileged. The hole left in her heart from losing her brother gradually closed but did not seal entirely. Day in and day out, Anna read and reread Bobby's journal. She knew he would have wanted her to read it. But she knew that just reading his tortured words was not enough. Anna knew what Bobby was hoping for her. Working that summer with the young kids and the teenagers who needed her had helped Anna realize what she was destined to do with the rest of her life.

After a year at the ranch, Anna returned to college and graduated with her psychology degree, followed by her masters. She earned her therapist's degree and certification and planned to spend the rest of her days helping youth understand they were the purest of souls who just need some guidance, reassurance, and trust. She might not have been able to bring her brother back, but she was hellbent on making sure other troubled kids wouldn't feel it necessary to throw their lives away by being there to help them find their way to acceptance and happiness with a future in front of them waiting to be fulfilled.

"So, Miss Cindy, tell me, how are you feeling today?"

Cindy beamed. She bounced in her chair with happiness, unable to contain herself. "Oh, Miss Anna, I had such a good day today. You know I'm in this program after school with some other students, and today, we had to talk about a club we might want to join."

"Yes, tell me more."

"Well, I wrote down the club in my notebook we keep for Mrs. Waverly and Mr. DeWitt, but I was too afraid to raise my hand."

Anna folded her hands in her lap and gazed at Cindy. Just admitting she was afraid was a leap for Cindy. Anna could see the droplets of sweat forming on her forehead from where she sat. "Cindy, being afraid is perfectly normal. What's the worst that could have happened?"

Cindy pushed her bangs over her forehead and tried to rub some of the sweat dry. "I . . . I . . . Everyone will laugh at me when I tell them my club, and I . . . uh . . . oh . . ."

Anna let Cindy take a breath, and then she said, "And then what? Are they going to laugh at you for wanting to be a part of something? Who will laugh at you?"

"I, uh, I really don't know. I don't know everyone in the group that well, and it's not like they say hi to me in the halls. In fact, Miss Anna, they totally ignore me when I walk by."

"Do you feel safe in this program?"

Cindy stared at the floor and didn't notice as Anna

picked up a cushy ball from her desk. She reached out to Cindy, who took the ball gratefully and began squeezing it nonstop. "I think so. I mean, no one else has said anything to me since we started, so I guess that means no one outside the group knows what we talk about in there. So yeah, I guess I do feel safe." Cindy laughed quietly. "You know we all swore that whatever we say in that room stays in that room? Mr. DeWitt said that's what they say in Vegas, but to tell you the truth, I don't understand what that means. I just know no one is supposed to post anything on social media after we leave."

Miss Anna watched as Cindy's small shoulders sank into the chocolate-brown faux leather chair. "So what worries you the most today?"

Cindy took a breath and stared at the poster on the wall. She read it slowly to herself. It was her favorite poster, and by now, she could recite the entire thing by rote.

You are brave. You are enough. Your words are meaningful. You have great ideas. You are the best at being you. Don't be afraid to be yourself. You are beautiful inside and out. It is okay to cry. You can say yes. You can say no. You are LOVED. Self-care is important. You don't have to be perfect to be great. We all make mistakes. You care not anyone's expectations. You are interesting. Nobody's perfect. You are worth it. You are important. Thank you for being you!!!

She finished reading it and looked at Anna. "I'm worried they'll hate me and I'll never have friends."

Anna had known this was coming. Their sessions always went down this road because Cindy was still anxious about having friends. Anna closed her eyes and nodded. Then she opened her eyes.

"Okay, so I hear you saying everyone will hate you. Who, exactly, will hate you?"

Cindy shrugged, not sure how to answer because she felt like everyone already hated her.

"Cindy, close your eyes for me, will you?"

Cindy closed her eyes. Miss Anna was doing her special thing with her, and it always made her feel better at the end.

"Now, let's go back to the classroom for a moment. Do you see yourself sitting in your chair?"

Cindy nodded, her eyes still closed.

"Okay, let's look around the group. You told me before you sit in a circle. Look at each person in your group. They are looking at you. And you know what, Cindy? They're smiling. They're smiling because you're all in this program together, and whatever you talk about is to help you be successful in your years at Wells. What are you hearing? Is everyone talking about the clubs they want to join?"

Again, Cindy nodded, sinking deeper into her large chair.

"Is anyone laughing, Cindy?"

Suddenly, Cindy opened her eyes. "No, Miss Anna, no one was laughing! But, then again, I didn't say what club I wanted to join. I was too scared."

Anna crossed her leg over the other and leaned back. "When I was in high school, there was this one girl I thought hated me. It took me a while to get my courage up, but finally, I went out of my way one day to talk to her, and—you're not going to believe this—I found out she was afraid *I* hated *her!*"

Cindy chuckled. "Boy, that's a turnaround, isn't it?"

Anna smiled. "So, before we finish, let's go over a few of our grounding techniques, okay? I want to make sure we talk about how you focused on the room and the other students today so you will be comfortable speaking up next time. You can do this, Cindy. I believe in you. Will you tell me what club you want to join?"

Cindy relaxed. She loved seeing Miss Anna every week. She would leave today filled with the confidence she needed, and she would speak up in her group and tell them what club she wanted to join. She had to. She had to because she wanted to be able to tell Miss Anna that she had. And damn to hell anyone who laughed at her.

CHAPTER 21

Riley looked at her watch. It was almost the end of period six. Mrs. Winewrought was busy at her desk pretending to do schoolwork, but Riley knew she was texting on her cell. Mrs. Winewrought was always texting when she wasn't yelling at the class or assigning work.

Riley's desk was matched up with Jilly's, and for once, they'd ended up as partners. Jilly was much faster with the assignment, but Riley didn't mind. Jilly was stupid smart, and after this year, they would probably never be in the same classes. This year everyone had to take ninth-grade physics—it was mandatory, just like all the other classes—but Jilly was destined to be in the advanced placement classes, and Riley, well, she would be happy to just get by.

Riley leaned forward, hoping Jilly could hear her whispering. "How is it going? After school, I mean."

Jilly looked up, confused. "What are you talking about?"

"You know, that special class you have to take every

week. That's your punishment, right? I mean, after you and Lucas, you know, got caught."

Jilly stared back at her paper, pretending to fill in some answers even though she was finished with the assignment. "Riley, you need to fill in the blanks on your paper." She ignored Riley's questioning. Jilly had not spoken to Riley in weeks, and since she was grounded both at home and from her cell phone, Riley had no clue what had been going on with her.

Jilly took out her favorite Hi-Polymer eraser and brushed it against her lips. She loved the smooth feel of the clean white eraser and let it rest on her lips for a minute before erasing the picture she'd drawn of a beaker on a balance. Jilly was too much of a perfectionist and wasn't happy with what she had on her paper.

She wanted to talk to Riley; she missed her friend and needed someone to talk to about, well, just about everything. Jilly cleared her throat. "Ya know, sometimes I think the class is stupid and a waste of my time. And I think Mr. DeWitt can be a real weirdo, if you know what I mean."

Mrs. Winewrought looked up. She'd heard Mr. DeWitt's name, and like a periscope on a submarine, her flag was raised. She walked over by the girls' desks to rearrange the textbooks and beakers on the lab table near them so she could hear more clearly.

"I kinda like Mr. DeWitt. What do you mean by *weirdo*? Is he a creeper?"

"Well, I'm not sure. He smiles at me all the time and always looks to me to respond to his questions. I have to fill out this notebook every week and leave it there. It gives me the willies to think he's looking through my personal book. He says he doesn't look at anyone's book, but . . ."

"What's in your notebook, anyway? Have you written about you and Lucas? Has Lucas called you yet?"

The bell rang before Jilly could answer.

"Okay, everyone. Scoot your desks back into the nice, neat rows you found them in, and class is dismissed. Be ready for the quiz tomorrow! Study your packets tonight!"

Beverly wanted to hear more from Jilly, but she had heard enough. She ran to pick up her cell phone before her next class started.

> Alisa, let's go over to Starbucks after school today. I want to tell you something but not here.
>
> It's going to blow you away! TTYL

Alisa was checking the kitchen areas in her room when she heard her phone buzz. It could only mean another text from Beverly. Lately, Beverly was texting her constantly, and Alisa was tired of the drama. It had seemed like drama always followed Alisa ever since she was a little girl.

Their new townhome had been so beautiful. Little Alisa finally had her own bedroom, and her baby brother, Antoine, had his own, too. She wouldn't have to listen to him cry and whine in his crib, and she could read on her bed without being disturbed. Reading was everything to Alisa when she was a little girl. She'd wanted to read every book she could find, from *Crickwing, Beezus and Ramona,* and *Harry Potter and the Sorcerer's Stone* to *Where the Sidewalk Ends, Coraline,* and even *Tales of a Fourth Grade Nothing.* But Alisa's most treasured book, which her daddy had read to her each night, was *One-Hundred-and-One African American Read-Aloud Stories.* Alisa knew from an early age that she was African American, and that meant she was very special. She was proud of who she was, even when her family moved from the inner city to the new townhome and Alisa was the only Black girl in her class.

"Alisa!" her mom had screamed one day. Mom was always loud, whether she was scolding you, calling you for dinner, or telling you to get up and get dressed. That was just who she was, and Alisa loved her no matter what. "Get down here and come to the front door. You have a visitor!"

Alisa had run down the stairs, almost tripping over her skates at the bottom of the steps, and came to a sudden halt when she saw the prettiest blue-eyed girl with long blonde pigtails standing at her front door. The girl held two Barbie dolls and a Ken doll.

"Hello," whispered Alisa shyly.

The girl hopped on one foot and then the other. "Well, aren't you going to let me in?" And without waiting for a response, she blew past Alisa's mother and walked right up to Alisa. "Do you want to play with me? I have two different Barbies but only one Ken doll, but we can share. Do you have any dolls? Are they Barbie dolls or do you have other kinds? Do you have your own bedroom? I have my own bedroom because I have two stinky older brothers and they share a room, so I get my own. Wanna go play now?"

Alisa smiled. She wasn't sure if it was a white girl thing to talk so fast or if it was because this girl was nervous or maybe she was just excited. "What's your name?"

"I'm Janice, named after my grandmother Janet, but she died a long time ago, and I don't remember her at all. What's your name?"

"Alisa. I have to ask my mother why she named me that. I think she just liked it and all. And I have Princess Tiana, do you?"

"Hmm, I don't think so. Can I see yours?"

And so began a special friendship between the two girls. Alisa missed Janice. She and her family had moved across the country when her father was deployed. There were occasional letters now and then, but as time went by, their friendship had faded. Alisa smiled at Beverly's text. It reminded her of Janice because Janice never stopped talking, and drama was her middle name.

"You know, Alisa," Janice had said one day as they washed up for lunch, "if I wash your hands a hundred more times, I can get you white like me! Should we try?"

Alisa looked at Janice in disbelief. "Janice Billing, I take a bath every single day. I am never going to turn white. I'm an African American girl for always. Don't you get it?"

Janice shrugged. "I guess so. I'm not sure what that means. I wasn't sure if it was a permanent thing or not. But if you're okay, then I'm okay. Just saying, that's all. C'mon, let's wash up and go eat. I am *starved!*"

Eating at Janice's house was the inspiration for Alisa's future career. She'd loved everything Janice's mom baked, fried, boiled, and toasted. She was an amazing cook. Not that Alisa's mom was a bad cook; cooking just wasn't her thing. She liked to make the same thing all the time—meatloaf or fried chicken. After that, it was leftovers and lots of noodles. Eventually, Alisa would go visit with Mama Billing, as she affectionately called her, just to watch her in the kitchen. Slowly but surely, Mama Billing began handing her utensils over to Alisa and letting her take over, always watching and teaching and letting her experiment. By the time the Billings moved away, Alisa was quite the accomplished cook and knew she was going to do something with food in her future.

Alisa smiled to herself. Learning the history of African Americans was not a subject in school back then, and being the only Black girl on the block for so long didn't help her classmates understand her culture any better, but her friendship with the Billings had helped shape her future.

Like Janice, Beverly was overly dramatic, and although there were times when Alisa thought Beverly was spreading more gossip than fact, she enjoyed their friendship.

Alisa finished cleaning the kitchen areas where some of her lovely students had "accidentally" missed spills and crumbs. *It's a labor of love*, Alisa mused, bending over on the counters and spraying and wiping until all the surfaces sparkled. Alisa gathered her gradebook and her files and shoved them in her brand-new leather pouch—a birthday gift from Beverly. She turned off the lights and locked the door behind her, then made her way to the parking lot.

She didn't see Beverly yet, but she noticed Carl De-Witt and Cassandra Conway walking shoulder to shoulder. *Hmm, that's not a casual "let's walk to our cars" kind of stroll.* Alisa laughed out loud. "Ha, good for them! We can all use a close encounter now and then!"

Alisa threw her belongings in her car, started the engine, and headed to the Starbucks she and Beverly always went to when they wanted to talk privately. It was far away from the school, in a different neighborhood, where there was no possibility of bumping into any students or hopefully any parents.

Beverly pushed open the school doors in a hurry to meet with Alisa. She and Alisa had hit it off the first day they met and became fast friends with no secrets between them. That is, almost no secrets. Beverly still kept the one dark secret—her husband's physical and emotional abuse—tucked deep down. *Maybe one day*, she thought, *but not today.*

Beverly was so busy with her own thoughts she almost walked right into Carl and Cassandra. "Oh, hey." Beverly chuckled. "I'm so sorry. I wasn't paying attention and almost clipped you right on your heels."

Carl turned around to find Beverly Winewrought close enough to count the hairs on the back of his head. "Hey, no problem, Beverly," Carl said, not quite sure what to say next.

Beverly smirked. "Oh, hello, Cassandra. Looks like you were able to get away from the office at a decent time today."

Cassandra was uncomfortable. The negative comments Beverly had said to her the other day and being seen leaving school with Carl made for a very awkward interaction. She laughed weakly. "Everyone was in a meeting, and Joanne told me it was okay to skedaddle since I have to work late tomorrow night."

"Well, you two," Beverly said in an evil and calculating tone, "enjoy the afternoon delight!" Without waiting for a response, Beverly reached her car, threw her belongings in the back seat, and took off to meet with Alisa.

Carl shrugged and looked at Cassandra. "She is one messed-up woman, I think. Now, how about grabbing that bite to eat?"

Cassandra smiled. She enjoyed Carl's company despite the gossip Beverly was spreading. *Maybe I should let Carl know about it? No,* she thought, second-guessing herself, *it's not worth it.*

CHAPTER 22

Beverly enjoyed socializing with Alisa. Alisa was easygoing, and Beverly loved sharing stories with her. Actually, it was Beverly who did most of the talking and very little of the sharing. Alisa never judged Beverly; she was a good listener. She had learned to become a good listener growing up with the family she did. It was not too often that Alisa got to jump in during dinner conversations, so she learned to listen and store it all away in her family memory bank. It was when she stayed over at Janice's house that Mama Billing would let Alisa go on and on about her day at school, the drama at her own house, what was going on in the world according to Alisa, and so on. So Alisa was comfortable letting her conversations with Beverly be one-sided.

"And that's why," Beverly said, "I think Carl DeWitt is a danger to kids."

"You know, Beverly," Alisa said softly, "I think you're going down a very scary road making these accusations.

How can you be sure you're interpreting what you're hearing from teenagers correctly?"

"I heard the word *weird*, and I know for a fact that's code for *creepo*. It has to be. We don't know what's going on after school, and those kids—"

"Wait a minute. Isn't Neva Waverly in there as well?"

"Yeah, so what?"

"Well, c'mon, then. You can't tell me Neva is allowing anything inappropriate to go on. Can you? Do you really think she would let that happen? Not on her watch. No way."

Beverly stared at Alisa. "How old is Neva? Do you realize she's probably totally clueless when it comes to this kind of thing? Neva is a widow, I think. I don't even know if she ever had kids, so how sharp do you think she is? For all we know, he could be texting the girls in the group."

Alisa shook her head and looked over Beverly's shoulder. It was getting dark. "Look, Beverly, I don't have anything against Carl. I hear he's a fairly good teacher. He gets along with his students, his department, and the rest of the staff. And now I think he might be trying to go out with Cassandra, who also has a good head on her shoulders. She wouldn't bother with a creeper. No, I'm not buying it. Not yet, anyway. And besides, kids say all kinds of things when they don't know what they're talking about. Maybe we need to ask around a bit more. Even Scott, who is always walking the halls and hearing what the kids are talking about, has never mentioned this."

Beverly smirked. "You think those guys would rat on

one another? They stick together like stink on poop, if you ask me. They would never . . ."

"And what about our administration? Surely they would have heard something by now. In fact, it was Barbara our Battle Axe Atkinson who picked Carl to head up that after-school program. She's way too savvy to have chosen someone with a shady character flaw."

"Yeah, ol' Battle Axe herself chose him and Neva, and if you want to know the truth, she picked the two worst teachers to be in charge. Neva is too old, and Carl is young and greedy. He wants it all. You know the type—teach for a couple of years, and then wham bam! It's time to move on up the ladder and leave the classroom. What kind of teacher is that? I should've been the one who was asked to lead those mentoring sessions."

Alisa sat back. She finally understood where this conversation was heading. Beverly was jealous. Jealous of Carl, of Neva, and pissed as hell she wasn't chosen for some special program. It had nothing to do with all the innuendos she'd described. Beverly Winewrought was envious, and her claws were coming out sharper than ever before.

There was another time when Beverly had gone after a popular teacher, spreading ugly gossip and lies. She caused so much turmoil that the teacher transferred to another school, where her outstanding teaching skills led her to win Teacher of the Year for the district. Alisa took a deep breath. Could Beverly be this manipulative, even evil?

Finally, Alisa stood up. "Look, Beverly, I think you need to dial it back just a little and think on this before you do anything you might regret. Let's meet again—same time next week? It's getting late, and I need to get going. Promise me you won't say anything to anyone else, okay?"

Beverly finished the last of her vanilla latte and put it down on the table. She licked her lips and gazed at the ceiling. "I guess I can hold off, but if I hear anything more, you and I need to talk about next steps. Do you agree?"

Alisa nodded. "Okay, I'll agree to that if you swear you'll chill for a bit. Deal?"

Beverly cursed softly to herself. "I didn't realize it was this late. Let's get out of here."

The two cleaned their table, threw away their cups, and headed out into the early chill of evening.

It didn't take long for Beverly to arrive at home, and she entered the house quickly, quietly, and with trepidation. She hadn't planned on staying out so long, but it was so good to sit and talk with someone like Alisa. She needed female companionship and comfort, and quite honestly, her current home situation was far from comforting and provided little to no companionship. Beverly had also texted a few of her non-teacher friends, but thus far, only Alisa—loyal Alisa—had responded.

She could hear Ted in the kitchen making a noisy racket with utensils. A cup shattered on the floor, and a round of curse words split the icy stillness in the air. Beverly placed her leather school bag and her jacket on the bench by the front door and walked carefully to the kitchen.

Ted stood by the stove, his rolled-up white starched shirt splotched with grease. Bits of flour dangled from the locks of his dark blond hair that spilled onto his forehead. He snapped his head toward the door when he heard Beverly amble in as though she didn't have a care in the world. His dark brown eyes filled with rage, and his lips pressed tightly together, as though if he were to relax them, an entire barrage of obscenities would escape.

"Hi, babe." Beverly spoke as jovially as she could, knowing anything, absolutely anything, could trigger an onslaught of threats and accusations. She was not looking for another fight. She was tired—tired of the arguing and tired of the physical confrontations that left her bruised and frightened.

But Ted wasn't going to let her off so easily tonight.

"And where the hell have you been?" he asked, his tone brusque and sharp and filled with daggers.

"Oh"—Beverly tried to sound nonchalant, which she definitely was not feeling—"I had a meeting with a teacher at school, and we had to go over."

"What's his name, Beverly?"

"Ted, really," said Beverly, her voice quivering as fear crawled into her veins like the ice chips on her windowsill. She knew she was treading on a slippery slope and wanted nothing to escalate their conversation.

"I'm going to ask you again, Beverly . . ." Spittle slipped over his lips as he stepped closer to her.

Beverly spotted the pan on the stove filled with hot oil Ted must have been about to use to fry something. On the floor, spices were strewn, along with the broken glass Beverly had heard shatter when she first came in.

"Can I help you with whatever you're cooking tonight, Teddy?" Beverly reached for a hand towel to scoop up the mess on the floor, and Ted grabbed for her wrist and yanked her to him. "Ow, Ted. That really hurts. Let go!" Beverly winced in pain as though a heated knife had sliced her skin in two.

But Ted did not let go, his anger taking over now, his brain slipping into another zone filled with hatred and disgust that blinded his rational thoughts. Ted could not find his words. Instead, his grip tightened on Beverly's wrist. For the first time, Beverly's body took over, and her other hand curled into a tight fist. She swung at Ted's face as hard as a weakened body could. Blood spurted out of his nose and onto his work shirt. He released Beverly's wrist from his deathlike grip, and in one fell swoop, his anger swelled up and burned white hot in his head. It was the culmination of anger, jealousy, and pride squeezed together that was now bottled up inside of him and needed to explode.

He could not control himself as both hands shoved against Beverly's chest like a snake striking violently at its victim. Beverly's eyes widened as she lost her balance. She stumbled backward, trying to regain her balance, but the shove was so savage her body crumbled to the hard ceramic tile. Instinctively, she reached out to cushion the fall, allowing her wrist to suffer the weight of her body. Ted heard the loud, unearthly snap and watched Beverly go limp. Her eyes rolled up, and her world turned black. Her head bobbed from side to side and then went still.

Grunting and groaning, Ted knelt beside Beverly. His

anger had dissipated, leaving him spent and exhausted. She was breathing but not responsive. Ted jumped up and turned off the stove before reaching into the drawer and grabbing a handful of kitchen towels. He dropped to his knees again and gently placed the towels under Beverly's unconscious head.

"Shhh, Beverly. I am so sorry." Ted's eyes filled with tears, and they spilled out and dropped onto Beverly's cold face as if the heavens were crying over her. "God, I can't believe . . . I'm so sorry. It's just that I . . . Beverly, wake up. Dear God, please wake up. I didn't mean to hurt you. I . . . I . . . I couldn't stop thinking about who you were with, and I got so enraged I couldn't see straight. I was trying to make us a special dinner tonight to celebrate . . . I . . . I got a promotion, and I wanted to share it with you, but you weren't here, and you weren't answering my texts, and I got scared, and I just kept thinking the most awful thoughts in my head . . . Oh, please wake up."

Ted got to his feet and soaked a washcloth with cold water. He squeezed out the excess and rushed back to place it on Beverly's forehead. His eyes followed Beverly's arm, which lay on the ceramic tile at an awkward angle. And then he saw her wrist. It looked lifeless, like a dangling fish on a hook. Ted reached over and touched her fingers softly, almost caressing them, but Beverly moaned, and he jerked his hand back for fear of hurting her again.

Beverly stirred, and her eyes fluttered open. She opened her mouth to speak, but no words came out—just a groan. Ted reached over to touch Beverly's wrist, and this time, she howled. It was a sound that ripped at Ted's insides. He had never heard Beverly make that cry before, and he winced knowing how badly he'd hurt her. He never meant to, and he didn't remember grabbing her wrist so tightly. But then she fell on her wrist. He did not break her wrist. He kept repeating that to himself. She passed out when she fell on her wrist. Passed out from the pain—the pain that he inflicted. Again.

Ted knew he had to take Beverly to the emergency room and quickly. He didn't want to call an ambulance because, well, he didn't want the neighbors to hear the sirens and start their questioning, which led to gossip and rumors. He leaned behind Beverly and helped her sit up. She moaned again so loudly Ted was afraid to move her more.

"Beverly, can you sit up?" Ted begged. "I need to take you to the ER. Do you think you can stand?"

Beverly was barely conscious. Her ears were ringing, and the room was spinning out of control. She felt like falling backward, but something supported her shoulders, so she relaxed her body against it.

The pain. The pain. The pain was so intense. Something had snapped, crunched, and cracked, and then her body gratefully went limp, and she had passed out. She didn't realize she had fainted; she only became vaguely aware of it when she tried to open her eyes and realized Ted was saying something to her. *What are you trying to say? What just happened to me? What is wet on my face? Am I crying? Why won't the room stop spinning?* And then the room went dark again.

Beverly didn't know how long she'd been unconscious. When she became aware of herself again, there was a humming sound, and it felt like someone had strapped her body to something hard. A breeze blew over her face, and Beverly tried very slowly to open her eyes. Lights flashed by. Houses, trees, cars. She was in a moving car. Ted was driving her. Where were they going? The pain. *Oh, God, please stop the pain. What's wrong with me? My wrist. My arm. My head. What happened?* And then the pain took over, and Beverly closed her eyes again.

CHAPTER 23

Neva and Carl sat side by side in Carl's classroom. They had been preparing for their mentoring program and had many packets in front of them. Before they had a chance to organize the stack, the students started to stroll in.

"Hi, Mrs. Waverly."

"Hey, Mr. DeWitt. What's shakin'?"

The students called out their individual greetings as they filed in, picked up their composition notebooks from the counter against the wall, and found their seats.

Carl and Neva looked at their delightful dozen as Neva liked to refer to them. They had been mentoring them for several months now, and the camaraderie that had blossomed was palpable. The students had become comfortable talking with one another, knowing that for some of them, this kind of conversation would never take place in their regular classrooms, the lunchrooms, or even the media center.

It was the beauty of the program, allowing the students to grow into successful and confident high schoolers.

Tommy looked up at Mr. DeWitt and said, "Ya know, Mr. DeWitt, you are one weird dude!"

Carl laughed. "Why do you say that?"

Jilly joined in. "Because one minute, you are so serious about us getting good grades and all, and then the next minute, you're goofing with Mrs. Waverly about her not being able to understand the game of football!"

"Yeah," said Cindy. She almost stuttered, then caught herself and slowly and confidently added, "But we know how much you care about us, so that makes you a little less weird!" Cindy beamed. She couldn't wait to share this with Miss Anna later in the day. *Yay*, she thought. *I spoke up, and I wasn't even asked to yet!*

Neva had to jump in the mix. "Now, you all know we want you to succeed, and so far, meeting with you has been the highlight of my days! And I want you to know, Miss Jilly, that I have been studying up on my football knowledge, and I am ready to tackle any question you have. And, yes, that was my pun of the day!" She laughed.

"Okay, okay, okay," said Mr. DeWitt. "Let's get down to the business of the day. I want to share an icebreaker with you. Now, the answers are private—just for you and no one else, right? So here we go . . . Take out your composition books and open them up to the next blank page. Put today's date on the top line, and the title for today's entry is *A Walk in the Woods*."

Carl continued with his lesson. It was important to him to share these special icebreakers because they allowed each student to reflect on who they were and ultimately to become more and more confident in themselves.

"So"—Carl's strong voice boomed across the room—"Here we go. Number one. Imagine you are in a strange forest, trees all around you. Someone is there with you. Who is it? Name that person."

Carl waited about two minutes before continuing. "Number two. You walk along and see an animal. What animal do you see?"

Again, he paused and looked around at his group to see when they had completed their answers. "Okay, number three. What do you do about this animal? Anything?"

This activity continued for another fifteen minutes. Then Mrs. Waverly took over.

"I am so glad none of you had trouble writing down your responses. Now, let me explain what your responses mean. Ready? Here we go. Number one. The person you listed as with you in the woods—well, that person is someone who is very special to you. What do you think?" Neva looked around the room. Some of the students were smiling, while others looked quizzical.

"It's okay if you don't agree with any of this." She soothed their worries. "It's just a game, and sometimes, these answers really make sense, and sometimes, they can be way out in left field, if you know what I mean."

Neva nodded as she saw that some of the worried faces relaxed and smiled at her. "Okay, I'll explain number two because that might be very interesting to you. The animal you selected—think about what this creature looks like. The size of your animal is supposed to represent the size of your problems in life. What do you think about that?"

Some of the students laughed.

"Oh, my goodness." Linette, a small perky Asian American girl with dark eyes, a petite nose, and long jet-black hair, cackled. "I picked an elephant! Oh. My. God!"

Some of the students giggled, but only because there was a bond among them that allowed the laughter without the judgment. And Linette knew she was not being judged and laughed right along with them.

Mrs. Waverly composed herself and continued with their icebreaker, stopping after each explanation to allow the students to share their responses if they wanted. Sometimes, there was laughter; sometimes, it was simply an "Ooooh! You are bad!" followed by a "You're a lover, not a fighter!"

And so it rolled on. The two teachers smiled and joked and prodded for more reflection when necessary, but by the end of the session, the group felt as though they had progressed. Milestones were not measured by feet or yards or miles or days, but rather on the way each student felt as he or she walked out of the room. More confident, more involved, more engaged, more willing to reach out and stand up for what they believed in. And hopefully, by the end of the year, ready to complete the next three years of high school successfully and with all the confidence they so desperately needed but had never had.

Before the afternoon session was over, Mr. DeWitt said, "Before we finish, I'd like you to do one more thing." There were a few groans, but they were good-natured and paired with a few laughs and giggles. "At the bottom of your page, I want you to write one word. Just one word. And that word should sum up how you feel about everything we do here. Remember, I don't want a paragraph, a sentence, or even a creative haiku! Just one word. Go ahead."

Mr. DeWitt waited for two minutes, and then, smiling, he put down the EXPO pen he always carried in case he was struck by something earth-shattering he had to share on the whiteboard.

"Well done!" called out Mr. DeWitt as the students packed up their belongings. "And most importantly, thank you. Each and every one of you. Today was awesome. You guys are totally amazing, and as you leave, remember who you are and where you're going, and while on your way, do something nice for someone today. Have a totally, inexplicably, and phenomenally awesome day! See ya, my favorite freshmen!"

Cindy looked down at her notebook where she had scribbled her one word—*SAFE*—with a little smiley face next to it. She closed her book and got up to leave with everyone else.

"See," said Jilly to no one in particular as she sauntered out the door. "Definitely a weirdo, but he is one cool weirdo!"

CHAPTER 24

Leland Memorial Hospital was only a ten-minute drive from Beverly and Ted's house, but Ted felt like it had taken him an hour to get there. He pulled up to the ER, jumped out of the car, and sprinted into the waiting room. He raced to the front desk and demanded someone come out to his car with a gurney as his wife had fallen and was still unconscious.

The nurse at the front desk sprang into action. Within minutes, two orderlies ran out of the hospital, pushing a gurney and heading straight to Ted's car. They lifted Beverly out of the car and onto the gurney, being extremely careful to hold her poorly bandaged arm with care.

Beverly had the oddest sensation she was being carried. Her eyes fluttered open to see overhead lights streaming above her, and she experienced the whirring motion of being transported. Transported? Where? Was Ted with her? Was she in a sci-fi movie?

The moving sensation suddenly stopped. She felt enclosed in some sort of room with large machines humming around her. Nothing was clear, and her eyes strained to stay open. Some man in a white coat leaned over her. He spoke gently to her, but her ears were still ringing. Was that a needle in his hand? What was he saying? She knew her name. She knew it, but the words would not come out. She felt her lips moving, but she did not hear any sound. Was that her groaning? She never groaned. Cried maybe, but what was that animal sound coming from deep within her? She felt a pinch, and then the room went dark again.

Beverly stirred. She felt groggy and numb and . . . heavy, as though her body were weighted down with soaked towels. She couldn't move her arms, and her eyelids seemed glued shut.

"Wha . . . ? Where . . . ?" she mumbled, but her mind wasn't functioning well enough to add more.

"Shhh. Bevvy, it's me. It's Ted. I'm here with you. We're at the hospital. You fell in the kitchen. Remember? I brought you here, and well . . ."

A nurse walked in and whispered something to Ted, who moved back toward the wall.

"Hello, Beverly. My name is Michelle. I'm your nurse. How are you feeling now?"

Beverly heard the voice, but her eyes remained sealed shut. She tried to force her mouth to utter something, anything, and while she thought she was coherent, all that came out was, "Umphhhh."

"It's okay, Beverly," Michelle said. "Your mouth is a bit dry from the morphine we gave you. You took quite a nasty fall. The X-rays showed a break in your radius, so the doctor placed a soft cast on your arm.

"You can't move your arms right now because we've restrained them temporarily. We didn't want you to disturb the cast till you were awake. Go ahead and rest some more. I have an IV with some pain reliever flowing in nice and slow to take the edge off. Let your body absorb that now." Michelle turned and said to Ted, "Try not to talk to her too much right now. She's too groggy to understand whatever you're trying to tell her. Especially if you're explaining what you want her to remember."

Ted narrowed his eyes, and with laser-like focus and a caustic superiority to his tone, he replied, "My wife fully remembers how she slipped on the wet kitchen floor, thank you very much."

Michelle said something under her breath and walked out.

• • •

Alisa sent and then resent the same text:

> Hey girl...where are you today? BA had to cover your 1st period and then they called for a sub.

She went down to the main office. Alisa tried to be nonchalant as she tiptoed over to Cassandra's desk and bent over so no one could hear their conversation. "Hey, Cassandra. How are you doing today?"

Cassandra looked up and smiled. "Well, hey, Ms. Saper. What's cooking today?"

Alisa laughed, and her deep copper eyes crinkled at the corners. Everyone used that line on Alisa, and it never got old. She was proud of her job, her skills, and her profession. "It's hot off the stove today, my dear!"

Cassandra chuckled. She held out both hands with her palms up. "So, where's my free sample, huh? Are you falling down on the job?"

"Funny you should ask, my favorite secretary in the office," quipped Alisa as she reached into the vivid purple apron she always wore at work. She pulled out two chocolate chip brownies with fudge topping wrapped in cellophane.

"Oh, my!" said a not-too-surprised Cassandra. "Why, thank you, Ms. Saper! I will definitely enjoy this with my lunch!"

Alisa took the opportunity. "And maybe, since I gave you two, you could share one with a special someone who, a little bird has told me, you may have spent some extra-curricular time with recently."

Cassandra blushed, the red spreading past her cheeks and up into the roots of her auburn hair. She looked at the numerous papers on her desk. Not reading any of them, she said, "Well, I might have spent some time with the teacher I'm guessing you suspect."

"Why, crush my garlic, Miss Cassandra. You are blushing, girl!"

Cassandra giggled. "He is the sweetest man! And quite a

gentleman! He took me out to dinner, and we never even discussed work. We were so caught up in talking about the environment and climate and saving the whales. Did you know he is totally into saving the whales? He wants to take me on a whale-watching tour up in Boston somewhere."

Alisa couldn't stop smiling. She was happy to hear Cassandra talking about Carl, and knowing he was a decent man only made her wish Beverly were standing right beside her to hear all of it, too. And that reminded her . . . "Hey, did you happen to hear anything about Beverly? I mean, she didn't call in this morning, and that isn't like her, is it?"

Cassandra sniffed and squinted as though she were trying to grab at something in the back of her memory bank. "Ya know, I don't ever remember Beverly forgetting to call in for a sub when she couldn't come to work. That does seem odd, doesn't it?"

"I thought maybe you had heard something. I keep texting her, but I'm not getting any response from her at all. And that's really odd, you know?"

Just then, Alisa felt her phone buzz. It was a text message. She took out her phone. It was from Beverly.

I'm okay, I guess. I won't be at school today or tomorrow. I will fill you in later. Can you let the front office know I will need a sub for tomorrow, too? I'm not near my computer right now.

Gotta go……TTYL……promise

Alisa's stomach tightened. Something was definitely wrong. This was not like Beverly. Not at all. She couldn't imagine what had happened from the time they left Starbucks till today. Unless . . . goddammit, was it that prick of a husband of hers? She knew they weren't doing well, and Beverly didn't have to tell her the bruises on her arm weren't from banging into the damn cabinets in her classroom. Alisa had seen those kinds of bruises too often a long time ago.

CHAPTER 25

Lucas sat slumped in his seat, looking miserable. Everything was going wrong for him . . . again. Football season was over, and his grades were so terrible he wasn't allowed to try out for wrestling. He loved wrestling, and he was good at it, but until his GPA came up, he was stuck. And he was angry. No, he was pissed off at the world.

Lucas stared at the girl in the front row. What was her name again? Judy? Janey? He couldn't remember. He barely remembered grabbing her hand and running down to the special hallway all the guys had told him about. Take a girl there, they'd said. Do whatever you want because no one *ever* goes down there. Hell, they'd said you could make out for an entire period, and no one would ever find you. *Yeah*, he thought. *Never find me. Really, they found me in a hot second, and then my whole world collapsed. Again.*

His mother had grounded him; his stepfather had given him *the* lecture about girls and where that would lead him. The guys had all slapped him on the back and given him high fives because he was so cool for trying to do it with a girl in the dark hall. *What the hell is "doing it," anyway?* He wasn't quite sure, and he was not going to ask his stepfather. If only his real father were around, but then again, just thinking about that night and reliving the nightmare made Lucas shake.

"Lucas?" asked Mr. DeWitt. "Lucas Cannon! Are you okay? Dude, talk to me, because it looks like you're no longer with us. Mr. DeWitt to Lucas, come in, please."

Lucas shook his head. It took a few seconds to focus on who was talking to him. "Huh?"

"Lucas, perhaps you want to go see the nurse for a few minutes. Can I have someone go with you?"

Lucas sat up straight. This was good. "Uh . . . I, well, I'm not feeling too hot. Is it okay if I go see the nurse like you said? I don't need anyone to take me. I know where her office is. I'll just be a few minutes."

Lucas stood up, grabbed his book bag, and walked out of the classroom, ignoring the snickers and quiet laughter as he exited. Jilly's inquisitive eyes followed him as he strutted out of the room. Every time she saw him, she felt a twinge in her chest, and she wasn't sure if it was embarrassment, humiliation, or maybe she still had a crush on a cute guy. *Whatever*, she thought, and she turned her head back to Mr. DeWitt. He was going over the American Revolution one more time in preparation for their test and never saw which way Lucas turned once he'd slipped out.

Lucas should have taken a right turn when he strolled out of the classroom, and anyone watching him would have known that, but he went left—the opposite direction of the nurse's office. Lucas jogged down the hall, knowing exactly where he was headed.

He spotted Mr. Sheldrake and the security team, who were escorting a few seniors probably to the security office. He had been down that road too often himself. Fortunately, because security was focused on another issue, no one noticed Lucas ambling down the hall trying his best to appear nonchalant.

He turned right and crouched down to relax in the dark hall where he could be alone—all alone to think and just veg without anyone bugging him about homework or asking him for the answers to the drill on the board or why he wasn't wrestling or what he was going to do over Thanksgiving break. *Damn*, he thought. Thanksgiving meant being stuck at home with his family.

Riley walked down the hall; her hand squeezed against her notebook filled with foreign words that illustrated cooking techniques. It was for Ms. Saper's class. She was focusing so hard on memorizing the list of words that she almost smacked straight into security guard Ms. Clifton—or PC, as everyone fondly called her for short.

"Well, hey, girl. What do you have going on today that you're out here walking the halls?" asked Ms. Clifton. "Aren't you supposed to be somewhere learning skills for your future?"

Riley liked Ms. Clifton. She was cool but strict, and she told you like it was, so there was no messing with her. If you needed help, she was there for you, but if you were doing something inappropriate or totally stupid, she wasn't going to let you slide. That is, unless there was a super good reason for it, like if you were in the bathroom because you got your period and forgot to prepare for it and absolutely could not go to class. Like she had ESP or something, she would appear in the bathroom checking for stragglers, and when she found you, she would run to the nurse's office, get what you needed, and be right back to save you. But if you were just skipping class because you couldn't stand one more minute of algebra—well, that was never a good reason. Not only would she drag you back to class and embarrass the hell out of you in front of everyone, but you'd have to serve detention with her after school.

Fortunately for Riley, today, she was in the halls with a pass from Ms. Saper.

"Oh, my bad, Ms. Clifton. Uh, I have a pass. Really, I do. Look." Riley quickly stuck her hand in her pocket and pulled out the school pass with Ms. Saper's handwriting on it:

Please allow Riley Maddox to pick up a package for me in the cafeteria.

Thank you,
Alisa Saper

Pauline Clifton looked at Riley's pass and studied it for a moment. There was no way Riley could have forged Ms. Saper's beautiful signature. She handed it back to Riley, smiled, and said, "Now you make sure you don't take too long going to the cafeteria and getting back to class. You have a lotta class time left, girlfriend!"

Riley nodded. "You got it, PC. I'm on it!" She hustled passed Ms. Clifton.

Riley *did* have a lot of class time left, so she was in no particular hurry. Ms. Saper wasn't going to check how long it took her to pick up her package. And even though she was warming up to Ms. Saper—especially since she had asked Riley to join her special club after school—Riley was still on the fence about the class.

And so, with Ms. Clifton long gone, Riley took a sudden left turn down the next hallway and meandered. Ms. Saper had asked her to be a part of a team that would be cooking in a competition in the spring. If that meant learning how to cook some really awesome meals for her mom, Riley decided to suck it up and become a positive and integral part of the team. She wasn't involved in anything else anyway, and this was a good way to keep busy. For now, she was given the charge of memorizing the names of some stupid knife cuts Ms. Saper was going to show the team that afternoon. Stupid or not, deep down inside, Riley kind of liked it. She was lonely after school, and Jilly had not been much for companionship lately.

Riley was so busy thinking and walking that she hadn't even realized which hallway she had stumbled into. She looked up, and a chill ran down her spine. Riley hated this dark hall because it reminded her of when her best friend became her not-so-best friend anymore. But part of her liked venturing down this way because it was always so isolated. Security rarely walked down here, so she knew she would be undisturbed.

"Julienne, brunoise, small dice, medium dice, large dice, paysanne, batonnet, chiffonnade." Riley repeated the list over and over and over again until it became rote memory in her head. She tried to make a song out of it as she kept walking, but she wasn't great at rhyming.

"Damn these knife skills," Riley said aloud to no one because there was no one in the hall—or so she thought. She turned the corner to sit in the notorious and very private dark corner of the building. There, sitting on the floor by himself, was the one person in the entire school she did not want to see: Lucas.

"Damn! It smells in this corner. Lucas Cannon, you're a pig! What are you doing? Sitting here farting all by yourself, feeling lonely?" Riley was angry that not only had she lost the opportunity to be alone like she'd wanted, but now she had to bump into who else but Lucas, and he must have been having a party by himself because it really smelled like rotten eggs!

Lucas looked up to see Riley Maddox holding a notebook with one hand and covering her nose with the other, her face all scrunched up like she was going to vomit.

"What the hell are you doing in my private office, Riley Maddog?"

CHAPTER 26

Beverly sat on the couch, TV remote in one hand and a Starbucks latte in the other. She stared at the television—some new movie on Netflix—but she wasn't watching. It wasn't even noon yet, and her wrist was throbbing something awful, but it wasn't time for another painkiller yet. Wonderful things, those oxycodone pills. No wonder people got hooked on them. Beverly could take them and just forget everything about last night.

Ted walked into the room. "How are you feeling, honey?"

Beverly wanted to ignore him, but she couldn't. It would have been so much easier to start a conversation with Ted, forget about "the incident," and move on. But truth be told, how could she move on with Ted? This painful confrontation was really the last straw. No number of apologies or explanations like, "I'm so sorry. Honest, honey, this will never ever happen again. I don't know what got into me. I just snapped," could ever excuse what had occurred.

Beverly pretended to look dreamily into Ted's watering eyes—he was good at that—and then said ever so sweetly,

"I'm feeling a bit tired, that's all. Why don't you go ahead and get to work? I'm just going to relax here and watch some television. Really, I'm okay. In fact, maybe you could bring me some soup for dinner tonight. How does that sound?"

Ted stared at his wife. He'd thought she was going to start another argument, accuse him of hurting her when she had hurt herself when she fell. He was in no mood for another disagreement. Beverly wore him out. She was always on him about something: dirty dishes in the sink, smelly socks left on the bedroom floor, the Amazon purchases of candy he bought only for himself. She complained if he didn't leave his briefcase exactly on the table by the front door saying she kept tripping over it in the hallway.

If Ted listed just a few of these complaints in his head, it certainly justified his Friday night drinks with his new secretary, Livvy. She was beautiful and carefree, and she laughed at all his jokes, no matter how corny. She didn't argue with him, and she thought whatever he said was filled with wisdom.

Ted was going to take the next step with Livvy. He'd work it out as a business trip that he would take without Beverly. Of course, he wasn't going to leave town, only his home. He'd make a reservation for dinner and a hotel room for the weekend in the next county. Beverly would never find out, and he needed this. He needed a break from his nagging wife, who never made him feel worthy of anything anymore. With Beverly on the couch and that huge soft cast on her wrist, well, this was a perfect opportunity to go away. She would be grouchy and ugly and demanding of him. Ted didn't want this anymore. He wanted fun and jokes and, well, perhaps something physical he was not getting from Beverly.

Beverly could barely focus on Ted with the way he was glaring at her. Did he think he was completely innocent of this accident? She was so tired of this selfish, immature, lazy man who always claimed to be so righteous. *Damn it to all hell. I'm in pain. You would think I'd be deserving of a little pity and maybe some coddling? But no.* Ted looked like he was ready to bolt. *Let things get a bit too hot for him to handle, and he's out the door. This is not what I signed up for, to say the least.*

"Uh, B-B-Beverly." Ted always stuttered when he was nervous around Beverly, nobody else. "I'm going to go into work now, if that's okay with you and you don't need anything from me today. I can pick up dinner on the way h-h-home for you." Ted wrung his hands together. "And, I-I-I think I may have told you, but my boss is sending me out of town this weekend. Some new client he wants me to wine and d-d-dine. That is, if you'll be okay without me . . ."

Beverly could always tell when Ted was lying. It wasn't just his stuttering that gave him away. He avoided direct eye contact until he was done talking, and then he would glance at her for a second, then scan the room as though he were searching for forgiveness from up above.

Beverly took the opportunity to squeeze some guilt out

of Ted. She had her suspicions about his Friday night meetings. That's what he called them, anyway, but Beverly could always smell something sweet on him that certainly was not the Tommy Bahama she'd bought him last Christmas.

"Oh, gee, Ted. I was hoping we could spend the weekend together and have some special alone time. But, hey, I understand. Whatever your boss wants you to do, I get it. I know what that's like. I have an administrator who is always on me about not getting grades and referrals to her in a timely manner." Beverly sighed. "Will you be gone the entire weekend?"

Ted almost backed out of his plans. But then he thought about it. This was one of Beverly's tricks, her tactic to make him feel remorseful. He would have given in only to despise the entire weekend while she guilted him into cleaning and doing laundry and waiting on her hand and foot.

"Look," said Ted, feeling bolder than ever before, "I'll tell my boss that I need to be home Sunday by lunchtime to take care of you. Will that work for you?"

Beverly knew he was only making a slight concession, not giving up whatever his shady plans were for the weekend, but she didn't want to fight. She didn't have the energy or the desire for another battle. Instead, she would enjoy the quiet time without him and deal with her anger another time.

Besides, she thought, *I need to go to work tomorrow and catch up on my lesson plans.* Even with a broken wrist, she could still teach. That way, she wouldn't get too far behind.

I'm sure if I ask Alisa, she will help me tomorrow. And then it would be the weekend, and Beverly could rest and take care of her body.

Beverly smiled at Ted. "You know what, Teddy?" She had not called him Teddy in a long time, and she noticed how his face relaxed when she did. "I plan on going to work tomorrow and then just resting all weekend. So you go ahead and do what your boss asks. I'll be just fine. Perhaps you could call or text, just to check on me. That is, if you have the time. I know how busy you get when you're entertaining a new client." Beverly's voice dripped with sarcasm, but Ted was oblivious to her tone.

Ted nodded in agreement, then awkwardly leaned over and gave Beverly a quick kiss on her forehead. "Okay, I'm gonna head out now. I'll check on you later. Bye." The stuttering disappeared as Ted found a new confidence in his courageous lie. He grabbed his briefcase and scampered out the door.

Beverly grabbed her phone. She texted furiously and nonstop.

> Alisa, I am home, finally. Maybe you could stop by after work for just a few minutes? I have so much to tell you, but not in a text. Did I get a sub yesterday and for today, too??? BTW, can you get the papers from the sub so I can catch up on the grading? I am going crazy here by myself. TTYL

Beverly waited a few minutes for Alisa to respond, but then the oxy kicked in. Beverly saw flying fish on her ceiling before she gave in to the dreamy effects of the drug.

CHAPTER 27

"Hey, I repeat—what the hell are you doing in my private office, Riley Maddog?"

Riley felt bilious and thought she might vomit right over Lucas's mop of dark curls. She took a few steps and shoved the exit door open, then stuck her notebook in between the door and doorframe so it would remain open. The sudden whoosh of fresh air gave Riley a short reprieve from her nausea.

She glared at Lucas. "Oh, so you think you own this little corner of the school, do you? I'll have you know it's my go-to hideaway when I need some private time."

Riley wasn't comfortable being nasty to Lucas. While it really upset her to find him there when she was hoping to chill with her notes, deep down inside, she always felt sorry for him. Not that she excused any of his bizarre, racist, and macho behaviors, but she pitied him. He must have had some awful things happen to him in his life to shoulder so much anger—so much anger that he never cared about the consequences of his actions. Detentions and suspensions. Hell, he was even at risk of getting sent to that special school no one liked to talk about where kids who served time in some juvey center transitioned until the powers that be let them back into the local schools with the regular kids.

Riley squatted next to Lucas. The noxious fumes that had emanated from his lower half seemed to have dissipated for the time being. Their shoulders touched, and if someone had walked by, they might have assumed they were a couple. Riley looked into the deep blue eyes that had mesmerized so many other girls. *Such power*, thought Riley as she struggled to feel what had puzzled her for years. *I wish I were Tracy Turnblad hearing the bells because Lucas touched me, but I don't feel anything, and that just confuses me.*

Lucas mistook Riley's gaze as something more romantic, and whether it was muscle memory on his part or wishful thinking, he reached for Riley's hand.

"What are you doing?" hissed Riley. "Get your large, over-athletic, wannabe a rockjock hand offa me, and I mean now!" She yanked her hand from Lucas's callused palm.

"Hey, I just thought—"

"You thought wrong, buddy. I'm not one of your little playthings you grab onto every week. Damn, Lucas. I thought we were friends. Nothing more."

Lucas shrugged. He thought Riley was pretty in a cute tomboyish way, with her short hair that made her amber eyes stand out like a lion staring you down. He always wanted to get closer to her, but Riley never gave him those *I like you, wanna kiss me?* vibes.

"So, now that we've established I'm not interested in smelly, farting, hiding-in-the-dark-halls kinda guys, what the hell are you doing here in the first place? I, at least, have a pass and was going to chill here for a few minutes. What's your reason?"

Lucas was nonplussed. No girl had ever gone toe to toe with him before. He liked it. He respected it. And he wished he could have done more with Riley than just grab her hand. She smelled good, too. He'd liked her since they were cubby partners back in elementary school. Sometimes, Lucas had this sneaking suspicion that Riley knew more about him than she let on, and maybe that was a good thing.

"I, uh, I'm not in the mood for history or math class. I'm failing math anyway, and I hate it when Mr. Tannereck makes snide comments about me. You know, like, 'So jock boy, if you can't angle left ninety degrees for a long pass on the field, can you calculate what the angle is in this problem?' and then everyone laughs. Then I have to listen to Junay tell the class that not only will she solve the problem, but that 'there's no helping Lucas and his angles because he only likes rounded parts.'"

Riley laughed so hard she almost wet her pants. Then she saw the look of astonishment on Lucas's face and covered her mouth with her hands. "Oh, Lucas." Riley pressed the words into her hands, still covering her lips. "Don't be upset with Junay. She is such a goody-goody. Maybe she's upset because you've never hit on her." Riley took her hands from her mouth and let herself have another good laugh. She relaxed with Lucas. She didn't feel threatened by him or worried that he would make fun of her for not liking him the way the other girls did.

"Hmph." Lucas didn't know how to respond. He liked being in command with girls, and Riley was definitely not someone he could control. He liked that about her. Lucas liked many things about Riley, but perhaps being her friend was more important than anything else.

"So," Lucas asked, "what were you going to do here, anyway?"

Riley smiled. No one ever asked her what was happening in her life. Not her too-busy-to-ask-her-anything parents or her BFF who was no longer her BFF, so she was left with nobody. "Well, if you must ask, Lucas the power jock, Ms. Saper asked me to be part of her foods team after school. We're going to enter a real cooking competition, and now I have to learn all these damn knife-cutting terms. I can't even pronounce half of them, let alone how to use them." Riley shrugged. "But you know what? I have nothing else to do after school. I like cooking, and I like Ms. Saper. I think she's pretty cool, so I agreed to join. Now I'm trying to memorize these funky words. Ya wanna help me?"

Lucas yawned, stretched, and reached into his pocket. He pulled out two granola bars. "Sure, why not? Here, have a bar to keep up your energy."

The two of them, with their heads pressed together,

talked and laughed. Anyone who might have walked by would have definitely thought they were a loving couple.

The bell signaling the end of the period was only a few moments away. Riley looked up and realized the door she had jerry-rigged was now inching its way closed, which was a good thing since security might've noticed the open door while on watch outside the building. Riley stood up, yanked her notebook from the doorjamb, and pulled the door all the way closed.

She turned to Lucas, who was now sprawled out as though he were in his living room watching a game on TV. "What goes on in the after-school program Jilly had to become a part of after the two of you . . . Well, you know . . ."

Lucas looked up, bewildered. "Who?"

Riley, astonished, said, "What do you mean, who? You know damn well *who*! The girl you brought here and . . . Well, I don't even know what you two did here, but you both got caught, and you were suspended from football, and she got stuck attending that yearlong program. Don't even tell me you don't remember. Jeezo flip, boy, how many girls do you hoodwink into coming down here to do whatever you do to them, anyway?"

Lucas smiled, his lips parted, and he winked at Riley. "Now wouldn't you like to know what I do to those girls back here, huh?"

"Give me a break till next Tuesday. You are slime. Now get off your hormones for one second and tell me what goes on in that program. After all, Lucas lover boy, aren't you supposed to be in that program with all the other rejects?"

"Why the hell do you even care?" Lucas got up off the floor, stretched, corrected his crotch, and slipped on his book bag.

"I care because you made it so my former best friend doesn't even talk to me anymore. She has totally taken herself off social media. And, well, I hear some creepy things about Mr. DeWitt."

"What could you have possibly heard about Mr. DeWitt that would be creepy?" Lucas put his arm around Riley's shoulder so casually one would think they did this all the time. The two of them started down the hall just as the bell rang. They saw Mr. Sheldrake and Ms. PC, and Riley and Lucas both nodded at security, smiling and acting very innocent. Scott and PC looked at each other, but since the halls were filling up with students, they decided to keep focus on their patrol since the unusual couple appeared to be heading to their next class.

Lucas and Riley walked very close together, their bodies almost pressed against one another.

Riley was on a mission. "Why do you think Mr. DeWitt is such a cool guy? I mean, you being a guy and all, maybe you don't notice things the way a girl does. I mean, I have nothing against him. I think he's pretty cool myself, and I really like his class."

"So, what's your beef?"

"I heard some girls talking, and they kept saying he was a weirdo, and I wondered. That's all. Forget it. Hey, I'll see you sometime. I gotta get back to see Ms. Saper and then get to my next class. Bye, Lucas."

"Later." Lucas stopped in the middle of the hall and watched Riley rush through the crowd, dodging students as though she were in a computer video game. He sighed. *No, never mind, not Riley.*

CHAPTER 28

It had been a long week what with grades due, endless phone calls to parents, plans for the next unit, and most importantly, seeing Cassandra again.

Carl rushed out of his classroom so he could spend a few more minutes with her. He'd been going out with her for over a week, and he was thrilled. He was only hoping she was as thrilled as he was, which meant he was praying very, very hard.

As he speed-walked through the hall, he saw Beverly Winewrought walking slower than he had ever seen her move before. And then he noticed the sling on her arm. And what was that? A soft cast on her wrist?

Beverly was looking down as he closed in on her. With no one else in the hallway, Carl felt it necessary to say something.

"Hello, Beverly."

"Oh, hello, Carl." Beverly was in no mood to have a conversation, let alone with Carl of all teachers.

"Say, I'm really sorry to see you're wearing a cast."

"Oh, this? It's nothing, really."

"Nothing? I'd say it's something. Has our nurse taken a look at it? I mean, she is really something else, and I'm sure she would want to see that you're okay. You are okay, aren't you?"

Good God. This man can talk, thought Beverly. "I'm just fine, thank you very much." Beverly picked up her pace, attempting to walk past Carl, but the big lug stood right in front of her.

"Uh, Beverly . . . I don't know how to say this, but I've seen you with bruises on your arm, and now you're in a soft cast. As your coworker, it's my duty to make sure you are okay. Safe, that is. Can I ask how you hurt your wrist? After all, when you see a kid with a cast on his arm, he can't wait to tell you all the gory details. So, shoot. Tell me the gory details. I'm a sucker for that stuff."

"You have no right to assume anything, Carl DeWitt. Who do you think you are, Mr. Detective or something? I was walking into my house with a boatload of notebooks to grade, and I dropped one of them. I slipped right on the damn slippery thing and landed on my wrist. There. Plain and simple. Went to the ER. They took an x-ray and found the radius was slightly fractured. Then they gave me this soft cast for a few weeks. Happy?"

"Wow. I didn't mean to offend you, okay? It's just I've noticed some things, and, well, I was only looking out for you. I didn't mean to insinuate that someone may have—I mean, well, hell's bells, never mind. I was trying to be nice, you know? You always seem to be angry with me, Beverly. Have I done something to upset you?"

"Look, Carl," said Beverly, a little softer in her tone, "I don't mean to come on so strong, but I've had a rough week. I'm tired and hurting quite a bit, and I'm really behind on my schoolwork, so if it's okay with you, please stop talking to me and let me get on to my classroom." She brushed by Carl as though she were walking away from roadkill that had splayed its innards all over the road.

Beverly turned sharply away, but because she was in such a hurry to get away from Carl, she didn't see Roland Burke and Aiden Sutton laughing and shoving each other as they pushed a large book cart, which collided right into her chest.

"Ummmpppph." The escaped air was all that came out of Beverly's mouth before she collapsed to her knees. The mountain of English novels on the cart came tumbling and crashing onto her already battered body.

Beverly's piercing primordial scream of agony came from such a deep place, one might've believed an exorcist was purging her body. Carl froze for what felt like forever, and then he sprang into action.

"Aiden, you run for the nurse, and Roland, hurry, man, go get Mr. Sheldrake and tell him to run here as fast as he can. Go! Now! Hurry!"

Carl crouched down and shoved the books off Beverly, who moaned. Tears flowed down her reddened cheeks, and pangs of sympathy for his colleague punctured him, leaving him feeling helpless and sick with worry.

"Beverly, shhh, it's okay. I've got the nurse coming, and more help is on the way." Carl reached into his pants pocket and pulled out his handkerchief. "Here, for your face."

Beverly, snot running from her nose and tears cascading over her burning cheeks, rolled over and tried to sit up, but she couldn't do it with only one hand.

Carl saw her struggling and reached over to help her twist her body so she could at least sit up. With Carl's handkerchief in her hand and her bottom planted solidly on the floor, Beverly asked, "Who the hell carries a handkerchief in this century?" Grateful for something to use, Beverly wiped the running mucus with the blue-and-green monogrammed handkerchief and then dabbed at her eyes.

"Oh, the pain!" Beverly moaned as she reached for her wrist. "I think I broke it again. Oh, shit on a stick! I'm gonna die right here, right now, and it's all because of you, Carl DeWitt. It's always because of you!"

Just then, the nurse arrived with her wheelchair. She took one look at Beverly and said, "Okay, everybody, easy does it. Let's get this woman off the floor and into my chair. Now!" Nobody argued with Nurse Kelly Arroyo. A rather large woman in her forties with short black hair and dark piercing eyes, she was someone everyone revered. Her word was God, and when any student argued with her, it was nothing short of sacrilege.

Scott Sheldrake, Carl DeWitt, and Nurse Kelly all crouched together, and on her command, they hoisted Beverly into the wheelchair. Roland and Aiden, both back from their emergency run, stood motionless and in awe as Nurse Kelly orchestrated the technique.

Once Beverly was in the wheelchair, still groaning in pain, Kelly wheeled her around. In a flash, she ran down the hall, her patient bent over in the chair holding on to her splinted arm.

The two men looked at each other and shrugged.

"What the hell happened here, Carl?" asked Scott, completely stunned by the situation that had just occurred. "Were you two fighting or something?" Then Scott realized the two boys were still standing there, their mouths wide open, their legs spread as if they might need to run somewhere else.

Carl laughed. "Okay, you two heroes. Collect all of Mrs. Winewrought's notebooks and her bag and take them to the nurse's office. But before you run off, pick up all these books that fell off the cart and get them to where they belong. Off you go, now. And, hey, thanks, men. You saved the day today. Don't know how you're gonna up your game from here, but I'm proud of you."

Roland and Aiden laughed and high-fived each other, then took off down the hall.

Carl turned to Scott. "I have no frigging idea what just happened here, but I'm glad you came along. That woman is certifiably crazy, if you ask me. Frankly, I'm clueless as to what she's talking about half the time. Anyway, I still have a few minutes before my next class, and there is an unbelievably cute secretary who happens to have the hots for me, so check you later, dude."

Scott stood alone in the hallway, shook his head, and said aloud to no one in particular, "Teachers are one crazy-ass group of people!"

CHAPTER 29

Alisa stood in the nurse's office watching Nurse Kelly adjust Beverly's splint.

"You are going to be just fine, Mrs. Winewrought," said Kelly somewhat unconvincingly. "Your soft cast cushioned your fall. Now, your butt might be a bit sore tonight since that area took the brunt of the landing on that wonderful foam-treated hallway floor! Not!" Kelly laughed. "*Dios mio*. Please take better care of yourself when you're walking through the school. Now, do you want to rest here for a while?"

Aiden and Roland flew into the office, both boys carrying a load of Mrs. Winewrought's notebooks and her bag. Not wanting to be involved any longer with the science teacher who looked like a glazed-eyed Medusa, the boys dropped all the materials on Nurse Kelly's desk, grabbed a Jolly Rancher each from her jar of goodies, and bolted.

"Well, thank you, boys," called Nurse Kelly as her door closed.

Beverly let her head fall back on the pillow. The school

cots were not the most comfortable, but for now, lying down was her only option. She was dizzy, nauseous, and above all, angry as all get out. "Just give me a few minutes, and I'll go back to class. My kids are watching a slide show today about their next lab, so I think I will be fine."

Alisa jumped in. "Oh, no, no, no, girlfriend. You stay right here, and I'll get one of the extra subs to sit in your class till later today. You hear me? Lie back down, and I'll go make the arrangements."

Kelly nodded in agreement, but before she could add anything, the door flew open to reveal PC holding onto a sobbing Cindy. Kelly went to Cindy's aid while Alisa sat down next to Beverly. She whispered something to Beverly, who nodded with her head still snug on the pillow.

Pauline Clifton murmured to Kelly, "She's having a bit of a meltdown. I found her sitting on the floor of the girls' bathroom sobbing. She won't tell me anything about why. I figured she might as well rest in here with you so no one finds her and makes her feel even worse than she must be feeling right now."

Cindy, her shoulders shaking up and down, could not stop sobbing. When Pauline guided her to the other cot in the room, Kelly deftly pulled the curtain to shield Beverly's bed and the two teachers in their close conversation.

Pauline sat down next to Cindy, her hand on her shoulder while her other hand rubbed her back. "Shhh, child, it's okay. PC is here with you now. Why don't you tell me what's making you so upset? I've heard just about everything that goes on in this school, so if someone is bothering you, all you have to do is tell ol' PC, and I'll take care of it. You got that?"

Cindy, her sobs subsiding, sniffed hard and long before she could talk. "It's not anyone in school." And then Cindy started crying again. "It's my mom. She found out last night that she has breast cancer, and I don't know how to fix her. I don't know how serious it is. I don't know what any of it means, and I'm . . . scared . . . so scared. I can't lose her. I . . . can't."

Pauline hugged Cindy hard. "Shhh, it's okay. I'm here. Look, Nurse Kelly is here with us, too, and she can help you understand what's happening with your mom."

"I knew something had to be wrong with my mom. I . . . I . . . I just knew it. She wasn't acting right, ya know? Snapping at me, especially when I was telling her about Mr. DeWitt and all."

Beverly sat up. She'd been listening to Cindy with half an ear while Alisa went on and on about her after-school chef team, but when Beverly heard Carl's name, she put her good hand on Alisa's arm and gave her the *Shhh* signal with her fingers. Beverly wanted to hear what Cindy had to say about Carl. She sat up and softly placed both her feet on the floor. Ignoring the pain in her wrist, Beverly leaned toward the sound of Cindy's whining voice.

Just then, the bell rang, and Alisa jumped up. "Damn, I've got to get to class. I have to set up the kitchens. Are you okay if I leave you here for now? I promise to get someone to cover your next class and more if you need me to. Text me, okay?" Alisa whooshed herself out of the nurse's office and raced down the hall to her room.

Pauline pulled out her walkie. "Hey, team. PC here. I'm in the nurse's office with a student. If there's an emergency, let me know. In the meantime, Scott, cover my area for me. I'll check in soon. Thanks."

Kelly brought Cindy a small bottle of water and a bag of crackers, then sandwiched her with Pauline on the other side of her. "Here, Cindy. Now let's talk about your mom. Start at the beginning."

Once Pauline saw that Cindy had calmed down and Kelly was ready to embark on a very serious but compassionate conversation, she said her goodbyes and left to focus on the traffic in the halls.

Beverly was done with her own physical injuries. She was tired of being babied and tired of not being in control of herself. She pulled the curtains aside, walked over to Cindy, and interrupted her conversation with Nurse Kelly. "Hello, Cindy. I hope to see you in class later today. Is everything okay with you and Mr. DeWitt? I heard you mention his name."

Cindy was startled to see Mrs. Winewrought, who was not her most favorite teacher. She was usually short with Cindy—short with most of the students, actually—and she definitely played favorites. Cindy had not realized Mrs. Winewrought was in the nurse's room, and having her stand there like some angry Greek goddess with her arm all bandaged up intimidated Cindy to the point of stuttering.

"I, uh . . . Just that M-M-Mr. DeWitt told me I c-c-could stay after school whenever I want to talk to him about my s-s-situation."

Beverly could not stand Cindy's stuttering. It reminded her of Ted, and that made her even more short-tempered than usual. "And why on God's green earth would you want to stay after school with Mr. DeWitt and talk to him about your problems? Didn't I read somewhere that you already see a therapist?"

Beverly regretted saying that immediately. Knowing what was in a student's personal file and throwing it in their face was the most unprofessional act a teacher could commit. "Um, I'm sorry, Cindy. I didn't mean to say that. After all, what you do on your own time is surely your own business. I just, well, I just—what I mean to ask is, are you okay sitting in a room with Mr. DeWitt after school all alone? I hope nothing inappropriate is going on in there. Is the door closed? Are there any other students? How long do you stay in the room alone with him? How many times have you done this? Does your mother know?"

Beverly's chest heaved from her nonstop babble, and Cindy stared at her in total disbelief. Kelly interrupted the barrage of questions. "Uh, Mrs. Winewrought, I think you have a class you need to attend to, isn't that right?"

Beverly recognized a brush-off when it was thrown at her. Kelly had no right talking to her as though she were an inferior staff member at the school. Beverly squinted in disbelief and disgust, clucked her tongue, and spit out,

"Mmmphhh." Then she turned around and walked out the door, letting it slam with a loud clunk behind her.

Since her class was being covered, Beverly decided to take on another mission that had been bothering her for some time. Her focused walk was so direct and her face so contorted in anger that anyone who crossed her path would have turned and raced in the other direction for fear of being called out for something.

Beverly wrenched open the door to the main office, marched past Cassandra, ignoring her sweet voice and cheery hello, and headed straight for Barbara Atkinson's office. The door happened to be open, and Beverly stormed right up to Ms. Atkinson's desk and waited to be recognized with a few "ahems" and a loud cough followed with a thunderous, "Excuse me!"

CHAPTER 30

Neva was not aware that her guttural moaning had startled Atticus, her beloved chocolate lab. It was a dark gray day, and even though it was not quite dinner time, without the lights on, the house looked dreary and foreboding, with afternoon shadows disguising themselves as villains. Neva was exhausted from teaching that day. It had been another intense discussion about *Jane Eyre* with her Advanced Placement students. The girls loved the romance, while the boys got a kick out of the creepy woman in the attic and jokingly trashed poor Bertha. After school, Neva had closed her eyes, snuggled under the cozy quilt, and sunk deep into her couch with thoughts of Mr. Rochester and his house going up in flames.

But sadly, her dreams—or night frights as she'd nick-named them—segued from Mr. Rochester burning up in his house to the infamous Triangle Shirtwaist Factory fire. Neva's great-grandmother Kathleen had escaped to the roof on that dreaded afternoon on March 25, 1911. She was finally rescued by none other than Neva's great-grandfather

Sean Depoli, a firefighter whose company was first on the scene that day. It was fate that the two of them met that day, and their love developed into a deep and true bond. They married two years later. Neva had the entire ancestry tree filled out, but she rarely dreamed of the fire.

That afternoon, in her night fright, Neva stood in Greenwich Village in front of the burning factory, sweating from the raging fire while the horror of bodies throwing themselves out of windows in desperation brought bumpy chills on top of her perspiration. Neva writhed in her twisted dream, hearing the shrill sirens coming closer and the odd sensation of water slathering over her face.

Neva threw her arms out, trying to catch a young girl dropping out of the sky, but the sensation of fur and something cold startled her, and her eyes flew open.

"Oh, Atticus, my love." Neva exhaled as she pulled her beautiful four-legged companion into her arms. "Were you worried about me? Did I scare you out of your own precious nap?" Neva flung the quilt off and let the cool air soothe her overheated body.

"Were you trying to wake me?" Neva asked Atticus as she rubbed her damp cheeks dry. "What noises must have been coming out of my mouth that you tried to save me!"

"Oh, no!" Neva exclaimed as she jumped off the couch and raced into the kitchen. The piercing sound coming from her teapot had served as a siren in her dream. She was grateful she'd set her stove to a low flame and that it had taken so long to heat up her pot.

Atticus followed her into the kitchen, his tail wagging

and his low whimpering signaling that perhaps he deserved a treat for saving his wonderful owner.

"Okay, you big baby! I guess I owe you a special treat after all, don't I?" Neva knew she talked to her dog as though he were her roommate, but being a single woman, she felt comfortable with their relationship.

"Here you go, my friend." Neva handed Atticus his favorite bacon bit chewy and then turned to fix herself some tea. She was about to sit down and enjoy her Lady Grey tea with a small piece of her favorite lemon cake when the doorbell rang.

Atticus shot out of the kitchen in a flash and barked at the door to let the visitor know he was in charge of the safety of the home. Neva put down her cup of tea and went to the front door. She pulled it open slowly to make sure Atticus would not eat her visitor, and the look of surprise on her face transformed into a warm smile.

"Well, good afternoon, Carl. How lovely to see you! And what brings you all the way to my house after school? Surely we can go over our mentoring lesson plans tomorrow, don't you think? Well, my, my, where are my manners? Please do come in and excuse my partner-in-crime, Atticus. Atticus, this is Carl. He is our friend and a good guy. Do not eat him. I repeat, do not eat this man, please."

Carl bent over and gently patted Atticus on his head. Atticus licked Carl's hand, letting him know he was acceptable to come in and visit—at least for a while.

"Hi, Neva," Carl said in a voice that was not his usual happy-go-lucky singsong. "I need to talk to you. I, uh . . .

Oh, Neva. I think I'm in trouble. Really, really big top-of-the-chart trouble. And the craziest thing is, well, I don't even know what I did!"

Carl followed Neva into the kitchen and sat down at her small mahogany table. Neva poured hot water into one of her large mugs, grabbed some rooibos tea, which she knew Carl loved, and sat down next to him.

"Now, Carl, tell me everything, my boy. And don't leave anything out."

Carl bobbed his tea bag and stared into space. He unconsciously kept his other hand on Atticus, as if the loving dog would give him the confidence to go on.

CHAPTER 31

Barbara Atkinson typed on her computer, her eyes focused on the screen, all the while chewing her gum like Coach Mike Ditka, making a loud, popping racket that sounded as though a ball were smacking into her window every few seconds.

Barbara despised being interrupted when she was so deeply involved in a project. She'd always had trouble concentrating on her studies when she was a young girl. She became the class clown and enjoyed the attention even though she suffered through detentions and parent conferences and numerous whippings from her strict father. Barbara might have been the smartest one in her class, but not being able to focus had hampered her education. She suffered with ADHD, but since that diagnosis was still a few years away, everyone simply thought she was a funny but needy, quirky little girl.

In college, Barbara discovered speed from a few of her edgy new friends. While she didn't abuse those little pills, Barbara did realize how much better she was able to concentrate when she used them. The world suddenly opened up to her in ways she could have never imagined. She raced through college and graduated at the top of her class. Barbara had wanted to be a lawyer but felt a different calling halfway through her sophomore year.

She knew she had to work with students and help them understand some of their inappropriate behaviors might be due to ADHD. There were many new studies since the first mention of it back in 1902, and by the time Barbara was in college, the philosophy of education was heading in an entirely new direction. Barbara wanted to jump on that train and, if she could, drive that speeding train right into her classroom.

When Barbara was a novice teacher in 1975, Congress passed the Education for All Handicapped Children Act (EAHCA). Public schools were required to provide "free, appropriate public education" for all students. Barbara had stood on the Capitol steps and cheered and cried and threw herself into teaching.

Years passed, and Barbara eventually found herself on adult ADHD prescription medication. While she tended to be more serious than her younger class clown days, she felt she was more focused with her work and accomplished her tasks efficiently. Her biggest pet peeve, however, was rude staff members or those teachers who lacked any semblance of compassion. Ironically, Barbara knew that behind her back, the staff felt those were her own characteristics.

As she sat zeroed in on the memo in front of her, Barbara was sharply aware of someone standing near her, talking loudly, and attempting to distract her from her task. Barbara typed in a few more words, reread her memo, hit the send button, closed her screen, and slowly—very slowly—turned to face whoever it was who had so disrespectfully entered her office.

Beverly Winewrought was about to say something that would have been not only inappropriate and unprofessional but downright wrong when Barbara Atkinson finally swiveled in her chair to face her.

"Did I hear you knock?" questioned Barbara. "I mean, after all, I was very involved in writing something, so perhaps I didn't hear you knock. I would assume anyone who wanted to come into my office while I was obviously otherwise engaged would have had the decency not only to knock at my door but then wait to be called in. Or did your mother never teach you any manners?" Barbara stared, squinting behind her thick glasses in anger as she waited for a response.

Beverly, feeling totally humiliated, stood in front of Ms. Atkinson's desk, her feet feeling as though they had weights attached to them. "I . . . I, uh . . . Can I sit down, please?"

"Actually, no, you may not. Now, tell me in thirty seconds or less what is so incredibly important that you had to burst into my office without being invited and stand there coughing and making guttural noises just to get my attention."

"Well, you see . . ." Beverly could feel her cheeks burning with embarrassment, and her wrist was throbbing. She wanted to sit down for fear of falling over. She took a deep breath, looked up at the ceiling as though she were asking for guidance, and began again. "You know, I have been teaching here for quite a few years now, and—"

Ms. Atkinson cut her off like a machete slicing a pineapple. "I know how long you've been here, Mrs. Winewrought. Now tell me something pertinent to this rude interruption."

Beverly shuffled her feet, swayed a little side to side, and forced herself to continue. "The truth of the matter is, I have been asking you year after year to be part of the mentoring program I knew you were developing. And then I return this year to find out that not only did you finally start the damn program, but you completely ignored my request to be included. I could have done so many wonderful things in that program, but no—*oh no*—you had other intentions. You already have your goddamn favorites in this building. Everyone knows that about you! Oh, yeah, don't act so high and mighty behind your desk!"

Beverly suddenly stared at the ceiling because she was afraid to see the look on Barbara's face. She remembered seeing Ms. Atkinson slice and dice another colleague during a faculty meeting, and it was horrifying. Beverly was about to crack and cry, but she was determined to stop this from going on any longer. She could no longer stand the humiliation. It was a nightmare at home too often now, and her workplace was her place of safety, but since Carl had been getting under her skin, her emotions had become raw and poisoned with hatred, even here.

So Beverly decided it was time to let it all out. "And

then to top it all off"—Beverly sniffed, snot from her nose sluicing down her lips while her eyes welled with tears threatening to run over—"and to top it all off, you asked Mrs. Waverly and that brand-new nerdy teacher, Carl DeWitt, to run it. He has no experience whatsoever! He's obnoxious, conceited, and he's full of himself. And . . . and . . . and I hear he's doing inappropriate things with our students!"

Beverly knew she had crossed the line. She knew deep in her heart that she was exaggerating beyond belief, but her blood was running cold, and the lies seemed to flow through her veins and right out of her mouth.

"And," she continued, starting to believe the dark, evil fabrications she was building, "I firmly believe that I heard he took a student—I'm not sure whether it was a girl or a boy—but I do believe—yes, I'm sure of it—that there was something very suspicious going on with him down that dark hall where no one ever goes. There! I've fucking said it all now!"

If she stood there one more second, Beverly would have passed out right on the goddamn Turkish rug that was the pride and joy of the ol' Battle Axe. The falsifications had tumbled over her tongue so easily that Beverly smiled triumphantly, sucked in the stale air, and turned on her heel while cradling her wrist.

Barbara, her mouth wide open in shock, stared after Beverly as she faltered for an instant, almost falling over, and then paraded out of her office.

CHAPTER 32

Atticus knew Carl was hurting, so he kept his head in Carl's lap for support. Carl, unaware of the dog's innate ability to detect sorrow, rubbed the top of Atticus's head in a rhythmic circle as though it were Carl who was soothing the compassionate canine.

"Gee, Neva, I'm not even sure where to begin. You know what? Let me start with Beverly Winewrought, because I'm super concerned about her. I've only known her for the three years I've been here, and quite honestly, she has never been very friendly toward me. I realize I'm the new guy and all, but I've made friends with so many of my colleagues—with the exception of Beverly. And today, I'm not sure what happened, but she said she was going to die right there on the floor and that I was the cause of all the trouble. I don't know what she is talking about, but Cassandra texted me that I needed to be very, very careful because she overheard Mrs. Winewrought yelling at Barbara Atkinson in her office today. And my name kept coming up. I have no idea what is going on, but I'm really worried."

Neva nodded. She understood exactly what Carl was talking about. "Beverly is one tough cookie, Carl. Don't take it personally. Beverly has a few friends in the building, and she isolates herself from everyone else. Her best friend, Alisa Saper, is her one and only true confidante."

Carl sipped his tea, contemplating his next thoughts. He wanted to share them with Neva, but once he shared these theories—once he let the proverbial cat out of the bag—well, there would be no turning back.

Atticus released a huge yawn, sighed, and plopped his body on the floor but remained pressed up against Carl's leg. Carl looked around the living room, stalling to think it all through. He loved the pictures on Neva's walls and could tell she collected many different artists. One day soon, he wanted to hear all about her collection. He stared at the famous Escher titled *Encounter*. Carl had always been intrigued by it, and now, looking at it as though for the first time, he wondered what that man was thinking.

"So, Carl," Neva said softly to bring him back from his deep thoughts, "tell me about your interactions with Beverly today."

Carl shook his head as he tried to climb out of the rabbit hole he'd slipped down into. "They've been uncomfortable at best." Carl took another sip of tea. "This is great tea, Neva."

"Yes, Carl, it's rooibos, your favorite kind of tea. Stop

avoiding what you want to say. Let it out, my friend, and you will feel so much better."

Carl looked at Neva. She was very pretty, with her soft green eyes, layered graying hair, and strong straight nose. She used to joke about having the words *Tell me your troubles* stamped on her forehead because everyone felt so relaxed around her. Most adults gravitated to her for advice.

After wringing his hands, Carl wiped them on his pants legs. "The past few weeks, I may have stepped over the line with Beverly. You see, I, uh, well, I noticed she had a few bruises on her arm a while back, and I asked her if she was okay—you know, in a friendly, nonthreatening sort of way—and man, she jumped all over me. I almost freaked out, and that's when Ms. Atkinson found me in the lounge and asked me to come see her."

"Oh, that must have been the day Barbara asked us to start the program."

"Yeah, it was. And when Ms. Atkinson left the room, Beverly gloated and smirked at me, assuming I was in some big trouble. Holy moly, it didn't feel good; I can tell you that."

Neva was deep in thought. Why *did* Beverly have those bruises on her arm? Come to think of it, she always wore long-sleeve shirts or her lab coat. "What made you ask about the bruises?"

Carl's chin dropped to his chest. He hesitated, took a sip of his tea, and stared into the cup. "My older sister, Emma, she was something else. Boy, was she a rebel. She wore short skirts and hoop earrings and lots and lots of eye makeup. Well, my dad was super conservative, and she drove him up a wall. Every day, the two of them had an argument. He refused to let her go out at night, so she climbed out the window and made me swear I knew nothing."

"Oh my, Carl. What did you do?"

"There wasn't much I could do to convince her to chill and listen to Dad. I even tried to get help from my brother, Chip, but Chip was—well, with a cool name like that, what help was I really going to get? Chip was totally into Chip, and he was absolutely no help at all.

"When Emma was a senior in high school, she stayed out all night pretending she was at sleepovers even though my father demanded she come home. A few times, Dad drove around the neighborhood looking for her, but he could never find her. My mom, she was the peacemaker, and she tried to get my dad to ease up on Emma, but he stuck his heels in the ground and swore she would never see nineteen."

With a distant look in his eyes, Carl said, "By the spring of her senior year, Emma was coming home high on marijuana. It seemed that was the only way she could function at our house. I was overlooked by my parents since I didn't cause any trouble. All their negative energy was on Emma. But that was okay. I didn't mind. I . . . I loved my sister with every ounce of me, but I was scared for her. All the love in the family was focused on Chip because he brought the family pride, whereas Emma and I were the outcasts, so to speak."

Atticus got up, stretched, and let out his unique guttural sound that only Neva understood. "Wait right here, Carl. I think ol' Atticus is letting me know he needs to check out the back yard for a moment of privacy."

Carl sat by himself, finishing his tea. His eyes had taken on a glistening look as his memory of Emma rushed through his mind. So many memories and most of them so incredibly sad, but he had to share them with Neva so she would understand why he was so concerned about Beverly.

Neva returned in a few minutes with Atticus, who was happily chewing on his favorite peanut butter cup made of indestructible rubber. "Okay"—Neva sank back into her chair and cupped her tea with both hands—"let's get back to your sister Emma and why you were so scared for her."

Carl stared at the floor for a moment as his brain flipped back the pages of his youth in rapid motion. "Well, as I said, Emma was getting wilder by the day between experimenting with drugs and staying out late. I didn't know the crowd she was hanging with because I was, well, you know, a huge nerd. She loved me, but I was not invited to hang out with her. Ever.

"And then by June, just before her graduation, all hell broke loose. I was in my room studying for finals. Duh, what else would I be doing on a beautiful June afternoon? Chip, of course, was at school hanging with his friends doing the jock thing. Dad came home from work and totally lost his cool when he found Emma in this guy's car in our driveway. Emma was practically naked with this jerk in the back seat, and when Dad saw this, oh jeez, he lost his shit."

Neva took a long sip of tea. She didn't want to rush Carl, and letting him talk at his pace was probably the safest thing to do. So she just nodded and encouraged Carl to continue.

"Dad grabbed his baseball bat and went right up to that dude's window and smashed it to smithereens. He was cursing and screaming; the entire neighborhood must have heard him. I did, and that's when I looked out my bedroom window. After seeing Dad look like something out of a Bruce Willis movie, I ran downstairs and out the door to save Emma."

"No, you didn't get in the way of your dad, Carl!"

"Hell, no! I would have been smashed in the head with that baseball bat. No, I managed to pull Emma out of the car and ran with her down the street to my friend's house." Carl started laughing. "You know, now that I think of it, I never found out what happened to that guy. I was so busy getting Emma to my friend's house and getting some clothes on her that I didn't pay any attention to my dad back at the house.

"Well, much later that night, I snuck Emma back into our house. I overheard my parents arguing about what they needed to do with her, what her punishment would be. My mother kept fighting my dad. What kind of punishment do you give an eighteen-year-old?" Carl suddenly looked exhausted.

"Do you want another cup of tea?"

"No, I need to get to why I'm talking so much about my sister. You see, after that night, Emma left. I mean for good. She wrote a note to my mother explaining that she was leaving to go find one of her good friends who had moved out of state the year before. Emma told my mother not to worry. She said she would be fine and that the family would be fine without her."

"Oh my God!" exclaimed Neva. "How could she do that to your mom?"

"Well, Emma felt she was no longer wanted. She thought she was only causing my mother anguish and heartache, and my dad was becoming more and more violent in response to Emma's actions, so she thought the easiest thing for her to do was to leave.

"Emma would send me postcards every now and then. I secretly shared them with my mom and sometimes Chip, but he wasn't very interested if it didn't have anything to do with him. Anyway, Emma never made it to her friend's place. Instead, she found this local carnival, and would you believe, she got a job with them and started traveling around the country with this company."

"Well, I guess that might have eased the burden on your parents and you as well."

"Unfortunately, no. Things did not go well with Emma. She married one of the carnival workers. I think she thought that would be her ticket out of her connection to her parents. I don't know. Anyway, here's the reason I told you so much about Emma. About two years after she left, Emma came back home for a visit. She was a changed woman. We met at the local coffee shop because she didn't want to see Mom or Chip and especially not Dad. So I met her there. We talked for hours. It was the summer entering my senior year in high school. I told her all about my upcoming internship as a teacher's assistant and how excited I was because I had found my future career.

"She was happy for me, but I could tell she wasn't happy. At one point, she rolled up her sleeves, and there they were—all up and down her arms were bruises. They were different shades of purples and blues and greens. Some were old, some new. She rolled down her sleeves and looked at me with the unhappiest eyes I'd ever seen.

"'Don't feel sorry for me,' she said. 'I did this to myself. I was a stupid girl who thought she knew it all. I should have listened to Mom and Dad. Please, sometime when you can, let them know it wasn't their fault. I loved them; I was just that difficult child who wouldn't listen. And this guy I married—those bruises are his love taps, as he calls them. Every time I didn't listen to him or give in to his demands or have dinner on the table, well, these are my reminders, so to speak. And that's why I'm here. To let you know that I walked out on him for good. I walked away. Again. It seems that's the way I handle my problems; I walk away and find a new path. Well, I've run out of paths, but I wanted to see you one last time.'

"I asked her what she meant by 'one last time,' but she only shook her head. She held me tight, kissed me, and told me to embrace my future because I had a special calling to help others. Then she left. I never saw her again. She took her own life in some run-down hotel by the beach. She loved the beach; she always said it brought her peace. I guess she has that peace now."

Neva clutched a tissue to her face and wiped her eyes. She wasn't sure at what point in Carl's narrative she had started to cry, but the tears were running freely down her face and down her chin. Atticus lumbered over to her, placed his paws on her lap, and licked her face. He always knew when she was sad. Atticus turned and looked at Carl. He tilted his head as though asking Carl what was causing his master to cry.

Carl lifted his cup and drained the last of the tea. He looked at Neva, who was crying unabashedly, and dropped his head onto his chest. "Neva," Carl whispered, "I didn't tell you all of this to make you so upset. I've dealt with Emma's suicide. It took my mother several years to accept what had happened with Emma. On Emma's birthday a few years ago, Mom asked me to take her to the beach along with Emma's remains, and while we were there, Mom released Emma to the wind and the surf. It was good for Mom. She cried, but in the end, she was at peace, finally.

"And now I want to bring in Beverly Winewrought. Neva, I've seen Beverly's arms on several occasions over the past few months, and I have to tell you, Beverly has the same kind of bruises Emma had. I asked Beverly if she was okay, and boy, did she get angry with me. Nasty, actually, and I'm assuming that's what she has against me."

Neva gasped. "What do you mean 'against you'?"

Carl thought for a moment. "I think her husband has been abusing her and she doesn't want anyone to know. And perhaps because I'm questioning her, she's on guard and outraged. I don't know. Maybe I'm wrong. Maybe she's just damn clumsy, but that's the only reason I can think of as to why she dislikes me."

"Have you told anyone else about your observations?"

"Well, that's just it. When Beverly left the nurse's office the other day, I went in and talked to Nurse Kelly. I shared my observations with her. I felt it was my duty to report it to someone."

"You had to, Carl. You had to. I get it. But why do you think you're in trouble?"

"Before I left the building, I saw Beverly, and she looked at me with the evilest expression on her face, like she couldn't hold it back. She squinted and hissed, 'You better watch your step, because Ms. Atkinson knows all about you.' Now what do you think that means?"

CHAPTER 33

L ila Libertino sat in her office, hands clasped behind her head. It was her processing style. She leaned back in her chair, closed her eyes, and a tiny sigh escaped her lips.

There were so many wonderful experiences in her role as principal. She loved it. She loved her staff, her students, her parents, and her community. She woke up every morning excited, refreshed, and ready to take on the challenges of teenagers. Even the angry parents weren't the worst, considering they were always just trying to do what was best for their child.

But today . . . today, shit, these are not the moments I look forward to, she thought. If the allegations were true, this was going to be devastating for so, so many.

The door to Lila's office was closed, but when she heard the soft knock, she unclasped her hands, brought her chair back to its upright position, and took a sip of her now ice-cold coffee. "Come in."

In walked Barbara Atkinson, Jeff Stineman, and Amelia, Lila's secretary. They each took a seat at the round table near the window as Lila joined them. Lila smiled to herself. *Such creatures of habit*, she mused. *They always sit in the exact same spots as though it would be a criminal act if they mixed up their arrangements.*

Amelia immediately opened her laptop. She never went into a meeting without it, and Lila was forever grateful for such a competent and keen secretary. There were times Lila lovingly called her "Radar" like the character in *MASH* because Amelia was always a step ahead of Lila when it came to having a letter ready or the most recent news in the community.

Except today. Nobody was ready to tackle this. Not Lila, and from the looks of the faces around the table, the others were not ready for this either. But Lila knew she had to start somewhere. "Good morning, team, and thank you for coming in so early for this meeting. I'm not quite sure where to begin, so I'll just jump in. Yesterday afternoon, Barbara came to me with some rather unsettling news. It seems that Beverly Winewrought approached Barbara to share something we all need to hear. At this point, Barbara, I would appreciate you taking the lead and letting us know what Mrs. Winewrought communicated to you."

Barbara looked at Jeff and Lila before she began. She was not comfortable with this entire scenario because, deep in her heart, she believed Beverly Winewrought was as vindictive, jealous, and shallow as a human being could be and thought even less of her as a teacher. Unfortunately, because of the sensitive nature of the information Barbara had been given, she had no choice but to bring it to Lila. At what point was Beverly just mouthing off because she was angry and jealous about not being asked to lead an activity she wasn't even qualified for?

Barbara took a deep breath and let it out slowly. "I'm not sure where to begin, so if I don't always go in chronological order"—Barbara looked at Amelia—"we can go back and fix our notes." Barbara closed her eyes, like she was reading a mental script. "It all began last year. Beverly came to see me about once a week, begging me to start a mentoring program she'd heard about in other schools. She wanted me to do all the paperwork, and then when it was ready to roll, she wanted to head it.

"I'd already begun researching and planning a mentoring program two years ago." Barbara looked at Lila for confirmation, and Lila nodded in agreement. "I spoke to several different jurisdictions in our area and, quite honestly, across the nation. Lila even sent me to a conference last summer where I was able to meet with other schools who had their mentoring programs up and running. I was ready for Wells to start."

Lila said, "Please understand, team, Barbara and I had been in communications about this program for quite some time. One of the items we spent a very long time on was who would be the appropriate staff member to head this up. We wanted two, not just one, because, well, all the research claimed that two leaders were more effective than one. Barbara came to me on several occasions to share Beverly's demands. By then, she was becoming quite belligerent about acquiring the job, even though Barbara had never let her feel that she was a possible candidate, even in the slightest."

"The day we announced the program at last year's staff meeting, Beverly came running into my office, demanding a reason for her not being the one to run it," Barbara said. "I explained as professionally and cordially as I could that our team would discuss it over our summer meetings and come to a decision early in the fall. When we finally announced at the beginning of this year that we had chosen Carl and Neva, well, you can imagine the hell I received in my office that afternoon."

Barbara sighed. "The constant accusations and negative remarks regarding the program became a weekly occurrence. I started asking Joanne to intercept Beverly each time she'd storm into the office. Sadly, the comments have been becoming increasingly slanderous. And that is what brings us here today."

Lila stood up. "I have to add something else to this conversation."

All eyes looked up at Lila. She never let her emotions get to her when she was in professional mode, but right now, Lila looked like a gentle breeze could knock her over.

Jeff cleared his throat. "Go ahead, Lila. We can help you deal with whatever it is that is ripping you apart right now."

"Thank you, Jeff." Lila placed both hands on the table as if to hold her up for her next comment. "Sadly, Nurse Kelly came to see me yesterday afternoon. It seems Carl went to her in private to share with her what he strongly believed was evidence of Beverly being physically abused. Carl mentioned that he had asked Beverly on more than one occasion if she was okay because he noticed her bruises, but she rudely brushed him off. He guessed it was her husband, but he wasn't sure. He told Kelly he'd noticed these bruises on Beverly's arms in the past, but more as of late and, recently, her broken wrist.

"Kelly did not share this part with Carl, but she told me that when Beverly was in her office the other day, Beverly confided that the bruises were from her husband. Of course, Beverly played it off like they'd been horsing around—wrestling with each other, even—but nonetheless, Kelly did not believe her bruises were from playing around. Even with this admission, Beverly still told Kelly she had tripped over the laundry basket in the kitchen and that's when she broke her wrist. But Alisa, Beverly's only good friend in the building, showed me her texts with Beverly because she was so concerned about her friend.

"Alisa wouldn't say for certain whether Beverly's husband was physically abusing her or not, but she did say things have not been going well between the two of them."

Barbara said, "I think things are beginning to make sense. The combination of Beverly's desperation for the mentoring position, dealing with problems at home, and Carl's questions about her bruises have driven her to become a very angry and disillusioned woman. I do not know if her disillusionment and jealousy led her to accuse Mr. DeWitt of behaving inappropriately with his students or she has fabricated this completely, but nevertheless we are required to act upon this situation immediately."

Lila sat back down, but her face was pinched with stress and sorrow. "We are saddened by these events; however, and more importantly, we are obligated to move on both these allegations. I will report to the authorities on behalf of Beverly, and I will also have to let human resources know about Carl. Barbara, I had hoped I would never have to ask you to do this, but I will need you to escort Mr. De-Witt out of the building and send him home. Please have Scott Sheldrake accompany you as well. Jeff, please follow up for me and place a substitute in his stead for the time being. Don't put a time frame on the substitute as this is a fluid situation."

Lila choked back a sob. "Thank you, Jeff, Barbara, and Amelia for being part of such a serious and heartbreaking meeting. I will update you when I know more. That's all for now." Lila rubbed her eyes and let the tears flow freely down her soft cheeks.

CHAPTER 34

Riley ran down the hall, enjoying a bit of freedom from her foods class. She loved the class now that she and Ms. Saper were buds. Riley was the first to get to her class and often stayed after just to talk with Ms. Saper. She was pretty cool. They talked about food, hairstyles, clothes, and really anything Riley would bring up. In addition, Riley stayed after school almost every day to practice her knife skills and work on some of the recipes they were thinking about making for a contest in the spring.

While Riley was on an errand for Ms. Saper, the rest of the class navigated their kitchens and assigned jobs for each person. Riley ended up floating from kitchen to kitchen to help her classmates. She loved the responsibility, loved the leadership, and most of all, loved the special attention she was receiving. For the first time in forever, she felt like she was important.

Each morning, Riley would wake up thinking about a recipe she had read the night before and wanted to share with Ms. Saper. From her computer to the food channels, Riley had become obsessed with all she was learning. She thrived on the new challenges and felt herself becoming more self-confident.

What used to pass for dinner now became new horizons each night. Instead of frozen dinners in the microwave, Riley thrived on experimenting with the numerous recipes she researched—always leaving samples for her parents. She would mention an idea to Ms. Saper, who loved to hear about the ingredients and steps Riley had memorized before she went to bed. Riley's parents, always absent at dinnertime, appreciated the change in their daughter as they gobbled down leftovers every night. Mom and Dad were delighted in the shift in their only child, but Riley kept her new passions close to the vest. She never divulged to her parents what was happening in school, who Ms. Saper was, or about the after-school cooking club or the future cooking contest. Riley wanted her relationship with Ms. Saper to be something special, and sharing it with her parents only made it sound pretentious and fake somehow.

Riley strolled down the hall, almost skipping. She was supposed to be going to the main office to pick up Ms. Saper's mail, but Riley had decided to traverse the entire building before finding her way to the main office. That was the luxury of trust. Riley made sure never to break that trust, but nonetheless, she thought a little sidetrack of the destination was totally acceptable.

Riley should have turned toward the right side of the

building that day. It might have made all the difference. Was it fate? Was it bad luck? Or was it fortuitous that Riley had scooted to the left? Before she knew it, Riley was walking by that dark hall. "Sometimes this corner of the building has some bad vibes," she mumbled to no one.

Then she heard a cry. *Huh? What the F? Is that a bird in the corner?* Riley should have kept going. Nothing good ever happened in that damn dark hall. *Stay away,* she warned herself. The stories of weird happenings in that hall might've all been true, but Riley kept walking, following the sound.

"Damn it to all hell!" muttered Riley as she rounded the corner of the hall. "Cindy, what in the hell are you doing here sitting all alone in the dark hall? Aw, shit, girl, why are you crying? Did someone hurt you? Did someone make fun of you?" Riley wasn't a huge fan of Cindy, but she hated seeing anyone sobbing, let alone by themselves.

Cindy, her head bobbing up and down as she bawled, sniffed up the glob of snot rolling down her upper lip. Riley squatted on the floor next to her. She was a mess. Cindy's hair was askew, with long strands stuck to her moist eyelids. She had taken off her glasses, and they'd been tossed aside next to her book bag.

"Ah, gross, Cindy," Riley said when Cindy, at a loss without a tissue, wiped away hanging boogers and tears with her sweatshirt sleeve.

Cindy's chest heaved erratically, and Riley thought for a minute that maybe she was going to pass out. Riley's mom had dealt with a kid who'd lost sight of her mother at the mall one time a few years ago. She'd really been freaking out—screaming, crying, hiccuping, and not breathing. Riley had watched in total amazement as her mother talked gently to her and had her breathing regularly in just a few minutes. She was able to calm her down until they spotted a mall security officer, who happened to have the hysterical mother in tow.

Riley tried to remember some of her mother's magical words and could only recall a few, but it was worth a try. "Cindy, okay, do you feel safe here?"

Cindy, still unable to talk, nodded—albeit very slowly and deliberately.

"Okay, good. I'm here with you. Let's take a slow breath together. Ready? One . . . two . . . and three. Good. Let's do it again." Riley repeated the technique several more times until she noticed Cindy's chest was not heaving as strongly as before. "Cindy, look around you. What do you see outside the window here?"

Cindy turned her head and looked out the window. She smiled. "I see the PE class I'm supposed to be in right now running around the track way over there."

Riley laughed. "Good stuff, girl. You're doing good. What else do you see?"

Cindy was enjoying Riley's company and felt totally at ease with her even though she'd snotted all over her favorite blue sweatshirt. "Oh, wow, there's Ms. Glenstone. I guess I'm going to have to come up with a good reason for why I'm not in class."

"Don't worry yourself about that. I've got it all under control. What else do you see?"

Cindy didn't realize Riley was using her mother's techniques, and the longer they sat there going over what Cindy saw and heard, the calmer she felt. Cindy looked over at Riley. "You really are special, you know that, Riley? I was almost passing out back here, and if you hadn't come along, I don't know what would have happened to me."

Riley smiled. "It's all good, girlfriend. Now, let's get up and go see Nurse Kelly. I'll help you explain what happened, and I'm sure she'll write you a pass excusing you from gym class. Me, I got my own pass, so I'm golden. But there's one more thing to set this deal."

Cindy looked startled at first, apprehensive about what Riley might ask of her. Cindy was always thinking way too much, and it caused her too much anxiety.

"I see that look in your eyes. Just cool it. Here, take my hand and let me help you up. You look like a sack of grain that spilled over on the floor here." Riley leaned down, put her forearms under Cindy's armpits, and hoisted her up. Cindy stumbled at first and then caught herself. She leaned over, scooped up her book bag and glasses, and followed Riley.

"Okay, Cindy, before we get to Nurse Kelly, give it up. What's the deal with you hiding in the dark hall and bawling your eyes out? Who hit you, hurt you, said mean things to you, what?"

Cindy shuffled her feet, trying to slow the walk to the nurse's office. "I . . . I think I totally messed things up."

"Yeah, right. Now that could mean a zillion things, Cin. Ya gotta help me out here. What exactly did you do to mess things up?"

Cindy squeezed her eyes tightly, forcing the last bit of tear remnants from the corners of her red puffy lids. "Oh, Riley, it was all an accident, you know? I mean, I never meant it to be anything serious, but it got all mixed up and twisted and jumbled, and I . . ."

Riley stopped walking and grabbed Cindy by the elbow. Riley looked up and down the hallway to make sure no security guards were wandering around. Satisfied, she turned Cindy to look her straight in the face. "You gotta stop beating around the bush here, girlfriend. Stop being vague and tell me exactly what you're talking about. And I mean now! Before the damn bell rings and everyone starts running out of the classrooms."

Cindy looked up at the ceiling as if the answers to all her problems were posted up there from the heavens. She sighed deeply. "It was last week, right after my mentoring class. You know, the one I'm in after school with Mrs. Waverly and Mr. DeWitt? So the class was over, and I'm heading to the parking lot to find my mom. Then I have to go to my therapist, where I always tell her—"

"Get to the point!"

"Okay, okay. So, I'm just about to leave the building, and Mrs. Winewrought walks right by me. She says hello, and I say hello, and she says, 'How was your day?' and I say, 'Good, thank you and I gotta go,' and she says, 'Can you wait a minute, because I have a question I want to ask you?'

So I look out the window to see if my mom is waiting for me, and she is, which means I really gotta hurry now, so I tell her to go ahead, and she says, 'What can you tell me about Mr. DeWitt in the mentoring program? You know I overheard you talking about him in the nurse's office, and I was just wondering.'"

Riley stared at Cindy. "What? What was that all about?"

"Exactly, that's what I said to Mrs. Winewrought—well, not exactly. I kinda said, 'What do you mean?' and she says, 'Does he ever do anything weird or inappropriate to the students in the group?' And now I'm really in a hurry, and I don't know what she wants me to say, so I just say that he's really weird toward everyone, but that's what we love about him, because of the stories he tells and the activities we do. Then she says, 'Stop! That's all I need to hear,' and she turns around and walks the other way. I mean, I never got to explain what I meant by 'weird,' but you know what I mean, don't ya, Riley? He's just the coolest teacher ever because he understands us and he wants us to do well. He's always making us write personal stuff in our books to help us learn about ourselves, but he's not a creepo or anything like that. Now, you tell me, Riley, what did I do wrong?"

CHAPTER 35

Barbara Atkinson walked down the hallway, her eyes staring straight ahead. This was not the destination she wanted; this was not the job she wanted. Being an administrator could be emotionally exhausting, especially when dealing with students and parents in a stressful situation, but this was a teacher, a colleague, and someone she respected.

Barbara had no choice; she was responsible for Carl. He was her charge. But the thoughts smashed around in her head: was he really inappropriate, or was this a vindictive move of Beverly's, who was angry on so many levels? Students would need to be interviewed, and some staff would need to be interviewed as well, but to what extent would she ever know the real truth of the situation?

The closer Barbara got to Carl's classroom, the slower she walked. And then she stopped altogether. It hit her and almost took her breath away. She remembered another time, another teacher, another school. He was a good teacher, strict but fair. And then the girls. Ah, sometimes girls could be quite nasty and downright evil at times. And they hated this guy. He wouldn't let them get away with chatting during class or copying each other's classwork, and they were jealous of a few students who had become the leaders in the classroom.

So they devised a plan—wrote it all down in neat, organized paragraphs in their little slam book. They wrote fake blogs about class interactions, made up detentions and assignments that went along with them, and then sadly, they wrote about physical touching. Touching that never happened. Touching that was never hinted at. But their details were extremely specific. Perhaps they had put together a few movie scenes to create these horrific scenarios.

The teacher was yanked out of the building, put on leave, and left alone to question his life. His quiet life had suddenly gone viral on social media; his girlfriend of five years left him; his friends distanced themselves. Pieces from the girls' blogs made the news and circulated social media throughout the country. He received death threats from people who believed he needed to be dragged and quartered in the town hall.

And then two years later came the court date. By this time, most people had forgotten the entire story and what vague facts existed. He was yesterday's news, and so the court details were hushed. And when the four girls appeared in court, more mature and now somewhat humble, they admitted they had lied. They cried and said they were angry at being called out, picked on, and made to toe the line, so they wanted revenge. And the only revenge they knew was to get rid of the teacher.

The teacher was cleared of all charges. He received back pay. He didn't want to sue for reparations. He was tired, depressed, and disgusted. His entire life had been thrown into the gutter for all to see, and when it was washed clean, there was no one there to apologize, to befriend him, or to help him regain his life.

And so he moved away. No one ever heard from him again. The girls were sent to different schools, contrite but with no real consequences. Their lives continued much the same as they had before.

Barbara shook her head as if to erase the memory that had whirled inside her head like an omen—an evil warning about what was about to occur.

• • •

Down the hall, around the corner, and past the main office, Jilly sat in the nurse's office. She was having severe cramps again. Every month for the past three years, she'd suffered from acute stomach cramps with her periods. She never told her mother and especially not their family doctor. He was so old—he had to be in his sixties—and she got the willies from the way he stared at her. He seemed to take too long when he looked at her breasts, so Jilly would look at the floor to ignore his creepy eyes. There was no way she was going to discuss anything private that happened "down there." She didn't want to give that old wart reason to investigate.

Jilly had asked her mom if she could go to a woman's doctor, but Mom had said Dr. Richton was good enough for the family, and besides, Jilly was too young to see a gynecologist. Jilly had searched gynecologists in the area and told her mother there was one in the same building as Dr. Richton, but her mom was adamant; she refused to take Jilly to another doctor.

Jilly was even more afraid to share with her mother because she felt there was something physically wrong with her. But today, the aching was so intense it felt like razor blades making zigzags throughout her lower stomach, and the pain reached a point where Jilly couldn't take it anymore. Jilly was in math class and could not concentrate any longer. She begged Mr. Tannereck to go to the nurse. Male teachers automatically allowed girls to go see the nurse because they were too embarrassed to ask why they needed to. Jilly knew this, and even though she hated leaving math class, she felt like she was going to fall down on the floor and curl up in a fetal position if she wasn't allowed to go.

Mr. Tannereck took one look at her and said, "Whoa, Jilly. You are looking a bit pale. Take your things with you just in case you're there past the bell. Feel better, okay?"

Jilly nodded, grabbed her things, and scooted out the door as fast as her legs could take her.

Jilly slowed down as she went past the girls' bathroom. She hesitated for just a second, thinking maybe she should go into the bathroom, sit on the floor, and wait out the pain. That way, no one would know how sick she really felt. But then another cramp ripped across her abdomen, and Jilly sucked in her breath. For a moment, she felt like she was about to pass out, and the dizziness caused her to sway.

Jilly shook her head and pushed herself to keep going. She was afraid that if she did faint in the bathroom, no one would find her and—she couldn't process any further than that. Jilly pushed open the door to the health room. She took one look at Nurse Kelly and was unable to hold back the tears. For too long, Jilly had kept this secret, afraid she wouldn't be able to have babies, get married, or be with a guy to do—well, she wasn't exactly sure what that was, but she was afraid that whatever it was, she wouldn't be physically able to do it.

Nurse Kelly rushed over to Jilly as the poor girl staggered in. "C'mere, my *niña*. Oh, baby, come sit down on the cot over here. Now tell me, *mi dulce*, tell me, *que pasa*? What's wrong, little one?"

Jilly collapsed onto the cot. After holding in the pain for so long and not just for today, it seemed like a huge brick wall was crumbling down all around her, crushing her emotionally as well as physically. Her shoulders rose and fell so swiftly, Kelly reached over and placed her hands on Jilly to steady her.

"Easy now, Miss Jilly. Nurse Kelly is here for you. Tell me, *mi preciosa*. No one else is in the room now, so let me hear. Tell me, *niña*, what hurts you? What can I fix for you?" Kelly walked over to her refrigerator, pulled out a bottle of water, and brought it over to Jilly. "Drink slowly, *cariña*. Drink slowly and tell me everything."

Jilly took a sip, coughed, and sipped again, slower this time. She looked at Nurse Kelly, with the darkest mahogany eyes, and felt that those eyes looked right into her soul. Jilly didn't want to hold the pain all by herself anymore, so she took a deep breath, let it out slowly, and began.

She told Nurse Kelly everything, from the incident with Lucas to losing her best friend, Riley, to being punished at home, the mentoring class, and then finally, suffering from menstrual cramps for the past few years but being too afraid to tell her doctor because she did not trust him. Jilly was exhausted when she finished her story, but it felt good to have released so much, as though a huge burden had been lifted.

Kelly held Jilly's hands. "First, *pobrecita*, I need to talk about your cramps. You are not alone when it comes to having such terrible pains every month. I will call your mother and tell her what she can buy for you over the counter, but more importantly, I want to let her know that at your age, you need to see a gynecologist if you are having such problems." Kelly smiled. "Ah, we women, well, we women have women problems, and sometimes, we need to share so we understand better, no?"

Jilly smiled. She took a deep breath and finished her water. The bell had just rung, but she was in no hurry to leave. Right before Kelly could call Jilly's mom, the door to the health room flew open, and in burst Riley and Cindy. Cindy had been crying from the looks of her red face and swollen eyes. Riley had her book bag slung over one shoulder, and by the looks of it, Cindy's book bag on the other shoulder. The two girls stopped dead in their tracks upon seeing Jilly on the cot, her face puffy and red.

Riley spoke first. "Oh . . . my . . . God! You are not going to believe what we just saw!"

CHAPTER 36

"Take it easy, Mr. DeWitt, my main man. You take it easy today." Then the student raced down the hall. Carl smiled at his students as they filed out of his classroom, but his mind had gone back to another time in his life with his dad.

"Son, sometimes life doesn't treat you fair, and that's all there is to it. It can suck big-time, and getting angry and throwing a pissing fit ain't gonna solve your problem. Now, if them bullies keep bothering you . . . Well, shit, son, you better stand up to them with all you got. You hear me? Boy, I said, do you hear me?"

The memory was crystal clear in Carl's mind. He had stared at his father who was sitting in his favorite recliner with his gun in his lap. It was a revolver, and it was Harry's pride and joy. It seemed like Harry was always cleaning it. He'd stopped going to the gun range because, well, *he* said he didn't like the boys running the front desk, but Carl had heard from his friends that Harry would cause so much commotion at the range that the owner had to ban Harry from coming anymore. It seemed Harry was always carrying on about the younger boys getting the lanes he wanted. And if he wasn't complaining about the target he wanted to use, he was arguing about the rising costs of ammunition. On top of it all, Harry couldn't hide the fact that he had been drinking before he came to shoot, and that was a major rule that screamed *No!*

Harry didn't like to follow rules, but he liked to make them for his family and coworkers. He liked to pound rules into Carl and Emma and his wife, Leila. And when they didn't adhere to his rules, he grabbed his six-pack of beer and his Glock and got busy cleaning it over and over again. Carl's younger brother, Chip, was Harry's pride and joy. Chip, the athlete. Chip, the golden-haired boy with all the girls. After all, who the hell names their kid Chip and expects anything but greatness?

Harry had bragged that the night he ran after Emma's boyfriend with a baseball bat, he had his gun hidden in his back pocket. That was just for effect, of course. Harry would never—so he said repeatedly—use it on another human being, but if push had come to shove and if his daughter were truly in jeopardy, well then, all bets would've been off.

This picture played in Carl's head that day at school when Barbara Atkinson walked into his room after the bell rang for the dismissal of his third period class. Barbara waited outside his room until the last student filed out after turning back for one more look at Carl DeWitt.

Barbara hesitated, then grabbed the door handle and pulled it closed as she entered Carl's room. Carl's room was her favorite. She loved his posters, his quotes, his encouraging statements, and the student work plastered on the walls and every ounce of open space. Barbara had mentored Carl from the first day and was impressed with his dedication, his professionalism, his passion for teaching, and his love of the craft. He was always there for his students, helping them, going the extra mile, staying after school, honing the new mentoring program, and doing whatever was asked of him.

Barbara sucked in some air. Did she really have to do this to him? Was Beverly truly being honest, or was she just being vindictive? Would they ever know the truth? The kids loved Carl; the staff loved Carl. Why was Beverly filled with so much hate?

Carl shifted his weight from foot to foot. It was odd to see Barbara in his room and then for her to shut his door. He was confused. And worried.

"Hi, Carl," Barbara said, concentrating on her choice of words. "Listen, I, um, I'm here on official business. I need you to collect your personal belongings and come with me. Your book bag and anything else that's personal. Oh, and shut down your computer, too, please."

Carl was taken aback. "Ms. Atkinson, what's going on? Is something wrong? Did I do something wrong? I don't understand. Here, wait a sec, let me gather my stuff. What about the rest of my classes today? What about tomorrow? Are you sending me home?"

Barbara tried not to get emotional, but her eyes filled with tears that spilled over and down her face. She quickly sniffed and wiped at her eyes, smearing her mascara. She didn't care. This was not a happy moment, and she hated doing this to Carl. Hated that she had to drag him out of his classroom knowing Lucas Cannon's stepdad, Officer Walter Young, was in the main office waiting to escort them to the parking lot.

"Carl, I need you to come with me, because . . . because I need you to go home"—Barbara's voice cracked, and she sobbed the rest—"and stay home until further notice. I'm . . . I'm so sorry I have to tell you this . . ." Barbara stood there, her arms at her sides, tears rolling down her cheeks. "I, well, I can't explain anything more to you right now, but if you come with me, there is someone waiting to talk to you in the parking lot. Please, Carl, don't make this any harder than it has to be right now."

Carl stood there, too paralyzed to move. "I . . . How . . . ? What is going on? Ms. Atkinson, what did I do? Can't you tell me anything? Did I say something? What—holy shit— what is happening here?"

"Carl, please, gather your things now, and let's head to the front of the building, to the parking lot. Please, Carl, before we have to encounter any students in the halls."

Carl stared at Barbara, dumbfounded. Without saying a word, he walked over to his desk and shut down his computer. He threw a few papers and notebooks in his book bag, grabbed his jacket, and stood in the middle of his room. He looked around as if seeing it for the first and, perhaps, the last time.

Barbara flicked the classroom lights off and opened the door. Carl followed her, mechanically, as though she had electric probes stuck in him and was directing him, forcing him to follow her through the halls. Carl did not look up; he did not look around. He didn't know if anyone saw him, nor did he care at that moment. His eyes burned a hole in the back of Barbara's head, and whether she felt the laser point or not, he did not care. Carl didn't know what was happening to him or where he was going or why; he only knew this was not a good omen of things to come.

At the main office, Officer Young fell in step with Ms. Atkinson and Carl. He nodded briefly to Carl and then looked straight ahead as the trio filed outside the front door into the parking lot. Standing in front of Carl's green Toyota SUV was a stranger to Carl.

"Carl," said Barbara, "this is Lemont Jacobs. He is your representative from the district, and he wants to talk to you now. Officer Young and I are going to leave you with him. We will be in touch through Mr. Jacobs. And, Carl, take care of yourself."

CHAPTER 37

When classes changed, Lucas spotted his stepfather walking out of the main office. It looked like he was escorting Mr. DeWitt. Lucas had seen enough police shows to know when there was something official happening, and this was not a casual conversation and stroll down the hallway.

Lucas ran toward his stepfather, who left the building with Mr. DeWitt and Ms. Atkinson. Lucas, out of breath and chest heaving, waited until he returned and yelled, "Stop! What are you doing? What the fuck are you doing with Mr. DeWitt?" He charged over to his stepfather.

At first, Officer Young thought something was very wrong with Lucas. Other students gathered around as the commotion built up like spilled money on the floor. No one was around to control the crowd emerging as fast as an incoming wave. Officer Young put his hand up to stop Lucas. When Lucas was on a rampage, he was totally out of control, and Walter was afraid of what could transpire in this crowded hallway.

"Stop, son. It's all okay. We just walked Mr. DeWitt out to his car. Slow down, Lucas. Easy, son."

Lucas felt that trigger in his brain snap as his vision turned red. "I'm not your fucking son, goddammit! And what the hell did you do to Mr. DeWitt? He's my favorite teacher in the whole fucking school! What is going on?"

Lucas was out of control, but he didn't care. If his stepfather had walked Mr. DeWitt out of the building, something god-awful had happened, and he wanted to know what that was. He pounded on Walter's chest. "Where did you take him? I want to know! What did you do to him? Tell me! You owe it to me! TELL ME! What did you do? I hate you!"

The two of them were pressed nose to nose in front of the main office, and the crowd had grown to well over two hundred students, all yelling and cheering as they watched a fellow student in direct confrontation with a police officer. Security guards Pauline Clifton and Scott Sheldrake pounced on the scene, pushing students and staff aside as they rushed in to assess the situation.

"Everybody clear the halls! Now!" screamed Scott. "Get back to your classes right now! I mean it! Anyone still here in thirty seconds will have to answer to me every day after school for a week! Now get out of here!"

The crowd reluctantly turned around and shuffled off to their respective classes, all the while still watching over their shoulders, their cell phones recording the entire incident.

In those few seconds, Walter had grabbed Lucas's shoulders, spun him around, and dropped him on the ground with his face on the floor. Lucas banged his nose on the floor, and blood spurted out, creating a small pond of scarlet under his face. Walter had one knee on the small of Lucas's back and his hands pressed hard on his upper back. He wasn't hurting Lucas, but he needed to keep him restrained.

Pauline radioed Nurse Kelly, whispering for her to come to their location with her special case filled with gauze and other appropriate medical items.

"Now, listen to me, Lucas," Walter said. "If you don't want me to put you in handcuffs in front of the entire school, you need to calm down. I ain't bluffing, son. This ain't the playground, and this ain't no joke."

Lucas struggled under Walter's massive grip. "Let me go! Goddamn you! You always ruin everything I love. Everything! I hate your guts!"

Scott walked over, crouched down on one knee, and put his face right next to Lucas's, carefully avoiding the oozing blood from his nose. "Easy, son. Your stepfather is just trying to control the situation. You're not in trouble as of right now, but boy, every minute you don't calm down gets you closer to a place you do not want to go. Do you hear me? Lucas, do you get me?"

Spittle mixed with a thin stream of blood bubbled on Lucas's lips, his uncontrollable rage barely easing in intensity. "Let me up! Let me up! Let me up!"

Scott did not move his position. He wiped Lucas's chin with a napkin and very deliberately stared into his bloodshot eyes. "I'm gonna ask your stepdad to let you up, but

I need your word that you're not going to do anything but stand here and look at me. Do you understand me?"

Lucas closed his eyes, mucous dribbling down his nose and pinkish spit pooling around his lips. He took a deep breath. His body went limp as he forced himself to relax. Walter slowly lifted his knee from Lucas while scooting his arms underneath Lucas's armpits. He helped him get off the floor. Nurse Kelly brought a large gauze pad to his nose and held it there for him. His eyes glazed over, and his shoulders hung limp. Walter held him tight, knowing that if he let go, Lucas would crumble to the floor in a heap.

"Lucas," said Kelly. "Look at me, sweetie. Look me in the eyes if you can."

Lucas shook his head.

"Don't shake your head, honey. Just look at me, please."

Lucas breathed in and picked his head up enough to stare at his school nurse. He smiled weakly.

Walter asked Kelly, "Should I bring him to your room now?"

Kelly thought for a moment. She still had three girls sitting in the health room. Perhaps that wouldn't be the best place for Lucas. He didn't need to be interrogated by three gossipy teenagers, and she knew that was exactly what would happen if she brought him back there.

"You know what, Officer Young? Let's go see Principal Libertino. She would be a wonderful person right now to talk to, and I think given the situation, it's best not to escalate this any further."

"Okay, if you think that's best. You're the nurse after all.

Let me escort Lucas to her office, and then I'm going to take off, if that's okay with you. My presence right now is not going to be productive for Lucas."

Kelly nodded as she fell in step on the other side of Lucas. Together, she and Officer Young walked Lucas down the hall and into the main office.

Cassandra dabbed her eyes. She didn't know exactly what was going on, but between the chaos in the halls and seeing Carl ushered out of the building, things were not looking good. Ms. Atkinson had instructed her to call in for a substitute teacher for Carl, but before Cassandra could even raise an eyebrow in question, Ms. Atkinson had shut her down: "Don't ask me anything right now. Just call in for a sub and let them know it might be long term." Then she'd turned and raced off to her office.

Barbara Atkinson stuck her head into Lila's office. "Carl is out of the building. Lucas is being escorted to your office by his stepfather and Nurse Kelly." Barbara couldn't hold back her emotions any longer. She choked, coughed, and shuffled into her office. She closed the door and sat in her chair, and she sobbed, tears sluicing down her red cheeks.

CHAPTER 38

Beverly sat in her room staring at the walls. Her students were in the media center doing research for their next lab project, and Beverly had convinced Donnie Skaler, the media specialist, that her kids were so well-trained she didn't need to be there to help them locate their information.

Donnie—who had always liked Beverly and thought that if she ever left her husband, he would definitely ask her out—had said to her, "Oh, no problem, Mrs. Winewrought. I know how good your students are. Gee, they are always so well-behaved. I don't know how you manage to get them to be so independent!"

Beverly had smiled. She knew Donnie had a small crush on her, and she used it to her benefit. "Mr. Skaler, you are so generous and so sweet! I cannot thank you enough for allowing my wonderful young students to roam through your scholarly works. I bet you must have some special girl who really appreciates your incredible kindness!"

Donnie had blushed from his forehead down to his neck. He didn't know how to respond to Beverly, so he shuffled his feet until she blurted, "Oh, my, look at the time! I really have to get that report completed and to the principal. Wow! Thanks again, Donnie. You're my hero!" And with that, Beverly had dashed out of the media center and down to her room as fast as she could, even with the splint still attached to her.

Now that she was alone, her emotions began to creep into her conscience and prick at her soul. *What have I done?* She kept justifying and rationalizing, and yet still, she was not totally confident in her actions.

Beverly snatched her phone off the desk.

> Alisa,
>
> Damn, girl…I need to talk with you as soon as you are free today.
>
> Wanna go to Starbucks with?
>
> I could use something stronger, but I'm afraid to right now.
>
> B

• • •

A group of Alisa's students prepared to complete their special Mexican dinner entrées. Each kitchen had designed its own menu, and Alisa was so proud of their work.

"You are the most awesome group of students! I am so proud of each and every one of you! As soon as your last dish has been cooked, feel free to collect all your entrées, head to your area, and enjoy your meal! Yay! You've made my day!" Alisa, still smiling, returned to her desk to find her phone coming alive and vibrating across the calendar mat.

It was from Beverly. Alisa had been avoiding Beverly for the past few weeks. Between the broken wrist and Beverly's uncomfortable remarks about another colleague, Alisa had been conflicted. Beverly had always been a complainer—Alisa knew that about her—but this new behavior was downright scary. Beverly never stopped texting and whining about Carl DeWitt. Alisa didn't know Carl very well; in a high school setting, it could be difficult to get to know other teachers in different departments. It was not the same as when Alisa taught middle school. In a high school, it became cliquish, and teachers stuck together around their own subjects. Maybe it was out of habit and comfort; maybe it was snobbery—who knew? At any rate, the reason Beverly and Alisa got to be such good friends was because they were in a professional training class together a couple of years ago and had hit it off. Since then, they enjoyed going to Starbucks after school and sometimes getting dinner at TGI Fridays and having a few drinks.

Alisa knew Beverly's marriage was suffering, but she didn't know the extent of it. She was not sure how to help Beverly; she was not sure who to ask for guidance either.

Alisa opened the text. She knew it would be from Beverly. After all, who else would text her in the middle of a teaching day? Alisa read over the text with an invite to meet at Starbucks. Why would Beverly want to go out right now? She needs to recuperate and rest at home.

In addition, Alisa didn't want to get involved. She was done with Beverly and her drama. This last round of complaints about Carl had left a sour taste in Alisa's mouth. Carl was a good guy, a great teacher, and the kids adored him. Was she just being jealous? Alisa was confused because Beverly was a friend, but she was exhausting to listen to.

> Hey, listen Beverly…I'm really sorry… gotta do a few things after school today. Will catch up another time. TTYL
>
> A

And with that, Alisa decided to turn off her phone and enjoy the delicious meals her students had prepared.

• • •

Lila looked up at the gentle knocking on her door. "Come," was all she needed to say as she stood. The door opened, and Lila smiled tenderly as she welcomed in Lucas, her security leader, Scott, and Officer Young. Walking in behind the trio was Nurse Kelly.

Lila was used to meeting with students, parents, security, law enforcement officials, and other government officials, but today, looking at this young man who was practically carried into her office, disheveled, tear-stained, bloodied, and broken, Lila's heart sank.

"Hello, Lucas. Why don't you come sit over here with me at my table?" She looked at the other adults, who stood awkwardly, waiting to be told what was expected of them. "Kelly, will Lucas need any other tending, or can he stay with me?"

Kelly handed Lila some gauze and gave her principal the thumbs-up sign before leaving the room.

Lila looked over at Officer Young. "Officer, I know Lucas is your stepson. Would you give me permission to speak with him privately, sir?"

Walter looked at Lucas, who sat at the table, his chin on his chest, shoulders sagging under his emotional pain. Walter hoped Lila would be able to save his stepson from the heartache he'd been suffering for so long. He gave Lila the smallest nod and left.

Scott Sheldrake remained. He had worked with Lila for years and knew exactly what she would do. His respect for her was immense, and her ability to take a raw and crushed teen and bring him back to life was breathtaking to witness. But Scott knew Lila needed her privacy and wanted to make sure Lucas felt as safe and secure as possible, so without a word, Scott smiled knowingly and left her office.

CHAPTER 39

Kelly hurried back to her health room, where she had left Cindy, Riley, and Jilly alone in her race to take care of Lucas. When she arrived, the three girls were huddled together in the back. Kelly was a bit taken aback by this scene. This triumvirate appeared to be deep in a serious conversation.

"Well, hello, girls. The three of you seem to be in much better shape than when I left you. Jilly, how are you feeling?"

Jilly always kept a secret stash of Midol in her book bag, and as soon as Kelly had run out of the room, she'd popped two in her mouth. Sitting on the cot with Cindy and Riley, Jilly felt almost human again. She hated her monthly bouts with severe cramps, and when Nurse Kelly left the room, Jilly had decided to do the most courageous thing she had ever done.

"Riley," Jilly had whispered, even though it was just the three of them in the room, "could you ask your mom if I could visit with her? I mean, you know, like a medical appointment? Uh, what I mean is, can she see me as a patient?"

Riley immediately went down a rabbit hole. "Are you sick? Are you okay? Why haven't you told me? Goddamn it, Jilly, ya got me so worried sick, and you haven't exactly been talking to me. I thought you hated me 'cause of Lucas, and I . . . Oh, God, Jilly, please tell me you're okay!"

Jilly's shoulders had sagged under the weight of missing her best friend for so long. "Oh, Riley, it's my period again. It hurts so bad, and it's getting worse, and my mom won't take me to a doctor. She thinks I'm still too young. And, well, if your mom could see me, I won't tell anyone, I swear it!"

Jilly had suffered with cramps ever since they both started their periods on the very same day while away at a school function. Camping, the school had called it. Learning and loving nature, they'd called it. Ha! It was more like torturing preteens, according to Riley. And then they both got their—oh, what did the older counselors say? Oh, yeah: *your cousins from Red River just came* and *Eve's loving legacy* and *womanly duties* and other such garbage. It had hurt, and thank goodness the two of them were allowed to stay in the smelly office they called a nurse's room for the rest of the "camping" trip.

But when they came home, Riley's mom had been right there to soothe her and help her each month with purchasing the best products and taking medicine that would help with her cramps. Jilly never talked about it, but Riley knew she really suffered from stomach cramps, and her mom wasn't much help. *Boys will never understand the pain we suffer every month just so we can have babies later on. Honest to God. SO. NOT. FAIR!*

"Jills, as soon as I get home today, I will talk to my mom. She'll know how to go about seeing you. I promise."

"Thanks, Riley. And, Riley, I'm so sorry I haven't been talking to you. It's not you; it's me, and I hate myself for it. I'm just . . . I don't even know what to say anymore."

At this point, Cindy had coughed to get their attention, and they both looked up to see Nurse Kelly had entered the room.

"Well, hello, girls. The three of you seem to be in much better shape than when I left you. Jilly, how are you feeling?"

"Good!" said all three girls at once.

Riley spoke up. "You know, Miss Kelly, I think all three of us are ready to head back to class. After all, it's almost lunchtime, and we have so much schoolwork to do. Can you write us a pass to get back to our studies?"

Kelly squinted. "Who are you girls?" But she laughed and filled out three passes. "Now get back to class right away because your teachers will be asking me what time you arrived and what time you left. Got me? And Jilly? Remember you can come talk to me anytime, okay?"

Jilly took the pass from Kelly and nodded. "I will, Miss Kelly. Thanks for everything."

The three girls slipped out the door as though they were on a secret mission.

And they were. Without speaking and without heading back to their individual classrooms, they headed straight for the dark hall where no one would find them. They had a plan—a secret plan—and they did not want anyone to hear them.

CHAPTER 40

Lila reached over to her desk and grabbed a large bowl filled with a variety of candy bars, Rice Krispies Treats, and granola bars of different flavors. She placed it in the middle of the table, then reached over and gently placed her hand on Lucas's arm. "Lucas, look at me, honey."

Lucas sniffed, used his sleeve to wipe snot off his face, and raised his head. He had never been in as much trouble as he had been that year. "My life sucks, Dr. Libertino. I hate it. I hate myself, and I don't want it anymore."

Lila knew the signs: depression, hatred, self-loathing.

"Lucas, do you want to hurt yourself? I have to ask that, you know."

Lucas stared into the most compassionate slate gray eyes and whispered in a husky voice, "No. I don't want to hurt myself. I'm just so sad all the time. And now I saw that Mr. DeWitt, my favorite teacher ever, was taken out of the building. He's the only one in this entire place who gets me. What did he do? Is he a bad guy? And of all the people in the whole world, my stepfather was the one to walk him out. How can I go home and sit at the dinner table? I hate that man. I hate him!"

Lila let Lucas talk. The less she said, the more he would share. He needed to let it out. Lila was savvy. Her counselors were well-equipped to deal with students in crisis, but there was something she needed Lucas to find out on his own, in her office. And so she waited. And waited. And listened.

Lucas reached for a candy bar. He hadn't realize how hungry he was, and damn, that bowl had all his favorite treats! He unwrapped a Crunch bar, a bag of Skittles, and a Reese's Peanut Butter Cup.

He didn't remember being here, but he guessed he must have at one point or another considering all the trouble he had been in this year. But this was different. He was automatically stuffing the candy in his mouth while staring at some photographs, big ones, on the wall and on the bookshelves. He recognized Dr. Libertino, but he did not know who all the people were in the pictures.

And then it hit him. She was standing with the same man. The two kids in the pictures changed as they obviously grew older, from very young to teens. They were family photos—he got that—but these struck him oddly.

Dr. Libertino was white. The man in all the pictures was an African American man.

Lila observed Lucas, waiting for the light bulb to come

on. She saw the recognition in his eyes and heard the click in his head as the reality of the situation thundered like a bowling ball knocking all the pins down.

"Yes, Lucas, my husband is a Black man. And I have two beautiful biracial children, Benjamin and Bessie. They are the loves of my life. It hasn't been easy for them growing up, but they are strong, and they are smart, compassionate human beings who know what it's like to live in two different worlds.

"We have had many, many talks about being biracial, about choosing one race over another. My son and I have talked about how to speak to a police officer should he be stopped for driving an expensive car in a white neighborhood. I was saddened to have to have that conversation, but it was necessary. And I hope you and your mother and stepfather will have some talks about your family dynamics as well."

Lucas stopped chewing as he listened with rapt attention.

"Lucas, I know it was you who wrote the racial slurs on the wall over the summer. I have been wanting to talk with you about that, but I've been waiting for the right time. That time is now. We need to have this talk, son, and you have to be honest with me. The truth can hurt, but we need to put it all out on the table. Everything about Mr. DeWitt, about why you are filled with such hatred toward Black people, and why you are so angry."

Lucas couldn't hold it in anymore. It was like a dam had burst wide open, and he allowed it to spill amok. He told Dr. Libertino everything about his dad and that awful night and how Walter had been the only one to come to his rescue and how he'd resented that. He confessed that he was embarrassed by having a Black stepfather, especially one everyone loved but him. Lucas told Dr. Libertino how he'd been waiting for his biological father to return but knew deep down inside he was a sick man, and that made Lucas angry—angry because he couldn't fix his father, angry because his mother didn't protect him from the things his father had done to him, angry because his mother loved Walter, angry because Lucas was afraid to love Walter, because if Lucas loved Walter, that meant he was cheating on his father.

Exhausted, Lucas put his head on the table and wept, deep racking sobs Lila felt in her heart. She pulled up a chair next to Lucas and cradled him and let him sob till he was spent.

CHAPTER 41

Carl opened his car door and sat inside for a few minutes, staring at the school building. *What the fuck just happened to me?* One minute, he'd been loving life, teaching kids, laughing with them, hanging with his colleagues, and now . . . What? How?

Carl hadn't realized how long he'd been sitting in his car till Scott knocked on his window. He rolled it down and looked at Scott as though he were a stranger.

Scott knew the protocol. Whenever someone from school had to be escorted to their car, that also meant they had to leave the premises. Scott's chest heaved as he stared into Carl's bloodshot eyes. He could tell Carl had been crying—not the crying one does after watching a sappy commercial; no, this was the kind that had you one inch shy of puking your guts up.

"Hey, Carl," Scott said as softly as he could. "Listen, man, I know this is one rough situation, but, well, damn it, Carl, I gotta ask you to leave school grounds."

Carl wiped his nose with a McDonald's napkin. "What

did I do, Scott? What in God's name did I do to deserve this? Did a kid complain? A parent? It couldn't have been a teacher, could it have?" And then, suddenly, as though a light bulb had just clicked on, shining so bright your eyes would burn. "Holy shit! It was Beverly, wasn't it? It was Beverly Winewrought!"

Scott looked down at the pavement and shuffled his feet. "Look, Carl, you gotta go, man. I can't stand out here any longer. Just head on home and get some rest. You're gonna have to wait this out before you know what's what." Scott turned around and, with sagging shoulders, walked back to the building. He couldn't stay there any longer. It was too painful. Carl DeWitt was the nicest, kindest teacher, and he sure as hell didn't deserve this kind of treatment. Scott wasn't sure if it was Beverly or not. He hadn't been in the loop to know, but he swore to himself that he was going to find out who was trying to take Carl down.

Carl stared after Scott as he headed back to the building. He turned his engine on, slipped his gear into drive, and headed out, aimlessly driving, not caring, not wanting to care.

Twenty minutes later, it seemed his car had automatically headed straight for Cold Stone Creamery. Funny, the things you remember when you're completely devastated. When his sister had come to him, crying hysterically and wanting Carl to solve all her problems with their dad, they had gone to Cold Stone. Sitting outside, letting the cool, creamy mountains of flavor slide down their throats, the two siblings felt they could conquer the world. Well, perhaps not the world, but their father.

They might not have had all the answers, but they'd had each other, and laughing and crying over Kit Kats, chocolate chips, and marshmallows seemed to make them feel like, for a few minutes, all was right with the world. And where was good ol' Chip during these intense family dramas? Nowhere to be seen. Dad would always cover for him and say he was at some athletic event or meeting.

Carl stared at the store. He didn't want to go in. He didn't want to imagine his world would be okay just by finishing a bowl of ice-cold heaven. And so he sat there in the parking lot and stared and thought and cried again, and when his head started pounding from the tears and horror of his situation, he blew his nose and pulled out a scrap piece of paper from his pocket.

On the piece of paper was a phone number. He called it. A deep, melodious voice answered. Carl hesitated for a second, and then in a somewhat gravelly voice, husky from emotion, he said, "Uh, hello. Is this Lemont Jacobs?"

"Hello. And to whom do I have the pleasure of speaking with this afternoon?"

Carl cleared his throat. "Hello. My name is Carl DeWitt, and I, uh, well, we just met a littler earlier today at my car in the parking lot. You gave me your number and told me to call when I was ready and, I guess, talk."

"Hi, Carl. Yes, I've been waiting to hear from you. We will set up a time to meet face-to-face, but for now, can I ask you a couple of questions? That is, if it's okay with you. I know you just left school, and you must be bursting with questions and—"

"YES!" screamed Carl into the phone. He couldn't believe he'd just yelled at a complete stranger, and this stranger was supposed to help him. *Oh, dear God. What am I doing?* "Oh, excuse me." Carl's voice trembled. "I apologize for that outburst. I am so confused and angry and scared right now. I don't know what's going on. I'm talking to a complete stranger, and . . ." Carl could not finish. He was spent. His body sagged in his seat.

Lemont waited a few moments before he spoke. "Carl, have you done anything—anything at all—that might be frowned upon at school?"

Carl's head shot up like a bullet exiting the barrel. "Frowned upon? *Me?* What are you talking about? No, no, no, no, NO! There is absolutely nothing I have done today, yesterday, last year, or ever that someone, anyone would frown upon. Jesus, Lemont, I don't know what you know about me, but hear me, I have never done anything inappropriate to anyone at any time. Ever, man. You hear me? Ever!"

Lemont took his time before responding. He had been doing this job for several years now, and it was never easy. It was his job to find out whether or not the teacher in question was in denial, lying, or in some cases, totally innocent of acting inappropriately or saying something totally unprofessional. "Carl. Mr. DeWitt. You and I will be meeting next week. In the meantime, I need you to go home. Relax. Think about what may have started all of this. You are going to get phone calls from different people. Hear me very carefully, Carl. You are not to talk to anyone without me present. Do you understand? I mean this in all seriousness. A person calls you, and you go spill your guts about whatever, and then before you know it, things are misinterpreted, and we are done. And I mean D-O-N-E, done.

"Wait for my phone call. We will meet. Just you and me. That's it. No one else. When we can talk face-to-face, I'll share more information with you. For now, please, go home. Turn off the television, stay off your internet, do not write any emails, and for God's sake, you may not—let me repeat that—you may *not* speak with anyone from school. Do I make myself clear?"

Carl mumbled into his phone.

"No!" shouted Lemont. "I need to hear you tell me loud and clear that you understand what I just said. Repeat it to me, Carl. I am quite serious. Tell me the rules."

His voice robotic and without emotion, Carl repeated what Lemont had just ordered him to do. Or rather, what not to do.

"Good," acknowledged Lemont. "That's good. Now hang up, turn off your phone, and go home. Tomorrow, at 9:00 a.m., I'll call about where and when we'll be meeting. Take care, Carl. And be careful."

Lemont clicked off, and Carl stared at his cell phone, which felt like it weighed one hundred pounds. He pressed the side buttons and slid the power function to off, started his car, and drove home, frozen and numb.

CHAPTER 42

Lucas's mom arrived at Wells, and Cassandra escorted her to Lila's office. Lila asked Lucas to wait outside in the office. He stood up, nodded, and walked out without acknowledging his mom who was standing by the door. Mrs. Young sighed and waited for Lila to beckon her to enter.

Lila waved Mrs. Young in. She noted that Lucas's mom had taken a married name but had not changed Lucas's last name.

"Mrs. Young," Lila said warmly, "please come sit down at my table, and let's you and I have a, well, what we in the educational field like to call a 'courageous conversation.'"

Mrs. Young was nervous and uncomfortable. How many times in the past few years had she been called into the principal's office to discuss her son's behavior? How many times had she been told they wanted to place Lucas in a special school for students with uncontrollable conduct?

But Lila had a very different approach than all the other administrators. Yes, her team was professional and kind but direct and looking for the conclusion of a situation. Lucas was growing emotionally and mentally, and he was nowhere near the finality of anything. Lila was not ready to jump to any conclusions yet. Julie and Walter had had a long talk last night, and they were awfully close to agreeing that maybe Lucas needed to go to a special boarding school—somewhere he could learn to better manage his anger and control himself when he felt he was at his breaking point.

Julie Young stared at Lila. She could barely process what Dr. Libertino was saying to her. She homed in on a few words. "Are you serious? You were able to talk about Walter and Lucas's biological father at the same time? And he didn't lose his temper? He didn't scream or stomp or bang on your table?" Julie took a deep breath and pushed herself away from the table. She walked over behind Lila's desk and pointed at the pictures. "Is this your family? Are these your children and your husband? Did Lucas see this? Did he understand? What . . . how . . . ? Please tell me what happened here. I need to know."

"Mrs. Young, I have a great deal I want to share with you. Please, come back and sit down, and let's learn more about Lucas together."

And so, during the next hour, Lila and Julie talked and shared and cried about their respective lives and marriages and children. In the end, however, Lila morphed back into the role of the principal. "And now, Julie, I need you to think about sending Lucas to—"

"I know, I know. You want to send him away to another

school, a school that will accept my son for what he is and not for what he's not, and—"

"No," Lila said reassuringly. "No, Mrs. Young, I want Lucas to remain here with me. I want to see him graduate. I want to see him grow and mature and see what life has to offer him and, more importantly, what he has to offer the world. But in order for him to achieve all of these things, I need you to consider putting him in therapy. Not leaving the area at all, but therapy here in town. Several of our students are seeing Ms. Anna Klug, and she is absolutely amazing with these young teenagers. She's getting married very soon and may be away for a while, but not for long, and I know Lucas will be very successful with her. Tell me you are willing to try it. Please, for his sake."

Julie stiffened and puffed out her chest. "And if I refuse? What then? Will you demand that Lucas leave your school? You will only keep him here on your terms? He has to give in to whatever you deem the panacea for his behaviors? Is that what this meeting is all about?" Julie stood up, swung her purse up and over her shoulder, and pushed her chair out so hard it crashed onto the floor. Julie walked around the chair without looking at it and headed straight to the door.

"Mrs. Young." Lila's voice was loud and authoritative this time. She was no longer sitting and sharing stories; she was the principal of a large high school, and she was not going to allow a parent to knock over a chair and walk out of her room without acknowledging the conclusion to their meeting. "Mrs. Young, I need you to stop where you are and turn around and look at me! We are not finished. And you, my dear, are making assumptions about our talk right now that I do not appreciate at all!"

Julie was shocked. No one had ever spoken to her like that, and she froze in place. "I will not allow my son to be manipulated into doing something he doesn't want to do."

Lila smiled. "Now, Mrs. Young, when did I say seeing a therapist was a deal breaker? I only strongly—and I do mean strongly—advise you to take Lucas to this therapist. If Lucas is not willing, then sadly, it will be his loss. But if he does see her—and I know he will like her—it will be a win-win for all of us. So, Mrs. Young, are you willing to give it a try? Are you willing to have Lucas see Miss Anna, even if it's only for one time? Afterward, you can come let me know how Lucas felt about his meeting. That is the only deal I see on the table."

Julie's shoulders sagged, and her purse slipped off her shoulder. She let it fall to the ground. Then she walked over, picked up the chair, and placed it back where it belonged. She hesitated, uncomfortable with her myriad of mixed emotions, and took a slow, deep breath. Julie knew what she had to do. In a single motion, she reached up and hugged Lila tightly. "I am so, so sorry," she whispered, trembling.

Lila reacted by putting her arms around Julie. "It's okay, Julie. It's going to be okay."

Julie left the office, and this time Lucas looked up at her. He stood up, reached for his mom, and the two of them hugged. Then together, they left the building.

Lila sat in her office. It was quiet for the moment. So much went on in a building that Lila felt her head was in a constant spin mode. Her mind raced back to Carl and his situation.

She was still numb from everything that had transpired, but she knew, sadly, that sometimes there were situations well beyond her control. She didn't like it; in fact, there were times she opposed decisions directly, only to be told point-blank that she was to follow the rules or she could find employment in another jurisdiction.

"Bah, damn the politics of it all! I know Carl is a good man, but how in hell am I going to prove that? All I have is this one conversation from a teacher stating they 'know' Carl DeWitt has been acting inappropriately with students, especially during after-school hours." *Ugh! Damn it all to hell!* Lila was talking to no one, but it felt good to hear herself talk out loud. It calmed her somehow.

Lila sat at her desk staring at the blank computer, too upset to turn it on. She turned in her chair to gaze upon her family pictures, thinking back to when she and Lucas had a long and powerful talk about interracial marriages and biracial children and feelings of racism and hatred. Lucas wasn't a bad kid, and she did not feel he was racist as much as he was angry at his biological father. Taking it out on Walter was natural, though hurtful.

Lucas had cried when he spoke of his biological father and the events that had sent him running into the night. Running away from his father and eventually into the supportive arms of Walter should have been a positive and reassuring one, but instead, it was the birth of a hatred so strong it pushed him to vandalize and destroy.

Amelia knocked and slowly opened Lila's door. "I brought you some hot coffee and a sandwich before you forget you haven't eaten today."

Lila smiled. "Bless you, Amelia. You made my day." Lila sipped the coffee and closed her eyes. "Oh, my, I needed that."

"My pleasure, Dr. Libertino. And while you take a moment to enjoy some nourishment, I do have three girls who have been pacing by my desk asking to see you. They say it's urgent."

Lila looked up to see the three girls who stood side by side outside her door, all holding hands. The tall one in the middle stuck up her chin and said in as convincing a tone as a fourteen-year-old girl could muster, "Dr. Libertino, we need to talk with you, right now! Uh . . . please."

CHAPTER 43

She knocked on the door. And knocked. And knocked. And knocked one more time as hard as she could, almost tearing the skin off her raw and bruised knuckle.

Alisa came to the door. "Who is it? It's 11:30 at night!"

Beverly said through tears, "Alisa . . . Alisa, it's me, Beverly. Please open up. Alisa, please."

Alisa unlocked her door and pulled it open. Her friend stood on her porch with two suitcases and her school bag hanging off her shoulder, looking as though she had just gone through ten rounds in a boxing ring and lost it all.

Alisa's mouth fell open as she stared at Beverly. "Beverly, what? Oh, girl, come in right now!" Alisa reached for Beverly and grabbed her before she collapsed on her front porch. "Get in here. Come sit down on the couch."

Beverly, supported by Alisa's strong hands, shuffled over to the couch and crumpled into a heap. She looked like a rag doll as her head fell to the side of the couch and her body tilted sideways. Alisa slipped off Beverly's pointed pumps and lifted her legs onto the couch. Beverly moaned when her arm, still in a sling, slid under her side, causing rivers of pain to slice through her wrist.

"Here, let me help you reposition yourself." Alisa very carefully pulled Beverly's body up so she could lay her down on the couch, taking care not to tangle her splinted arm again.

Beverly moaned and closed her eyes. Alisa took that moment to run back to her front door and grab the two suitcases and Beverly's school satchel and drag them into her foyer. Alisa then closed and locked her door. Surveying the scenario, she shook her head. *This is gonna be one long night.*

Alisa took a few long steps over to her recliner, grabbed the afghan her mother had always said would be the warmth to her soul, and covered Beverly tenderly with it. Alisa cradled Beverly's non-slinged hand with the bloody scrape marks and broken nails.

"Oh, baby." Alisa's voice was heartbroken. "What happened to you tonight? It's okay, girlfriend. You're here with me now."

Alisa touched Beverly's forehead with the palm of her hand and, as light as a feather, soothed her knitted brows until she heard the even breathing of her friend. Every now and then, Beverly jerked her bruised hand and made a noise filled with pain. Beverly's eyes twitched, and her shoulders wrenched a few times, but she did not wake up.

Alisa got up after a while. She turned off the living room lamp and tiptoed into her office and closed the door. Alisa turned on her computer and waited for the humming to subside. The Wells High School home page opened up, and Alisa typed quickly and efficiently. She scrolled down to the substitute tab, and clicked on the request for a substitute for Beverly and herself. She'd have to deal with Beverly in the morning, and getting up and dressed for school was not an option right now.

The computer screen was too bright, and Alisa squinted at the intense glare. "Damn you, Theodore Winewrought. I don't know what you did to my friend tonight, but just be glad I'm not coming after you myself. There's a place in hell for wife beaters like you, and I hope you don't have to wait too long to go down to your next home!"

The computer seemed to moan as Alisa turned it off again for the night. She turned off the lights and climbed the steps to her bedroom to go to sleep. Again.

Tomorrow, she'd sort this all out. She sighed. For now, she needed to get a good night's sleep. *I have a feeling there's a lot more to this story than coming for a sleepover.*

Alisa crawled into her bed and fell into a restless, disturbing sleep filled with dreams of violence and unease.

CHAPTER 44

Lila recognized one of the three girls: Jilly Castings. Ironically, she was the girl who'd been involved with Lucas in the dark hall a few months ago. (Lila hated that section of the building and silently swore to reconstruct the area one day.) Jilly, as part of her restorative justice for her inappropriate actions, had become a part of Carl and Neva's mentoring program.

Lila smiled at the girls and invited them in. Amelia Goddard, Lila's personal administrative secretary, came rushing in behind them.

"Oh, my goodness, Dr. Libertino! I apologize profusely! I am so sorry! These three girls walked right past me and ignored my requests to stop and make an appointment with you." Amelia was out of breath and red-faced. Her shoulders jerked up and down while her hands circled in the air in front of her.

Lila put her hands on Amelia's shoulders and guided her out of the office. "It's quite all right, Amelia. These girls are obviously quite upset over something and probably never heard you ask them to stop. Don't be upset with them. And I am certainly not upset with you. Now, be a dear and bring me some more coffee, because my head is going to burst. Oh, and Amelia, cancel my other afternoon appointments. If I get a reminder call that I'm supposed to be at the central office at the most important principals' meeting, just take a message or let whoever's calling know that I have a major crisis on my hands and cannot under any circumstances be interrupted. Are you okay with that?"

Amelia looked at Lila with her big Irish green eyes—which were quite watery right now—and nodded. She rushed past the other secretaries' desks and into the break room to prepare Lila's coffee and, if she could find one, perhaps a sweet snack for her beloved boss.

Cindy, Riley, and Jilly threw themselves into the chairs surrounding Lila's round table. Cindy was crying; Riley was rubbing Cindy's back; Jilly was staring into space. Lila walked over to the table and said rather harshly, "Now, what could be so incredibly dramatic that all three of you had to rush past my secretary and demand an audience with me?"

Riley, who was the calmest of the three, blurted, "Why are they arresting Mr. DeWitt? We demand to know because, well, he is absolutely the best teacher in this whole entire school."

Lila glared at the three innocent faces staring at her wide-eyed and wanting answers. Answers she was not sure she could provide at this very moment. Lila walked around to her desk and fell into her seat, mentally and physically exhausted. *This has been one hell of a day. You cannot make this shit up.* She contemplated her response. *Sure, they want answers. I want answers, too.* Lila wanted to know why they thought Carl was the best teacher since Annie O'Sullivan, since Maria Montessori, damn, since Jaime Escalante!

Amelia knocked and entered with a steaming cup of coffee.

"Bless you, my dear. And Amelia, make sure we are not interrupted. I know I already told you that, but I have a feeling there might be some chaos happening soon, and I need to stay put. Okay? And one more thing, Amelia—thank you for all you do."

Amelia smiled and looked at the girls sitting there with tear stains on their faces and candy from Lila's famous candy dish in their hands. *They're all yours, Doctor. And that's why you get paid the big bucks around here*, she mused. "Thanks, Double L. If you need me, all you have to do is call." And with that, Amelia disappeared as quietly as she had come.

Lila took a long sip of her extra hot and sweet coffee and sighed while the girls filled their faces with Kit Kats and Skittles. And then it was silent. The girls stopped chewing and looked at each other nervously.

Lila took a slow, deep breath. "Now, one of you—not all at once, mind you, one of you at a time, and slowly please—tell me about your favorite teacher, Mr. Carl DeWitt."

Riley sat up tall in her chair and raised her hand. Lila

smiled. "This isn't class, sweetheart. Tell me your name and start talking."

"Dr. Libertino, my name is Riley Maddox. I am a freshman. I am a really good student. I do not get in trouble, and I do not lie. Jilly, here, well, she has been my best friend for, like, forever. And Cindy over here, well, honestly, we are just becoming good buds. You know how it is—we're still learning about each other and about being in high school, 'cause I gotta tell you, it's really, really different from middle school, and I—"

"Riley, thanks for all the great background, but can you focus on just Mr. DeWitt?"

Riley blushed from the bottom of her neck all the way to her forehead. She had never been in the principal's office, and here she was, chowing down on the woman's candy dish and relaxing at her table like they were chilling at the mall together. Now she'd been called out.

"Oh, gee, I am so sorry. Okay, okay, let me get back to why we are here. Like I said, high school can be scary. The upperclassmen are huge, and the girls are so, well, confident about who they are and all, and well, Mr. DeWitt makes you feel so comfortable with who you are. Did you know he sends home postcards to our parents when we have a good day? Did you know that when Cindy was having a breakdown—sorry, Cindy, I don't mean to bring that up—but when she was having a bit of a meltdown in class, not only did Mr. DeWitt send her to the counselor, but he sent me with her to make sure she got there. And then he made sure she was okay, 'cause after class, guess who came straight to see our counselor, Ms. Lozak? That's right, Mr. DeWitt. What I'm getting at, Dr. L—can I call you that? Is that okay?"

Lila smiled and nodded. "Go on."

"Well, it's just that Mr. DeWitt is always saying the right things to us in class, whether he is talking history or how it relates to us. He has a way to make it all clear and understandable, not just facts and sh—I mean, stuff."

Cindy raised her hand. "Dr. Libertino." Cindy spoke so softly Lila had to lean forward to hear her. "I know I have some issues. I do see a therapist every week. And I am always talking about Mr. DeWitt and how he m-m-makes me feel comfortable and all. But you have to know, when I say c-c-comfortable—'cause my therapist is very strict about this part—I mean comfortable in a professional way, like he never embarrasses me when I'm stuttering or if I don't know the answer. But—and this is what's bothering me, 'cause I think I got him in t-t-trouble—Mrs. Wine-wrought overheard me say, while we were in the nurse's room, that Mr. DeWitt was weird, and she came over to me and kept asking me what I meant when I said he was weird, and—"

Jilly jumped in. "Mr. DeWitt is weird only because he's so cool. He knows how to relate to teens. He knows how to make his class relevant. And most importantly, he knows how to make us feel good about who we are. But teachers like Mrs. Winewrought, well, she twisted what Cindy and some of the other kids were saying. *Weird* is actually a good thing. He's not evil, Dr. Libertino. He's not a perv and doesn't touch anyone. He's one of the good ones. So why was he arrested? Cindy, she can't sleep at night because of the way Mrs. Winewrought was all over her when she was dipping into her conversation. Dipping where she shouldn't have been swimming, and now he's gone. It's her who should be gone!"

Lila took down copious notes. The girls talked longer and longer and without any hesitation about what they felt about Mr. DeWitt and Mrs. Winewrought. Jilly claimed the after-school mentoring class with Mrs. Waverly and Mr. DeWitt was the best thing that had ever happened to her.

"The two of them are so incredible together, and they make us feel okay with being teenagers. They teach us lessons about social media and how to handle so many other things. If I hadn't had that class, I would be a wreck, especially because of, well, you know what happened to me with Lucas."

Lila nodded. She couldn't believe what was happening, but after an hour of listening, Lila knew what she had to do. But first, she needed to contact these phenomenal girls' parents to let them know why they would be coming home on a late bus and how proud they should be of their daughters.

CHAPTER 45

"I left him. I left Ted. We fought. And you know why we fought? Because he claimed I was having an affair. Me. An affair. And you want to know who I was having an affair with, Alisa? Are you ready for this? Are you really ready, because I almost threw up when he said it. He said I must be having an affair with some guy named Carl because I'm always mentioning him when I'm on the phone with you."

Beverly and Alisa sat at the kitchen table. Alisa had let Beverly sleep in, and when she'd finally woken up, Alisa had explained she'd called in a sub for both of them because there was no way they were mentally or physically capable of teaching that day. Beverly needed time to share everything, and Alisa needed the day to help her friend heal.

Alisa looked at Beverly as though she were staring at a stranger. Who was this woman? She'd always had a gut feeling that Ted was abusing her, and this last time, when her wrist was broken, well, she knew it was because of Ted. And now, there were still unanswered questions.

Alisa was almost too afraid to ask her next question because somewhere down deep, something sinister was happening, and it was because of Beverly. She sipped her coffee and picked at the croissant in front of her. She had to ask. "Beverly, you know yesterday at school, there was a great deal of commotion. In fact, there was almost a riot at the front entrance. Did you happen to see any of it?"

Beverly ate her scrambled eggs so voraciously one would think she hadn't eaten in days. She shoveled the food into her mouth and slurped down the hot coffee. Alisa was afraid she was going to choke.

"Beverly, slow down, girlfriend. There's no fire to put out. Now, back to school yesterday. Did you see any of the chaos?"

Beverly nodded but kept stuffing her mouth.

Alisa reached over and placed her hand on Beverly's arm. "Stop. Right now. Stop eating, stop drinking, and look at me. Beverly Winewrought, what involvement, if any, did you have in the Carl DeWitt situation? I say *situation* because I don't have a clue as to what happened yesterday other than that the poor man was walked out of the building with a police escort and sent away. Now, what in God's name can you tell me? And don't beat around the bush here, baby. I need to know the truth."

Alisa sighed. "And I need to know why you haven't been honest with me about Ted hurting you. Instead, I have been told lies and falsehoods and innuendos. What am I supposed to think? You text me these cryptic notes but never really tell me what's happening. You come to school in a frigging sling and lead me to believe that you fell. Really? Now come on, spill, and I mean now!"

Beverly stopped chewing. Her eyes filled with tears and spilled over, landing on her half-eaten eggs. Alisa handed her a napkin, but she wasn't going to fall for the sympathetic routine. Oh, no—that kumbaya train had long rushed through the station. It was give-all time.

Beverly sniffed back snot and dabbed her eyes. She swallowed hard. She pushed the plate aside and looked at Alisa for a long time. Alisa stared back. She was not falling for any of it, and Beverly knew it.

"Ted has been hurting me for the past few years. I have secret pictures of it on my phone with dates so I remember. He has a short temper. When he'd lash out at me, he always made sure it wouldn't show—well, at least not too much. I would wear long sleeves in the middle of summer and pretend I was always cold. I would wear long pants and avoid the pool because I had bruises on my thighs where he would grab me in anger under the table.

"I thought he would get help. I thought I needed to be more understanding because I needed him. At least I thought I needed him. I thought I could cure him. Ha! Isn't that a laugh? How many times did I ask him to go for help? How many times did I threaten to leave him? And he would only leave another bruise on my arm and then cry and say how much he loved me and needed me. Needed me? Ha! To tell you the truth, I think he's the one having an affair! And yet he blasts me, trying to guilt me into confessing something. He should be the one praying for forgiveness!"

Alisa scoffed. She tried not to show any judgment, but she hated Ted for hurting her friend and was disappointed Beverly had not confided in her sooner. And she was angry at herself for not coming to the abusive husband conclusion sooner. She also felt guilty that she'd sometimes ignored Beverly's texts because she didn't want to deal with the drama.

Alisa wanted Beverly to get it all out on the table. She had to, because it had come to a boiling point, and it was dangerous. She reached out and held Beverly's hands, this time more tenderly. "Beverly, it's all right. It's going to be okay, but you need to keep going. Tell me more, honey. Tell me everything."

And Beverly did. She talked about how she had met Ted and how magnanimous he'd been to her. Considering her terrible upbringing, Ted was truly her knight in shining armor. The physical abuse didn't raise its ugly head till a few years into their marriage, when Ted was getting passed over for promotions and spent more and more time on the road with no significant increase in salary or compensation. This resulted in a newfound rage of jealousy toward Beverly. Everything Beverly did was somehow in competition with Ted. Every friend, every event, every place she went without Ted was either because she was embarrassed by him, didn't want to show him around, or worse, because she was involved with another man.

"And Alisa, I was never involved with another man. I . . . I thought about it. Hell, I dreamt about it because there was nothing for me at home. I stayed away as often as I could. I pretended I had so much schoolwork I had to be there for hours after school. And then, and then . . ." Beverly started choking and spitting, and Alisa rushed to the sink to get her some water. Beverly took a sip and controlled her breathing.

"Alisa, I did something awful. I hate myself for it. I really do. I don't know how I could have stooped to something so absolutely horrific. I'm so embarrassed to even discuss it, let alone confess it to you."

Alisa stood up and poured herself and Beverly another cup of coffee. When she sat back down, she knew what was coming next. Alisa had a feeling she knew exactly what had transpired over the past few weeks, and now she was certain of it. "Go on, Beverly. Tell me. There's nothing you can say that will end our friendship. I'm here for you. I always have been, and now it's time to rip open this ugly wound that's been festering inside you for weeks."

Beverly took a long sip of coffee. Her eyes were watery, but she was no longer crying. "I'd wanted to be a part of that mentoring program for so long. I did all the research. I contacted other schools to see what they were doing for their mentoring programs. I even made a list of potential students who should be involved in the program. I went to a seminar last summer on how to motivate students and how to help those at-risk students. I read. I studied. I wanted it more than anything else.

"I thought that if I were involved in the program Barbara Atkinson was putting together—well, somehow, I thought it would put my personal life back on track. I really thought it would. And then, goddamn it all! That bitch Atkinson went ahead and assigned it to Neva and that freak, Carl. And all I heard from every kid I asked was how much they loved the program and how much they loved Neva and Carl. I couldn't stand it anymore. I couldn't breathe any time I heard the kids talking about it."

Alisa listened and nodded and tried not to show any emotion. Her instincts had been right; this all centered around some illogical ill-conceived hatred for Carl. "Was Carl ever unprofessional toward you?"

Beverly shook her head. "That's just it. He was always sweet and generous and kind and—oh, Alisa, I know I did the wrong thing. But when I got bumped in the hallway, and Carl was there, and I was rushed to the nurse, well . . .

"I know it was Carl. I know he spoke to Nurse Kelly about my wrist and indicated it was maybe more than an accident. Who the hell was he to talk to anyone about my personal life? How dare he? Who does he think he is? Some frigging hero? I don't need a damn hero; I needed that program, and he took it from me. It should have been mine! I was the qualified one; I was the one who did all the work ahead of the inception. It was me! And this little know-nothing teacher who'd hardly been teaching gets such a gem of a reward. Why? And why not me? Hmm? How come, Alisa? How come I didn't get it?"

Alisa's eyebrows shot up. "I have no idea, Bev. It's not

up to me to figure out why administrators make the decisions they do. I haven't the foggiest idea why Barbara didn't include you. Did you ever ask her why?"

Beverly shrugged. "She gave me some lame-brain excuse, and I could have screamed. But I did it, Alisa. I did it."

Alisa scrunched her eyes at Beverly. "What do you mean, Beverly? What did you do?"

Beverly walked over to the kitchen sink and dumped her coffee in it. She reached for the bottle of scotch sitting at the end of the stone counter and poured herself half a cup.

"Uh, Beverly, it's only ten o'clock in the morning, girl."

"Shit, with what I'm about to tell you, I need this sip of courage no matter what time it is."

CHAPTER 46

arl finished speaking with his representative. He was numb; he was light-headed; he was angry. And to top it all, he wasn't sure what had just happened. What had he done to anyone to deserve this?

"Daddy, Daddy, please stop! I'm sorry. I'm sorry. Please don't hit me. I promise I won't spill the milk ever again. Daddy, ow! Please, stop!"

The memories came flooding back, too many to separate as they ran together like a movie out of control.

"Mom, Mom, don't tell Daddy. Don't tell him, because he's gonna be angry with me. I promised him, Mom, and I'm afraid. I'm so afraid of him. Please!"

"Daddy, Emma didn't break that glass. She didn't do it. I did it. I broke it. It's my fault! Punish me, Daddy, not Emma!"

"Ow! Not the strap! Don't use the strap! It hurts, Daddy. Oh, ow, it hurts so much. I'll be careful next time. I promise, Daddy."

"Emma, it's okay. It doesn't hurt too much. Really, I'm okay. Why don't you go out to your friend's house till Daddy calms

down? Where's Chip? Can you find him and go hang out with him? I'm sure he'll watch you. I got this. I'm good. I love you."

"Daddy, is that a gun? You have a real gun? Is that really a real gun? Can I touch it? Can I hold it? Can we shoot it? Can we go outside and shoot something? You let Chip shoot the gun, Daddy. He told me all about it. Said it was super cool and he was the best shot in the family."

"Mom, where does Daddy hide his gun? Tell me. I need to know. I need to know in case . . . in case, well, I need to know, Mom. Tell me."

"Emma, what are you doing with Dad's gun? How? What? Oh shit. Go put it back. Now! Emma, please, if Daddy comes home and sees you with his gun—hell, you gotta put it back!"

"Mom! Mom! Where's Emma? I can't find her. And I think Daddy's gun is missing. I can't find it in his hiding place."

"Dad, Dad, listen to me. Leave Emma alone. She's not responsible for these problems. She just likes to do things her way. Dad, c'mon, man, leave her be."

"Emma! Emma! Please don't go. Please don't leave me. I love you!"

Carl drove recklessly, the images and sounds and screams flooding his brain like water through a busted dam, rushing to find freedom. Carl didn't know if he stopped at red lights or stop signs; he didn't remember getting on and off the highways.

Before he realized it, he was at his old house. He had a key, and while his parents were at their summer home most of the year, Carl still took care of the house and even stayed there on occasion. Even good ol' Chip used the house as his free B and B when he was in town to see his buddies. But today, Carl was not there to check the mail or the condition of the house.

Carl walked up to the house, his thoughts scattered, dark and sad. He unlocked the door, and his eyes scanned over everything familiar. Some of it was comforting, but most of the house only brought back painful memories. Memories he had blocked for years.

He'd promised himself he would never treat a child the way he'd been treated. He wanted youth to be confident and positive. He didn't want negative thoughts to sway them down a dark path like the one his sister had gone down. And he'd worked so hard to be the best teacher, the best colleague, the best friend, and the best brother, until he'd lost that role.

Carl walked into his father's den, his private sanctuary. On his desk were pens and old pictures and scattered papers. His dad had never been an organized man, and things like family photos held little interest for him. Rearranging the framed images of his past, Carl moved the picture of Chip in his football uniform behind the one and only family picture, in which, oddly enough, everyone was actually smiling. Carl snickered. He didn't remember where it was taken or why, but it was the perfect example of how fake a smiling family picture could be.

The bookcase was filled with biographies of great men—there were no great women, according to his father—along with books on world disasters and wars of different nations. There was even an old collection of encyclopedias Mom had purchased each week from the local grocery store.

But Carl wasn't interested in the books or the pictures. He took his time making his way to his father's closet. He opened the door. He pushed aside hanging jackets and old sweatshirts until he could see the back wall. There the safe hung, staring at him, teasing him, daring him.

Carl turned the combination lock: twenty-four right, six left, thirty-two right, and finally, ten left. The door clicked and hissed, and Carl tugged at the handle. It was tight, as if it didn't want to be opened. *Leave me be. Don't do it. Don't open this door. There is only danger inside. It's not worth it. Go away. Go away!*

Carl ignored the voices in his head. He tugged again at the handle, and it swung open reluctantly. Inside was cool to the touch. Carl reached in farther, ignoring papers and small boxes filled with coins and wills and other insignificant materials. And then, there it was. His father's gun. Cold, hard, menacing. It was *the* Glock. Carl had only held it one time before, but how many times had Chip bragged that he'd held the gun, how many times had he gone to the shooting range with Dad?

Now it was Carl's turn. He pulled the gun out of the safe. He held it. It was heavier than he remembered. He turned it over and over in his hands. Carl closed the safe door, turned the combination lock, and backed out of the closet.

He sat down at his father's desk and placed the gun

gently on the desktop. He straightened the pictures that were askew and collected the papers into one neat pile. Carl stared at the gun. He wasn't even sure it was loaded, but it felt heavy.

How could he face his students again? Would they ever trust him? He loved his job. He loved his school. Why would someone say such evil things about him? It wasn't fair. It just wasn't fair.

Carl picked up the gun and caressed the handle.

Emma, what were you thinking during those last few moments? Were you sad? Did you think you had no way out? Was there never a time when you thought you would be happy again? Will I ever be happy again?

I don't know.

I just don't know.

ACKNOWLEDGMENTS

A book cannot be realized without the help of so many. I want to thank the following:

Irene Elder for being a phenomenal therapist who shared her wisdom and insight with me.

Dr. Tyler Gonzalez for his technical and expert medical advice.

Mickie Trapani Rivest for helping me with specific background knowledge on physical trauma.

Dr. Renée Brimfield for being my grammar champion.

To my loyal readers, Robin Wilpon and Ilene Tockman—you are always spot on.

To Connie Ornstein for sharing personal stories with me.

Chelsea Cambeis for her incredibly careful editing and wonderful insight.

Karen Robinson for her keen editing and helpful suggestions.

Victoria Griffin for her support and comforting emails.

To my children, who know I must write and who understand me:

Arleigh—for always supporting me and finding ways to help me with my passion and never letting me give up.

Daniel—I am always proud of your love of literature and how you share that love with your own children. Keep reading, always—especially your mom's books!

Jason—Believe in yourself, believe in the good you do for your students and your children every day, and never, ever stop dreaming.

To my husband:

> To your infinite love and unwavering support
> for me, I am truly blessed.